The complete guide to becoming
pregnant

Dr Firuza R. Parikh

EBURY
PRESS

EBURY PRESS

USA | Canada | UK | Ireland | Australia
New Zealand | India | South Africa | China

Ebury Press is part of the Penguin Random House group of companies
whose addresses can be found at global.penguinrandomhouse.com

Published by Penguin Random House India Pvt. Ltd
7th Floor, Infinity Tower C, DLF Cyber City,
Gurgaon 122 002, Haryana, India

First published by Random House India 2011
This revised edition published 2014

16 15 14 13 12 11 10

ISBN 9788184001174

Typeset in Sabon by R. Ajith Kumar
Printed at Replika Press Pvt. Ltd, India

www.penguin.co.in

For Rajesh,

best friend, husband, Renaissance man,
neuropsychiatrist, photographer, painter,
poet, pilot, trekker, clairvoyant, linguist,
and walking encyclopaedia

Contents

Acknowledgements

GOd's blessings and the incredible opportunities that I
have to serve my patients make this book possible.
It is they who make me the doctor and the person I am.

My parents, Sheru and Minocher, and in-laws Shobha
and Mahendra Parikh, have been guiding forces in my life.
My husband Rajesh and children—Swapneil, Manish, and
Nikita—make everything worthwhile.

My teachers Drs Manu Kothari, Lopa Mehta, Rhoda
Minina, Usha Krishna, Rusi Soonawalla, Mahendra
Parikh, and B.N. Chakravarty in India, as well as Drs
Alan DeCherney, Brian Rigney, Gabor Huzar, and Fred
Naftolin at the Yale University School of Medicine in
the United States have trained me with dedication. Dr
DeCherney's rounds would begin at 5:30 am every day,
weekends included. My seven-day work week is relatively
easy.

Nita and Mukesh Ambani, Sushma and Anand Jain,
Reena and Subrata Mukherji, Anu and Vidhu Vinod
Chopra, Hanifa and Anjum Bilakhia, Alka and Marezban
Bharucha have been fully supportive of my unavailability
while working on this book. Yet, as always they have
been there for me. Shamsah Sonawalla, Ishita Pateria and

Salomi Aladia have done invaluable work in ensuring the psychological well-being of our patients.

The trustees of the Jaslok Hospital and Research Centre—the late Mr G.K. Chanrai, Mr M.K. Chanrai, Mrs Kanta Masand as well as Col. Masand and Dr R.D. Lele have fully supported the work that has led to this book.

My team of forty dedicated individuals has made our centre what it is today. They are: Drs Prochi Madon, Trupti Mehta, Anahita Pandole, Neeta Warty, Sujata Reddy, Arundhati Athalye, Sangeeta Deshmukh, Sapna Agarwal, Madhavi Panpalia, Mamta Katakdhond, and Shonali Uttamchandani, Nandkishor Naik, Dattatray Naik, Smita Gawas, Suresh Dhumal, Mangesh Sanap, Chaya Ranade, Linette Dias, Arvind Shirodkar, Vijay Bandkar, Mahadev Kawle, Prashant Padyal, Rupesh Sanap, Vasant Dhumal, Mahendra Sute, Dhananjaya Kulkarni, Latha Jayakumar, Panamma Phillip, Shailesh Sakapal, Pradeep Tambde, Priyanka Lajnekar, Abhijeet Shirsekar, Yashwant Pangle, Kalpesh Sawant, Poonam Arya, and Ravi Nachikar. My special thanks to Dr Neeta Warty for brilliant endoscopy work, some of which is reflected in the photographs. I also thank Dr Chander Lulla for his sonography pictures.

I am especially indebted to Shonali Uttamchandani and Maherra Khambaty, who, in addition to everything that they do with such amazing efficiency, have worked with me through every word of this book. Arvind Shirodkar, Lourdes John, and Lynette Dias have MS worded this book.

A big thank you to Farah Khan who has been kind enough to write an entire chapter for this book, despite being incredibly busy with her family and professional commitments.

Thank you Milee Ashwarya—editor, syntax sentinel, and surrogate mom of this book, and Chiki Sarkar, my lovely publisher who stormed into my life one December evening, urging me to write this book. Things have not been the same since.

Finally, thank you readers. But for you, there would be no writers. May you be happy parents.

Foreword

When you spark a smile you make a positive difference, and when you help sustain that smile you make a profound one. This book, *The Complete Guide to Becoming Pregnant* by my dear friend Dr Firuza Parikh, is about sustaining smiles by showing pathways to parenthood— dreams that bring new hopes and new life, dreams that will be cherished for a lifetime.

Assisted reproduction is about science and technology, and Firuza is an accomplished and widely respected professional in this domain. Through the book, Firuza has effortlessly demystified this complex subject into an extremely understandable and handy piece of knowledge, with vivid illustrations and lucid language, while fully resonating her depth of expertise in her profession. Capturing the step-wise approach to treatment, and the numerous case histories which tell inspiring tales of conquering the challenge of infertility, this book will surely open the eyes of innumerable patients to the immense possibilities of finding a medical solution to a human problem.

I am writing this foreword not only because Firuza is among the finest doctors in the world, but also because she is a great human being. Mukesh and I have known her and her husband Dr Rajesh Parikh for over twenty years and consider them much more than friends. They are an intrinsic part of our lives and our family. Besides being godmother to our children, Firuza is more than a sister to me. I have observed her at close quarters for many years.

That Firuza works virtually non-stop, seven days a week, reflects her devotion to her vocation. Her patients run the gamut of society, from international celebrities to the poorest in our country. But Firuza treats everyone with equal compassion, grace, and care. In that she is blessed many times over by thousands of grateful patients from around the world.

One of Firuza's favourite activities is to lovingly go through the numerous albums of 'my babies'. Not surprisingly, some couples have named their daughters after her. There are baby Firuzas scampering all around the world: in New York, Paris, Rio de Janeiro, Johannesburg, Chennai, and Srinagar!

I wish this enlightening and empowering book the success it deserves. Let it help celebrate the beauty of parenthood, and bring about more smiles for couples across the world.

Nita Ambani
February 2014
Mumbai

Introduction: A Book is Born

The literature on becoming pregnant is anything but sterile. The health section of any large bookstore is overpopulated with books on pregnancy, and it would seem that everybody is keen to have a baby, including those who have already had one.

In many cultures the birth of a child is heralded as the most significant achievement of a couple. Sometimes, the lack of a child in the family is considered to be a harbinger of unhappiness. Hence, childless couples may go through humiliation and years of agony.

The causes for infertility are usually simple and need minimal treatment. When I started practising fertility twenty-five years ago (let me clarify—fertility treatment of my patients—my own practice of fertility started a couple of years later with three children over the years), I would have never imagined that one of the causes of infertility would be inadequate knowledge of sex. Yes, believe it or not, I do come across couples who are infertile because of sexual ignorance, but more of that later.

Infertility is usually treatable either through medical or surgical intervention. Seldom is the infertile status irreversible, and even in such situations the couples may have alternative avenues of treatment. As a fertility specialist, I have seen and shared the pain experienced by women and men faced with infertility. Often they do not know where to turn and squander precious years trying ineffective treatments. Yet, fertility treatments, while not exactly child's play, are not, as the cliché goes, rocket science. Hence the book.

When I was about to return after four years of training in fertility management in the US, some of my colleagues at Yale would ask, 'But why are you returning to India to practise infertility management? India is overpopulated!' Usually I just smiled. On other occasions I pointed out, 'Sometimes that's what makes it distressing for those who do not have children.'

So when my publisher, the amazing and irrepressible Chiki Sarkar, approached me to write this book, I hardly needed persuasion. Even if the pregnancy shelves are overcrowded, I believe that this book will have incremental value. The book starts with an explanation of what goes into the miracle of creating a human being. Next I have dealt with the causes of infertility. Assisted Reproductive Technology (ART) has been discussed, including alternative therapies. I have frequently drawn upon real life examples but with the names changed, to maintain the confidentiality of my patients. The only exception would be my friend Farah Khan. The becoming pregnant chart encapsulates a step-wise approach.

A comprehensive glossary helps the reader whenever an unfamiliar term is encountered. We have also tried to assist readers in a better understanding by providing black and white pictures within the text and coloured inserts at the end of the book.

Finally, I hope that Chiki, my well wishers, and I are not the only ones who look at this book lovingly. Some of you will hopefully take it home and get on with becoming pregnant! Do write in with your feedback, questions, and suggestions.

Firuza R. Parikh, MD
firuzaparikh@gmail.com

1

Fertility: Basic Concepts

- Sperms in an Olympic race
- The conception timeline
- The timeline changes after thirty-five
- What is infertility?
- What can go wrong?
- Some types of infertility
- Diagnosis, diagnosis...

Sperms in an Olympic race

Think sperm. You have the long and arduous task of climbing through hostile barriers within the female reproductive tract before winning the prize. Michael Phelps had it easier at the Olympics! At the time of ejaculation, hundreds of millions of your competitors are released into the vagina. Here, you battle an acidic environment, and most of your competitors perish. Only a few million that survive, like you, climb through the niches and crevices within the cervix.

On the way, many are lost or are engulfed by the white blood cells present in the cervix, similar to those hidden dangers in a Playstation game. Zap! Gone! Of the survivors many are immobilized in the cervix. Only a brave few race towards the uterus. The cave-like uterus has many blind alleys and your competitors often run into numerous dead ends. But not you! You know exactly where to go. You are truly focused. Even Phelps would have been distracted by now!

A few thousand competitors wiggle their way through two tiny openings called the ostia. These lead into two long conduits called the fallopian tubes. In one of these, the precious egg floats, cushioned in the warm currents of the tubal fluid. While others are dazzled, distracted, and fatigued, you get your second wind and zoom straight towards the golden ovum. And what's your reward? You get beheaded. Just like that!

But you do not give up. Not you. Your head keeps racing on inside the ovum. The whistle blows. The stands erupt. The race is over. You will soon become the greatest creation of nature—a human being. What is an Olympic medal in comparison?

Interestingly, a 'no entry' signal now flashes vigorously, preventing the entry of the remaining hopeful sperms. The ovum secretes chemicals, precluding the entry of the other sperms. 'Go home guys. The race is over.' What follows is the fusion of the maternal and the paternal genetic material, which takes approximately sixteen hours to be completed. The result is a one-celled zygote, which then continues to divide into a multi-celled morula and finally expands into a ball of hundreds of cells that eventually becomes a baby.

The zona—outer shell of the egg—starts thinning in preparation of the blastocyst (an embryo with more than a hundred cells) hatching out of the shell and invading the warm bed of nutrition provided by the womb.

When we look at this entire phenomenon of conception, a miracle of nature, it is not difficult to understand how this delicate balance can be deranged by small discrepancies and hurdles.

Let us look at the race in perspective. Proportionate to size, the race from the vagina to the ovum would be a 10 kilometre dash for Michael Phelps. A little humility would not be out of place for you, the lucky winner. A little compassion for those who lost would be truly outstanding. Later in the book we will talk about those who did not make it.

Okay, snap out of it. You are no longer a sperm. You are that incredibly marvellous, beautiful, complex and amazing creature—a human!

The life of the human egg is about thirty-six hours long whereas a sperm can survive in the woman's body for about forty-eight hours. Hence, there is a narrow window of time during which one can become pregnant.

A few weeks ago, a couple, who were both in their twenties and married for just three months, visited me. They were convinced that they were infertile since a baby had not 'happened' in three months. Only after I had explained the complex physiology of reproduction to them, did they leave my office hopeful, happier, and relieved of their anxiety. I haven't heard from them since other than getting a lovely thank you note. So I guess they are busy becoming pregnant.

The conception timeline

As a broad rule, if a couple has unprotected sex at least three times a week, their chances of conceiving every month, add up to about 25 to 30 percent. In other words, if a hundred couples plan for a baby, then within a year of trying and having unprotected intercourse, 60 to 65 of them would have a baby. Within two years about 75 to 80 would have a baby, and at the end of two years only about 12 to 14 would be childless. A couple is said to be infertile if there is no conception, in spite of having unprotected sex for two consecutive years.

The timeline changes after thirty-five

As women age, the chances of conception keep on diminishing. A woman's fertility peaks between the ages of twenty-four and thirty-four and hence it is advisable to have the first baby during this time. When a woman crosses thirty-five, doctors cut down the waiting period to one year. I urge women who are approaching their mid and late thirties to be on the fast track when planning a baby.

Kirti, a practising dentist, was thirty-two years old when she came to me. She was starting her career and wanted to defer childbearing for another two to three years. I suspect she came just to get my reassurance. I advised her not to wait that long. She was insistent that her career came first. She returned four years later. By then she had developed problems in the uterus, including small harmless tumours, which were removed and now she was impatient to conceive. We tried two cycles of intra cytoplasmic sperm injection (ICSI) for Kirti but she did not conceive as her ova had aged. She finally became pregnant using donor ova.

What is infertility?

The definition proposed by the American Society for Reproductive Medicine (ASRM) states: 'Infertility is a disease or condition of the reproductive system, often diagnosed after a couple has one year of unprotected, well-timed intercourse or if the woman suffers from multiple miscarriages.'

What can go wrong?

Pregnancy is a complex process dependant on a number of factors, some of which can go awry. Sperm formation may be inadequate (oligospermia) or completely absent (azoospermia). Sometimes, the sperm may be 'lazy' and lack movement (asthenospermia) like couch potatoes, or they may also have abnormal shapes and sizes (teratospermia). In some cases, there may be a blockage to the passage of the sperm, resulting in the condition of obstructive azoospermia. The presence of a varicocele—a condition where the veins, which normally surround the duct called the spermatic cord, get engorged with blood—and diabetes can contribute to oligoasthenoteratospermia (a bonus word for Scrabble addicts). Lifestyle related factors such as smoking and stress are also sperm busters.

Arti and Pratap had long standing infertility due to the male factor. Pratap smoked all day long and often at night. When they came to see me recently, I noticed his smile. I told him that some of the damage from smoking is seen in the discolouration of one's teeth. The damage that this does to the sperm can be seen only under the microscope. Smoking decreases motility of the sperm and also damages their genetic material. Pratap promised to kick the habit. He has not smoked for six months now, and his sperm count and motility are already significantly better.

Some of the common causes for low sperm count in Indian men are infection in the testes (usually due to childhood mumps) and genetic factors, which prevent the formation and maturation of sperm.

Now think ovum. Tough? Never mind. I, too, would rather be a sperm than an ovum, like in El Condor Pasa (the Simon and Garfunkel version). By the way, music too can help one get pregnant.

Some types of infertility

For women, there may be mechanical, chemical, or hormonal problems resulting in infertility. There may be obstructions in the vagina, cervix, uterus, fallopian tubes, ovaries, or in the area surrounding the fallopian tubes and ovaries. These blockages can prevent the sperm from reaching the egg. Mechanical blockages can arise due to infections, tumours, and birth defects. The secretions of the vagina, cervix, uterus, and the fallopian tubes may be hostile to the sperm and deactivate them. Endometriosis—a disease causing infertility—can secrete chemicals that can harm sperm, eggs, and also the embryos.

Hormonal

A hormone is a type of protein which is secreted by one organ and has an effect on another organ. The entire reproductive process is controlled by several hormones and is comparable to an orchestra playing a delightful symphony under the direction of the conductor. The pituitary gland—a pea-sized structure located at the base of the brain—along with the hypothalamus, another master gland in the brain, secretes many hormones responsible for thyroid, uterine, and ovarian functions. A glitch in the cascade of these hormones can have a ripple or a storm effect on the menstrual and reproductive process.

Genetic

Men and women are born with twenty-three pairs of chromosomes—thread-like structures that bear our genetic material. Of these, one pair, called the sex chromosomes, relate to the reproductive process. An increase or decrease in these numbers or a change in their shape can cause infertility and repeated miscarriages.

Immunological

Our immune system protects us from harmful diseases and degenerative changes. Sometimes the body's protective cells can turn treacherous and harm the body rather than protect it. When this happens, the autoimmune disorders affect the thyroid, pancreas, ovaries, and adrenal glands, resulting in their performing either sluggishly or not at all.

Diagnosis, diagnosis...

I once interviewed a couple in their late thirties who had tried several cycles of intra-uterine insemination (IUI)—the process of placing enriched sperm into the uterus with the help of a fine tube. After a thorough check, we found that her fallopian tubes were blocked and hence the treatment had not worked. What was required was the procedure of intra cystoplasmic sperm injection (ICSI) instead of the series of IUIs that she had undergone with various doctors. In ICSI, a single sperm is injected into the centre of the egg with the help of a fine glass tube. The lady conceived in the first attempt.

The first and foremost step should be to identify the root cause of infertility. Treatment is important but it should be prescribed only after the reason for the lack of conception has been established.

When my husband, Rajesh, was a resident doctor in psychiatry in the early eighties, his favourite professor, Dr Doongaji would ask, 'What are the three most important steps in medicine?' Without waiting for a reply he would holler, 'Diagnosis, diagnosis, and diagnosis.' To this day

Rajesh does a superb and affectionate imitation and I try to pass this on to the young doctors who train with me—diagnosis should always precede treatment.

2

Pregnancy on Our Own

- Avoiding the negatives
- Focusing on the positives
- Awareness of one's fertility potential

Sashi and Amish had been told by three gynaecologists that they should consider adoption. However, they were clear about having their own biological child. Moreover, Sashi had philosophical issues with taking any 'unnatural treatment'. I am embarrassed to confess that twenty-five years ago I might have responded by asking them why they were seeking my help in the first place. However, being older, and possibly a little wiser, I have learnt to become a patient listener and did not lecture them about their odds.

'Doctor, can you guide us about trying to have a baby without IVF (in vitro fertilization). We know our chances are slim but we want to give it a shot,' said Sashi. I told them that they could try naturally for a period of six months and suggested the methods of increasing the odds of conception.

They implemented everything I had suggested—a healthy diet, no smoking for Amish, no late nights, more sex, more positive thinking, using an ovulation predictor kit, and occasional sonography exams to determine the size of the growing follicle. I put Amish on antioxidants and Sashi on Arginine sachets and DHEA tablets—both these medications are believed to improve the quality of the eggs. I also suggested that they go on holiday to a place such as the Maldives. To my great surprise they went. That is the extent of them following instructions! Within three months, Sashi surprised me by conceiving. She had a difficult pregnancy with multiple hospital admissions, but finally delivered a healthy son.

In order to understand what it takes to make a baby, we must first realize that nature is resourceful. Not everybody needs IUI, IVF, or even a follow up with an infertility specialist in order to have a baby. There are simple guidelines, which when followed, optimize one's chances of conceiving naturally.

The creation of a baby calls for an interplay of the mind and body of both the man and woman. It may be worthwhile to explore the possibilities of conceiving naturally before initiating infertility treatment, particularly if the female partner is young and there is no male factor infertility.

Planning a baby can be an exciting project. Both partners should be open to discussing the issues related to parenthood as well as articulating their fears and expectations. Couples yearn for babies for different reasons—some want a child to bond with them, others to love and to be loved, some due to pressure from the family, and yet others because it may improve their interpersonal relationships. Most couples are caught unaware of the responsibilities that having a baby brings. A baby on the way may also put careers on hold. This has to be adequately thought through. Ambivalence about having a baby is not conducive to conception.

Avoiding the negatives

1. Alcohol

Excessive alcohol may inhibit the body's absorption of nutrients such as zinc, which is one of the most important minerals for male fertility.

2. Pollutants

Xenoestrogens are estrogens present in pesticides and plastics. They can cause infertility and miscarriages.

They may also be present in food products subjected to pesticides. Hence, it may be a good idea to consume organic foods.

3. Smoking

It has been linked with infertility and early menopause in women. In men, smoking is associated with decreased sperm count, sluggish sperm motility, and abnormal sperm.

4. Food additives and processed foods

They may cause birth defects.

5. Stress

It is important to identify stressors and to minimize them. A few minutes spent away from work or household chores, quick telephone calls to loved ones, relaxation, and breathing exercises, all help to relieve stress. Massages can also be relaxing. Music is therapeutic. Well, sometimes.

My assistant, Dr Trupti Mehta, was counselling Vaneeta and Sudhir in the techniques of de-stressing. She suggested that they listen to music together. Ten days later, Trupti got an exasperated call from Vaneeta. 'Doctor, why did you not specify the type of music that we are supposed to enjoy together? Now all I hear at home is Pink Floyd and Deep Purple at 2,500 decibels. Sudhir insists that I should relax to it. I have just bought him a pair of headphones.' So much for their musical evenings together!

Focusing on the positives

1. Regular frequent sex

Couples who want to conceive should have frequent sex, particularly between the tenth and seventeenth day of the period, if the cycle length is between twenty-eight to thirty days. Day one of the cycle is the first day of the period.

2. Folic acid and Vitamin B complex

Regular intake of folic acid can prevent neurological problems in the baby, such as spina bifida. The B-complex family of vitamins is essential for producing the healthy genetic materials—DNA and RNA. Research indicates that administering Vitamin B6 to women who have trouble conceiving increases fertility, and that Vitamin B12 has been found to improve low sperm counts.

3. Zinc

This is necessary for the functioning of the reproductive hormones—estrogen and progesterone. It is also a necessary component of the sperm tail. Zinc deficiency can cause low sperm counts and miscarriages.

4. Selenium

This antioxidant protects the body from chemical fragments called free radicals, and is vital for sperm formation. It prevents chromosome breakage, which can cause birth defects and miscarriages.

5. Essential fatty acids (EFAs)

These are essential for the reproductive system and for normal hormone function. Low intake of EFAs can cause poor sperm quality, abnormal sperm, poor motility, or low count.

6. Vitamin E

The antioxidant activity of Vitamin E improves the fertility potential of sperm.

7. Vitamin C

This antioxidant protects the sperm from DNA damage. A study has shown that Vitamin C, when added to clomiphene, leads to better ovulation rates.

8. L-Arginine

An amino acid found in abundance in the head of the sperm, it helps to increase both the sperm count and quality.

9. L-Carnitine

This amino acid is essential for normal functioning of sperm cells, and it also improves sperm vitality.

10. Trace minerals

Magnesium, manganese, and chromium are required in small amounts for various reproductive processes within the body.

11. Exercise

A couple trying to conceive should go for walks together; it gives time to unwind and discuss the day's activities as well as plan for the next day. Exercise improves the immune system, gives a sense of well being, and can correct irregular ovulation. However, excessive exercise can be counterproductive.

12. Yoga and meditation

It is important to have a healthy body and mind in order to increase the odds of becoming pregnant. One cannot emphasize enough the importance of yoga and meditation in attaining such a state.

Awareness of one's fertility potential

For the female partner

1. Menstrual cycle

A menstrual cycle is about twenty-eight days in length. The first day of the period is considered day one. The ovulation time is usually fourteen days before the next menstrual period. This information can help plan sex around the most fertile period. Many women sense their ovulation time by a peculiar pain called mittelsmerz, which they get in the pelvic area prior to ovulation. Maintaining a diary and noting down the cycle lengths over three to four months helps to identify the time of ovulation. Many women complain of a clear mucous discharge around the time of ovulation. Observing and noting this discharge over three to four months also helps in identifying the fertile days.

2. Body temperature

The body gets warmer after ovulation as progesterone increases the body temperature. If one takes one's temperature daily on waking up (Basal Body Temperature), it will be slightly lower than 98.6 degrees Fahrenheit in the first fourteen days of the menstrual cycle. It shows a further dip at ovulation, and then as the progesterone builds up, the body remains warmer than the basal temperature until menstruation. Keeping a chart of these temperature changes over three to four months is useful in identifying the ovulatory zone. It is important to use a special fertility thermometer, which has a special graph paper to note down the morning temperature. However, monitoring temperature may not help if there is no ovulation. This technique can also have other flaws.

Mithili called us in a panic saying that her temperature chart was very erratic. When I analysed it, I was surprised to see that her temperature remained high throughout the entire cycle. We soon identified the culprit—hot tea that Mithili would drink on waking up. It is important to take the temperature prior to consuming any hot or cold beverage.

3. The surge of Luteinizing Hormone (LH)

Ovulation is triggered twenty-four to forty hours after the sudden peak in LH. This phenomenon is useful in detecting ovulation. Home detection kits are available. The testing starts by day nine of the period. A paper strip is dipped into a morning sample of urine to detect the LH surge. In case of impending ovulation, the paper strip changes colour. Charting the colour changes of the paper strip over a period of three to four months helps to predict the peak fertility time. However, the test can be falsely positive.

4. Tell-tale body signs

Some women can predict ovulation within two hours of its occurrence. Many women say that they feel different around ovulation time. They complain of heavy breasts, water retention, and a change in bowel habits for a day or two around ovulation. If one experiences these changes, one can be in a better position to get the fertile period right.

For the male partner

1. Frequency of sex

Conventional thought entails abstaining from sex for more than a week, to increase sperm count. However, current research shows that frequent ejaculation increases the sperm mobility and vitality. So there is no need to slow down on sexual frequency.

2. Exercise

Exercise is healthy for the heart and brain. However, excessive exercise such as weight lifting can lower the sperm count. Men indulging in excessive endurance exercises have lower sperm counts.

3. Other factors

Spermatogenesis thrives in cool temperatures. Men should avoid hot showers, steam rooms, and saunas. Tight briefs reduce blood circulation through the testes.

Sudhir expected Prajakta to stay awake for him when he returned from work every night at 1 am. He kept long hours, as did his colleagues at the bank. There were constant arguments between the couple, to a point that they started sleeping in separate bedrooms to maintain their individual sleep patterns. Then they came to consult us for IVF. Somehow they expected to have a baby without regular sex. One session of counselling was all it took for them to have a baby.

When couples approach us, we try to understand their situation prior to suggesting the optimal way for them to have a baby. Sometimes they need us to tell them how much they do not need us. When Rajesh and I were medical students, our beloved professor Dr Manu Kothari, would tell us, 'A good surgeon is one who knows when not to operate.' I like to paraphrase that aphorism to teach my students, that a good IVF specialist is one who knows when not to conduct IVF.

3

The Male Factor

- The male reproductive system
- The penis and its role in fertility
- The testes and their role in fertility
- The epididymis and its role in fertility
- The vasa deferentia and their role in fertility
- The ejaculatory ducts and their role in fertility
- The seminal vesicles and their role in fertility
- The prostate gland and its role in fertility
- Cowper's glands and their role in fertility
- Stress and its role in fertility

The male factor accounts for about 40 percent of all infertility cases. With a better knowledge of human physiology, subtle defects in the male reproductive system have been understood more clearly. Thus, what was often attributed to unexplained infertility in the past, is in many instances identified as caused due to the male factor.

The male reproductive system

The male reproductive system consists of the external and internal genitalia (Figure 3.1). The external genitalia consist of the penis and testes. The internal genitalia consist of the epididymis, vasa deferentia, ejaculatory ducts, the seminal vesicles, the prostate, and Cowper's glands.

The penis has been described in more ways than one. Human penile length varies, but on an average is 4 inches in the non-erect state and about 6 inches when erect. Much has been written on the length of the male penis. One of the largest industrial enterprises in the world sustains itself on this obsession—the pornographic industry has an annual turnover of $14 billion, according to *The New York Times*. However, as far as fertility is concerned, size does not matter. The penis consists of three compartments. The two lateral compartments are called the corpora cavernosa and the central compartment, through which the urethra runs, is called the corpus spongiosum. The tip of the penis is known as the glans penis and has numerous nerve fibres responsible for sexual pleasure.

The skin of the penis is folded on itself at the tip to form the prepuce. This fold of skin is the centre of one major debate—to circumcise or not to! Its undersurface is rich in sebaceous glands, the secretions of which form the

External structures	Internal structures
penis	epididymis
testes	vasa deferentia
	ejaculatory ducts
	seminal vesicles
	prostate gland
	Cowper's glands

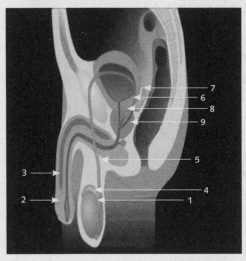

1. Testis
2. Penis
3. Corpus cavernosum
4. Epididymis
5. Vasa deferentia
6. Ejaculatory duct
7. Seminal vesicle
8. Prostate gland
9. Cowper's gland

Figure 3.1 The male reproductive system

smegma which facilitates sexual intercourse by acting as a lubricant.

The corpora cavernosa is made up of spongy bands of tissue, called the trabeculae, as well as nerves and blood vessels. During sexual stimulation these spaces fill up with blood, resulting in penile erection. This process is usually initiated by sexual arousal. Stimulation of the erotic centres in the brain stimulates the penile nerves causing a rush of blood into the blood-filled cavernosal spaces, resulting in turgidity and erection of the penis.

The male orgasm, which is under the command of the nerves of the autonomic nervous system, occurs at the peak of sexual stimulation. The sensory stimuli from the genital skin, and from the central nervous system, trigger signals, which in the first phase of ejaculation cause contractions of the muscles surrounding the epididymis, the vasa deferentia, and the prostate. In the second phase of ejaculation, the perineal muscles contract pushing the semen out of the urethra.

Men are endowed with a pair of testes. Each testis is approximately the size of a walnut. The testes contain thousands of thin tiny tubes called the seminiferous tubules. They would stretch up to half a kilometre if joined end to end. These tubules produce about two hundred to five hundred million sperm during each ejaculation. Men retain their ability to produce sperm throughout their lives though in the later years the production is reduced in number.

The process of sperm formation is known as spermatogenesis. It begins at puberty, decreases slightly with advancing age, and continues till death. Spermatogenesis occurs within the seminiferous tubules of the testes, and progresses to the epididymis where the developing sperm mature and are stored until ejaculation. The maturation of the sperm involves the acquisition of a tail and thereby motility. The antecedent of the mature spermatozoa is the spermatogonium. This cell goes through several phases in order to reach maturity as a spermatozoon.

A mature sperm consists of a head, neck, and a tail

(Figure 3.2). The sperm, in its entire length, is about 58 μm, the head being 3 to 5 μm, the neck 8 μm, and the tail 45 μm. Without the tail the sperm is one-twelfth the size of the ovum (thus about a tenth of the size of the period at the end of this sentence). The head is oval with an acrosomal cap—the acrosome being an important structure for fertilization. The nucleus of the sperm resides in the head. The neck, or the mid piece, contains the mitochondria—the sources of energy for the sperm. The tail contains the microtubules which give the unique quality of motility to the sperm.

The seminiferous tubules are lined with Sertoli cells. These create the right environment for the maturing sperm and also protect them from immune attacks by the body. In between the seminiferous tubules are the Leydig cells, which produce the male hormones. Millions of sperm pass from the seminiferous tubules to other fine tubules called the rete testes, from where they negotiate their way into the epididymis via the efferent ductules (Figure 3.3).

Prior to birth, the testicles are tucked away in the abdomen. At birth, they move outside the body and are secured in a sac called the scrotum. This is because sperm need a cooler temperature (34°C) than that of the body (37°C) in order to survive.

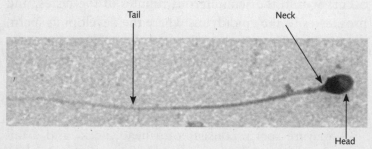

Figure 3.2 A normal sperm

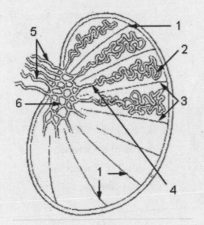

1. Testicular septa
2. Convoluted seminiferous tubules
3. Testicular lobules
4. Straight seminiferous tubules
5. Efferent ductules
6. Rete testis

Figure 3.3 Diagrammatic representation of the path of the sperm in the testis

The epididymis (Figure 3.4) is a tightly-coiled tube, approximately 5 to 6 m long, formed by the convergence of the ductules from the testes. It connects the testis to the vas deferens. The effort made by sperm from the testes finds them homing into this tortuous network of tubules. The epididymis has a head, body, and tail. The head of the epididymis receives spermatozoa. From here, the sperm progress to the body and finally reach the tail where they are stored. It is during this transit that the sperm undergo maturation. The epididymis leads to a thicker single tube called the vas deferens.

The vasa deferentia transport sperm from the epididymis to the ejaculatory ducts. Each tube is 30 centimetres in length and is surrounded by muscle fibres. These fibres contract during ejaculation, propelling the sperm forward. The vasa deferentia, along with the nerves

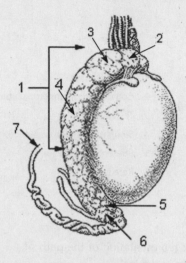

1. Epididymis
2. Head of epididymis
3. Lobules of epididymis
4. Body of epididymis
5. Tail of epididymis
6. Duct of epididymis
7. Vas deferens

Figure 3.4 Diagrammatic representation of the epididymis

and blood vessels, pass through a protective sheath called the spermatic cord.

The seminal vesicles are a pair of glands located close to the urinary bladder. They are approximately 5 centimetres in length and occur as an out pocket of the wall of the vasa deferentia. The seminal vesicles secrete fluid which ultimately becomes semen. The alkalinity of this fluid helps to neutralize the acidity of the vaginal tract, thereby prolonging the lifespan of sperm. The fluid also provides proteins, enzymes, fructose, mucous, Vitamin C, flavins, phosphorylcholine, and prostaglandins. The high fructose concentrations provide nutrient energy for the spermatozoa. The ejaculatory ducts are paired structures, each being about 2 centimetres in length. Each ejaculatory duct is formed by the union of the vas deferens with the duct of the seminal vesicle. The ejaculatory ducts pass through the prostate and empty into the urethra. During ejaculation, semen passes through the ducts and exits the body via the penis.

The prostate gland (Figure 3.5) is a walnut-sized gland located just below the urinary bladder and surrounds the opening of the urethra. The prostate comprises of thirty to forty glands, which secrete a milky fluid into the ejaculate. The prostatic fluid helps to neutralize vaginal acidity and makes sperm motile.

The Cowper's glands are two pea-sized glands located at the base of the penis. They empty out their secretions into a connecting duct which opens into the urethra at the penile base. During sexual arousal, the glands secrete fluid called pre ejaculate which neutralizes the acidic urine

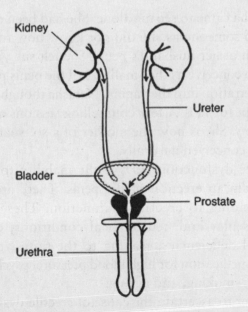

Figure 3.5 Diagrammatic representation of the prostate gland

in the urethra. This fluid helps to lubricate the urethra to facilitate the passage of the spermatozoa.

Semen is a creamy whitish fluid containing mature and immature sperm, a few white blood cells, and epithelial cells. It contains water, proteins, sugar, chemicals, and minerals, including calcium, chlorine, magnesium, nitrogen, Vitamin B12, and zinc. It also contains a trace of cholesterol and sodium.

The penis and its role in fertility

The penis occupies considerable space in medical texts and erotic literature. Its malfunction has perhaps caused more distress to both men and women than that of any other organ.

Natasha came to see me alone. She had been desperate to talk to someone as she did not know how to react to the length of her husband's penis. She felt she would not be able to conceive as the small size of the penis prevented deep penetration into the vagina. Natasha thought that she should opt for IVF. A few counselling sessions alleviated her anxiety. She is now the mother of a six-year-old boy who was conceived naturally.

Erectile dysfunction (ED) is the inability to develop or maintain an erection of the penis. There are several causes leading to erectile dysfunction. These include cardiovascular and neurological conditions, diabetes, hormonal deficiencies, trauma to the testes, penis, or prostate, medication for high blood pressure, psychological disorders, smoking, and ageing.

In order to ascertain the cause of erectile dysfunction, doctors might require some tests to be conducted. These include an ultrasound to check the flow of blood to the penis, and nerve testing. During sleep, it is normal for a man to have five to six erections. This is called nocturnal penile tumescence, and can be studied overnight. Magnetic resonance imaging (MRI) can help to detect issues in certain conditions of vascular blockage leading to erectile dysfunction.

The treatment of erectile dysfunction is based on the treatment of its causes. Medical conditions such as heart disease and diabetes can contribute to erectile dysfunction, and need treatment. In the presence of hormonal deficiency, testosterone supplements are given. Viagra or Sildenafil is used frequently to increase the flow of blood to the penis. Topical creams, such as Alprostadil, are currently being studied for their efficacy. Penile pumps help to engorge the penis. Injections of Papaverine provide temporary relief. In rare instances, a penile prosthesis may be inserted in the penis.

Dhaval and Sanyukta were in a sexual relationship for several years before they got married. While premarital sex was enjoyable, the houshold responsibilities of settling down, paying monthly bills, and dealing with absentee help took a toll on their sex life. Dhaval got a promotion, which made him plan his life on Singapore time. Sex became sporadic and eventually Dhaval stopped having erections. That is when they came to me. Sanyukta said to me, 'Doctor, we were happier when we did not have all these luxuries. Dhaval can't even perform.' Many couples lose their libido under duress and men develop performance anxiety. Several sessions of counselling rectified their condition.

Delayed ejaculation is the inability to ejaculate or persistent difficulty in achieving an orgasm despite the presence of normal sexual desire and sexual stimulation. Normally a man can achieve an orgasm within two to four minutes of active thrusting during sexual intercourse, whereas a man with delayed ejaculation either does not have orgasms at all or can have an orgasm only after prolonged intercourse, which might last for thirty to forty-five minutes or more.

Lack of sufficient sleep, psychological causes, worries, strained marital relationship, anxiety, stroke, diabetes, prostate enlargement, high blood pressure, use of antide-pressants, antihypertensive medicines, and recreational drugs can all contribute to delayed ejaculation. Pramod, in his late thirties, was experiencing a lack of libido and delayed ejaculation. Meena and he knew that a second baby would be difficult without medical help. His history was typical of a man suffering from diabetes. Pramod had joined the forty million Indians who suffer from diabetes. It took about four months of medication and lifestyle modification for Pramod to get his blood sugar level under control and enjoy sex again. In such situations, sex therapy, hypnosis, counselling, and therapy intended to enhance emotional intimacy might be required as a preliminary step. Open discussions of anxieties and fears contribute to better sexual relationships.

Most men will experience premature ejaculation (PE) at some point in their lives. It is a condition in which a man ejaculates within two minutes of sexual penetration. PE occurs when a lack of ejaculatory control interferes with the sexual or emotional well being in one or both partners.

Depression, stress over financial matters, unrealistic expectations about performance, a lack of confidence, unresolved conflicts, or extreme sexual arousal can all contribute to PE. This can also lead to other forms of sexual dysfunction and intensify the existing problem by creating performance anxiety. It is usually psychological in origin and can easily be treated with counselling and medication.

The testes and their role in fertility

Shitij was diagnosed by the urologist to have cryptorchid, or hidden testes. A CT scan showed that both testes were lying in the abdomen, and one of the testes appeared larger than the other. When Shitij and Maya came to me for their infertility problem, I explained to them that as the testes had remained in the abdomen since birth, the chances of finding sperm in them would be minimal. In fact, such testes are more prone to cancer and need to be removed by a procedure called orchidectomy. Shitij underwent bilateral orchidectomy a month later. They now plan to opt for donor sperm insemination.

Normally, each testis is approximately 2 inches long and an inch in breadth. The development of the testes depends on the follicle-stimulating hormone (FSH) and the luteinizing hormone (LH), secreted by the pituitary gland. In their absence the testes remain infantile, and the man does not develop the characteristic changes of masculinity such as facial, pubic, and body hair. He tends to have a low sex drive, and the semen is devoid of sperm.

In some instances, even though the testicular size may be normal, sperm may be absent in the semen. However, azoospermia is often accompanied by small testicular size and high levels of FSH and LH. Such conditions may be genetic in origin. They could also occur as a result of mumps and other infections in childhood.

The epididymis and its role in fertility

The epididymis may be inflamed (epididymitis) due to an infection with mumps, tuberculosis (TB), or filariasis. Sometimes the testes are also affected—a condition called orchiditis. The infection causes blockage of the delicate tubules of the epididymis resulting in obstructive azoospermia requiring TESA and ICSI (see pp 129–133). The treatment of orchiditis includes the use of appropriate antibiotics.

The vasa deferentia and their role in fertility

The vas deferens may get obstructed following an infection or surgery. During a family planning operation, they are usually tied to prevent the passage of the sperm. In rare instances, the vasa deferentia may be absent from birth although the testes and the epididymis develop normally—a condition called congenital absence of the vasa deferentia (CAVD). If the vasa deferentia are absent, the sperm are trapped. This causes an enlargement of the epididymis. CAVD is sometimes associated with a genetic disorder where the man is also a carrier for the cystic fibrosis gene—a serious illness, causing progressive damage to the respiratory system and chronic digestive system problems. In the rare event when the female partner is also a carrier, the baby can also be born with cystic fibrosis.

Fertility treatment of CAVD involves obtaining the sperm from the epididymis by the technique of percutaneous epididymal sperm aspiration (PESA) (see p 132).

The ejaculatory ducts and their role in fertility

The obstruction of the ejaculatory ducts is an acquired or congenital pathological condition, in which one or both ejaculatory ducts are obstructed. In case both ejaculatory ducts are obstructed, there are symptoms of aspermia or azoospermia. Surgery to correct prostatic hypertrophy may destroy these ducts, resulting in retrograde ejaculation. Sometimes this obstruction can be tackled by opening the roof of these ducts using an endoscopic procedure. Absence of ejaculatory ducts can be treated by the techniques of PESA and TESA (see p 132).

The seminal vesicles and their role in fertility

The seminal vesicles are glands which produce fluid rich in fructose. Sometimes these glands may be absent from birth, resulting in the lack of fructose in the semen, and cause obstructive azoospermia. This condition can be treated by the techniques of PESA and TESA (see p 132).

The prostate gland and its role in fertility

Being alkaline, the prostatic fluid enhances fertility. The fluid flowing from the testes and the seminal vesicles is acidic, and sperm are not optimally motile unless their medium is relatively alkaline. The prostate gland is prone to acute and chronic infections, which can be painful. Prostatitis can result in bacteria and pus cells in both the urine and semen. Prostatitis can be caused by escherichia coli (E coli), enterococci, staphylococci, and sexually transmitted diseases (STDs) such as Ureaplasma urealyticum, Chlamydia trachomatis, and Mycoplasma hominis, contributing to male factor infertility.

With advancing age the prostate enlarges, a condition called prostatic hypertrophy. Sometimes the result of an enlarged prostrate is pressure on the urethra and the bladder, which interferes with urination, precipitating urinary retention and kidney disease. Benign prostatic hypertrophy (BPH) can be treated with medication (Finasteride) or with surgery. One must ensure that the prostatic enlargement is not cancerous.

Prostate cancer usually occurs in older men and often begins in the outer part of the prostate. It is a slow-growing tumour originating in the outer part of the posterior prostate gland. Sometimes it can originate in the prostate close to the urethra. It occurs due to hormonal, genetic, dietary, and environmental issues.

The cancer spreads by stimulation with testosterone. Inhalation or ingestion of chemicals such as cadmium—a mineral found naturally in certain foods, cigarette smoke, plastics, paints, nickel-cadmium batteries—increases the risk of developing prostate cancer. A diet high in animal fat has also been implicated in the increased risk of prostate cancer. After the age of forty it is important for men to check for the presence of increased blood levels of prostate-specific antigen (PSA), which is elevated in the presence of prostatic cancer.

Cowper's glands and their role in fertility

Cowper's glands decrease in size with advancing age, diminishing the lubricating effect of the pre-ejaculate. Cowper's glands also produce some amount of PSA, and

Cowper's tumours may increase PSA to a level that is suggestive of prostate cancer.

Stress and its role in fertility

Purnima and Mitesh were a young and dynamic couple. Mitesh was deeply committed to the stock market and, to a lesser extent, to his wife. His daily life was full of stress! When Rajesh evaluated them, he found Mitesh to be anxious and Purnima depressed.

On examining their medical records, Rajesh was intrigued by the enormous fluctuation in Mitesh's semen analysis reports. They went from a few thousand sperm to several million per millilitre in a matter of weeks, and then came down again. Rajesh pointed out to them that stress has a negative impact on sperm production. He gently enquired if the periods of low semen counts coincided with the stressful periods in Mitesh's life. He also commenced Purnima on antidepressant medication.

The following week, Mitesh came to Rajesh's office and barged in without an appointment exclaiming, 'Dr Parikh, you are a genius! Let me show you why.'

To Rajesh's amazement, Mitesh had plotted a graph covering the past two years of the Sensex in blue, his financial gains in green, and his semen counts in red! And lo and behold, the three graphs synchronized almost perfectly! In other words, when the Sensex went down, and the bullish Mitesh lost money, his semen count went down too. The one time his count was at its highest was during a holiday in Australia.

Rajesh phoned me and said, 'Firuza, this couple needs a vacation more than our treatment.' Sure enough, they went to New Zealand for a month and returned with a positive pregnancy test. But the story doesn't end there.

The day they received the pregnancy report, Mitesh came with a big cake for Rajesh. As usual, in his excitement, he wanted to barge into the office without an appointment. This time Rajesh firmly requested him to wait while he attended to his other patients. Suddenly Gita, Rajesh's secretary, called him and said, 'Sir, I think you should see him immediately. He is excitedly telling everybody that you got his wife pregnant!' Rajesh stepped out, hugged Mitesh, accepted his cake, and told everyone present, 'I did not, repeat, did not, make this man's wife pregnant. He alone is guilty of the act!'

Purnima and Mitesh are among the most grateful patients we have had. They have a lovely son and daughter, and every Diwali and Parsi New Year, they shower us with their blessings and gifts. Mitesh also regularly offers Rajesh stock market tips, which are always ignored—we love reading Pablo Neruda more than the pink pages of newspapers. The only bonus issues we know of are twins!

4

The Female Factor

- The female reproductive system
- The vagina and its role in fertility
- The cervix and its role in fertility
- The uterus and its role in fertility
- The fallopian tubes, the pelvis, and their role in fertility
- The ovaries and their role in fertility
- Other factors contributing to infertility
- Stress and its role in fertility

Infertility has traditionally been perceived as a woman's problem. However, recent research has shown that it is only in 40 to 45 percent of the cases, that the cause of infertility is due to factors in the female. These factors may lie along the route that the sperm traverses on its way to the ovum, or they may be due to imbalances in hormones. Let us take a quick overview of the female reproductive system.

The female reproductive system

The female reproductive system comprises of the external and the internal genitalia. The external genitalia or the vulva (see Figure 4.1 in the insert pages) consist of the mons veneris, labia majora and minora, clitoris, introitus, hymen, and Bartholin's glands.

The mons veneris is a fatty pad overlying the pelvic bone—the area which is barely covered by a bikini. The opening of the vagina has two folds of skin with fat called the labia (Latin for 'lips') majora. The labia majora have glands that secrete fluids for lubrication which facilitate sexual penetration. Nestled in the inner folds of the labia majora is a pair of skin folds called the labia minora. It is devoid of fat but has a few glands which also secrete a lubricating fluid. Furthermore, the labia minora provides a protective cover for the clitoris. The clitoris is a small, 2-centimetre long organ, rich in sensory nerve endings which are instrumental in causing excitement and pleasure.

The hymen is a fold of skin that covers the entrance to the vagina. It is usually a thin membrane but sometimes can be thick enough to require surgery in order to permit intercourse. Far too much nonsense has been written and believed about the hymen and, historically, perhaps, it is the most over-rated fold of skin in the female body.

The Bartholin's glands, on either side of the entrance to the vagina, secrete a mucous-like fluid that acts as a lubricant.

The internal genitalia (Figure 4.2 below and 4.3 in insert pages) consist of the vagina, uterus, two fallopian tubes, and ovaries.

The vagina is like a passage—upstream for the sperm, and downstream for the birth of the baby. It is a tubular, elastic, muscular structure that can increase from a diameter of 4 to 5 centimetres during the non-pregnant state, to almost 10 centimetres or more during the birth of a baby. The vagina has the cervix protruding into it before it reaches a blind end.

The cervix is a deep well containing natural secretions and mucous. These form slender tunnels, which facilitate the passage of the sperm. It is here that the sperm get

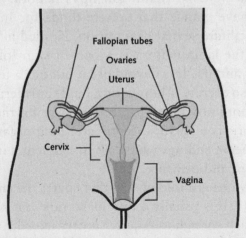

Figure 4.2 The female internal genitalia

'capacitated', that is, they obtain the ability to penetrate and fertilize the egg. They get this ability due to enzymes which change the chemicals present in the head of the sperm. These enzymes enable the sperm to actively recognize the ovum. The cervix has a small pin-point opening called the external os, leading into the uterus.

The uterus, in its normal state, is of the shape and size of a medium-sized pear. It is about 8 centimetres in length, 6 centimetres in breadth, and 4 centimetres in depth. It is about 75 percent of the size of a female fist and weighs about 50 grams. However, it can weigh up to 1.5 kilograms during the final stages of pregnancy, excluding the weight of the baby. In the pregnant state, it grows many-fold due to its highly elastic properties. The inner lining of the uterus is filled with blood vessels making it receptive to the implantation of the embryo. The process of implantation occurs as a result of a chemical reaction between the uterine bed and the embryo.

The two fallopian tubes are delicate, muscular structures. From one end to the other, they are about 10 centimetres each. Each tube has a trumpet-like outer end with many finger-like processes called fimbriae that engulf the ovum as it emerges from the ovary, at the time of ovulation. It is here that the sperm meets the egg and fertilization occurs. Once the embryo is formed, it makes its way into the uterus for its final housing over the next nine months. The muscles in the fallopian tubes contract to facilitate the movement of the embryo towards the uterus. The tubes also secrete fluids rich in nutrition, in order to nourish the embryo during its two-day journey to the uterus.

The ovaries are located close to the fallopian tubes, and

are about 8 grams in weight and 3.5 x 2.5 centimetres in dimension. The outer shell of the ovary is called the cortex, which houses follicles that contain ova in various stages of development. The inner core is the medulla—rich in blood vessels. Every month one egg is usually released from an ovary due to the coordinated activity between the pituitary gland and the ovary.

During childhood, the ovary is the size of an almond, which blooms to the size of a walnut during the reproductive years, and subsequently shrivels around the time of menopause.

The human egg is formed when the foetus is six weeks old and stays with the woman till ovulation or menopause. Unlike sperm, which are born every ninety days, eggs are not replenished. At birth, the eggs are called primary oocytes. A girl is born with one million to two million eggs in her ovaries. These are reduced to half a million by puberty. Only five hundred of these will have an opportunity to mature during a woman's active years and, with luck and a little help from her friends, very few will become babies. Cheer up and celebrate being alive. You truly are one in a billion if you also consider the humongous number of sperm that resulted in your existence.

Each cycle of activity of the ovary, lasts one lunar month. The cycle is divided into two phases—the follicular and the luteal phase—each of approximately fourteen days; the intervening event between these two phases being ovulation. The oocyte is housed in a fluid-filled space called the primordial follicle. It is here that the oocyte grows and the single layer of granulosa cells (cells present in the follicles of the ovary that surround the oocyte) multiplies into several layers (see Figure 4.4 in insert pages).

The enlarging oocyte secretes a protective coat called the zona pellucida. At the same time, the granulosa cells start secreting estrogen. As the granulosa cells multiply, they secrete an alkaline fluid called the liquor folliculi. The granulosa cells start projecting, at one point, into this fluid-filled cavity. This projection of cells is called the cumulus oophorus and the entire follicle is called the Graafian follicle. We will cover the importance of these cells when we discuss Cumulus Aided Transfer (CAT)—a technique that our team developed, which improves the chances of pregnancy.

The Graafian follicle continues to enlarge and produces an abundance of estrogen. This rise in estrogen triggers a rise in the LH from the pituitary gland, and this is called the LH peak, which heralds the process of ovulation. Just before ovulation the theca cells start producing progesterone in preparation for an ensuing pregnancy. The levels of progesterone peak following ovulation.

The ovaries act under the direction of the pituitary gland, which is located at the base of the brain. The pituitary gland secretes FSH in pulses or bursts, and with every pulse, the ovary produces estrogen.

Cut to Zubin Mehta. The pituitary gland is often called the conductor of the endocrine orchestra. I promise to give you a break from these pseudo-poetic medical expressions for some time! As the level of estrogen rises, many of the tiny follicles inside the ovary start developing. Eventually one of these gets selected for the process of ovulation. Soon the ovary receives pulses of LH. When the LH peaks, ovulation occurs and the ovary starts producing progesterone in preparation and anticipation of a pregnancy. If pregnancy does not occur, the uterus does not receive the signals of pregnancy and the uterine bed, or lining, sheds.

Ovulation is a gradual discharge of the ovum from the Graafian follicle. A thinning of the wall of this follicle helps the ovum to escape into the welcoming arms of the fimbriae of the fallopian tube. The fimbriae embrace the ovary in anticipation of the event. Imagine the process set to the music of *Thus Spake Zarathushtra* by Strauss, filmed in 70 mm by none other than Stanley Kubrick.

The theca cells within the follicle now multiply further and increase in size. This gives rise to wavy folds on the surface of the ovary forming the corpus luteum, which appears distinctly yellow, for it is loaded with cholesterol and carotene (the substance which gives colour to carrots). The cells continue to secrete progesterone in anticipation of fertilization and the implantation of the embryo in the uterine cavity.

If pregnancy does not occur, the corpus luteum will degenerate and the levels of estrogen and progesterone will fall. This will cause degeneration of the cells of the endometrium. This is the bleeding phase called menstruation. Our gynaecologic texts, in rare moments of lyricism, sometimes call menstruation, 'the weeping of an empty uterus'. My husband, Rajesh, in not so rare moments of humour, refers to it as the exuberant blush of a young woman discovering that she is not pregnant!

To recapitulate, the ovaries produce several hormones responsible for menstrual, reproductive, and endocrinal functions of the body. The two master female hormones— estrogen and progesterone—are produced in the ovaries. Estrogen is important for the proper growth and maturation of the eggs, whereas progesterone helps to maintain and nurture the pregnancy. Besides estrogen and progesterone, the ovaries also secrete small quantities of other hormones such as testosterone, relaxin, and inhibin. In women, testosterone provides a feeling of well being. Relaxin and inhibin are needed for the growth of the follicles.

The vagina and its role in fertility

Many women consider the secretions that gather in the vagina after intercourse to be unhygienic, and prefer to wash up or douche immediately after intercourse. This is not necessary and, in fact, should be avoided by those desirous of becoming pregnant, as it can kill the sperm. Sometimes a woman may produce copious amounts of thin mucous, which she may mistake for an infection. This kind of discharge is not abnormal and is seen just prior to ovulation.

Problems that can occur in the vagina

Vaginal infections

Conditions such as vaginitis (vaginal infections) can adversely affect the vaginal secretions, thereby inactivating or killing the sperm.

Vaginismus

Vaginismus is a condition of involuntary or voluntary contraction of the vaginal opening resulting in painful intercourse (dysparunia in Latin). In some cases, it can even prevent sexual intercourse and, hence, contribute to infertility.

Vaginal septum

Rarely, there may be a vaginal septum (Figure 4.5)—a division or partition in the vagina—causing a mechanical obstruction. A young couple once approached me saying

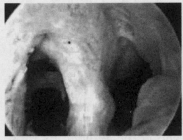

Figure 4.5 A vaginal septum

that intercourse was very painful for the husband. When I examined the wife, I noticed that there was a thick band of tissue in the vagina, which was practically blocking the entire vagina. We removed the vaginal septum and within two months the couple started enjoying regular sex. Six months later, she conceived naturally.

Absent vagina

Rarer yet is the condition called the 'absent vagina'. This may be associated with some other genetic defects, such as an absent uterus and ovaries and malformations of the kidneys. One such case was that of Manjri. Her mother started panicking when, at fifteen, she was the only one among her peers who still had not started menstruating. We asked for a sonography; the uterus was small and the tiny cervix ended abruptly. There was no connecting passage. Manjri had the condition of 'absent vagina'. Fortunately both ovaries were normal. We explained to the family that since Manjri had ovaries, but virtually no uterus or vagina, we could offer her a baby through surrogacy. I assured the family that once Manjri got married we could create an artificial vagina so that she could enjoy all the pleasures of a married life. Isn't that a quaint and marvellous euphemism!

The cervix and its role in fertility

The cervix (see Figure 4.6 in insert pages) is the mouth of the uterus. The glands in the cervix produce mucous, which facilitates the upward climb of the sperm. If the mucous is too thick, then the sperm get imprisoned. The cervical mucous may occasionally have antibodies which can immobilize the sperm. If the cervix is dry and shrunken, as in perimenopausal conditions, the sperm will find difficulty climbing up.

In the presence of an infection, the cervix secretes substances to counter the infection and inflammation. These could also inactivate and kill the sperm. The cervix may be very narrow and the external os—opening of the cervix, which leads to the uterus—may be a pin point with many blind ends, causing an obstruction to the passage of the sperm. If the cervix is very small, it may be fused with the vagina causing difficulty for the sperm to penetrate.

Problems that can occur in the cervix

Amputations

Operations of the cervix such as amputation of the cervix for cancerous and pre-cancerous conditions can cause a mechanical obstruction. Such an amputation may also destroy the mucous glands causing dryness and inability of the sperm to penetrate the cervix.

Floppy cervix

A floppy cervix is one that starts opening up prematurely during pregnancy. This condition is called incompetency of the cervix and can lead to repeated miscarriages.

The uterus and its role in fertility

The uterus changes its normal shape in many disease conditions. Failure of the embryo to implant may be due to the abnormal shape of the uterus (unicornuate, septate, subseptate) or due to an abnormal size of the uterus (uterine fibroids, adenomyosis, or a poor endometrial lining). Such abnormalities can also cause miscarriages. In India, one of the common reasons for a poor endometrial lining is genital TB. In 60 to 70 percent cases of genital TB, the uterus is affected.

Problems that can occur in the uterus

Uterine fibroids and polyps

Uterine fibroids or fibromyoma (see Figure 4.7 in insert pages) are growths which develop within the uterus. These are made up of fibrous tissue and muscle cells. Although they can range from a few millimetres to the size of a watermelon, or even bigger, they are usually harmless. They may be submucous (occurring close to the cavity of the uterus), intramural (within the normal muscle tissue of the uterus), subserous (close to the outer coat of the uterus), or pedunculated (hanging separately from the uterine wall). Very rarely, a fibroid may extend towards the boundaries of the pelvic wall as a broad ligament fibroid. These may or may not result in symptoms. It is believed that a hormonal imbalance in women with a predominance of estrogen can trigger the formation of fibroids. Recent research indicates that fibroids have a genetic basis.

Fibroids can result in symptoms such as frequent urination or difficulty in passing urine due to pressure.

There could be pressure on the rectum or in the lower abdomen. There may also be some back pressure and pain that might radiate to the legs.

Marissa noticed that she had to pass urine at frequent intervals. She took several courses of antibiotics without any relief. When the frequency increased to the point that it started disturbing her sleep three to four times in the night, she consulted me. Marissa wanted to have a baby and her history suggested that she probably had a mass which was growing fast enough to put pressure on the urinary bladder. When I conducted an internal examination, I could feel a distinct mass arising from the uterus. A sonography showed a large fibroid, the size of a grapefruit, between the urinary bladder and the uterus. This explained her frequent visits to the toilet. Removal of the fibroid gave her relief and set her on the path to motherhood.

Uterine polyps are ball-like growths of the glands, within the uterine cavity. They are usually the size of peas but sometimes can occupy the entire uterine cavity, thereby causing bleeding, obstruction, and irregularity of the uterine lining. These can prevent implantation of the embryo. Polyps usually develop due to hormonal imbalances, particularly in women who have high circulating estrogen and less progesterone. Polyps can be mistaken for submucous fibroids.

I underwent my third and final caesarean when our daughter Nikita was born at Yale. Having been given spinal anaesthesia, I was wide awake and could see Dr Mamta Bharucha's skillful hands getting ready to deliver my baby. But just then something caught my attention and I gasped loudly. I said, 'Hey, I can see two fibroids jutting out of the fundus. They were not there the last time around!' Their reflection was clear to me in the light reflector above the operating table. My husband murmured apologetically, 'Sometimes she forgets that she cannot be a gynaecologist all the time.' And then he affectionately added, 'Honey, right now you are a patient.' Everyone in the operation theatre had a good laugh.

The fallopian tubes, the pelvis, and their role in fertility

The fallopian tubes can get partially or completely blocked due to diseases such as TB, gonorrhoea, and chlamydial infections. Endometriosis is another condition that can cause adhesions to form, and lead to the blockage of the tubes.

Pelvic adhesions are one of the major causes of female infertility in India. Pelvic adhesions form between the uterus, fallopian tubes, ovaries, intestines, and the pelvic wall. These are abnormal strands of thin or thick tissue between the organs.

Some of the common causes for pelvic factor infertility are internal infection, endometriosis, surgery, and ectopic pregnancy. Infections can occur due to pelvic inflammatory disease (PID), caused by organisms such as the TB bacteria, chlamydia germs, and other bacteria.

Problems that can occur in the pelvis and the fallopian tubes

Genital TB
Genital TB is a widespread cause of uterine infection in India. In fact, cases of genital TB in India have been steadily on the rise. The World Health Organization

(WHO) estimates that each year there are two million new cases of TB in India. A large study by N.N. Choudhury, pointed out that in 92 percent of the cases, genital TB was secondary to TB in the lungs, lymph nodes, urinary tract, bones and joints. In India, pelvic tuberculosis is the major pelvic factor causing blocked tubes (see Figure 4.8 in insert pages). Women who have suffered from pelvic tuberculosis are more prone to ectopic pregnancy.

Women with genital TB may suffer from infertility, miscarriage, ectopic pregnancy, irregular bleeding, or decreased menstrual blood flow. However, the disease can also be without symptoms.

Ranjana had abdominal TB before she was married. She had taken the entire TB treatment and was declared completely cured at the end of it. But she could not understand why she still wasn't being able to conceive. Ranjana's laparoscopy results showed that her tubes were damaged and distended, and the ovaries were caught in adhesions with tubo-ovarian masses (TO masses). The only option for her was to disconnect the tubes from the uterus and have IVF or ICSI. She subsequently had twins.

Harini suffered from abdominal TB as a child. She had taken complete treatment for TB for nine months. When she did not conceive for four years, she and her husband, Abhijit, came to see me. Her sonography results showed that both tubes had hydrosalpinges—a condition commonly associated with pelvic TB, where the fimbriae get blocked, leading to the tube ballooning and getting dilated (see Figure 4.9 in insert pages). We performed a laparoscopy and found that both tubes were swollen with hydrosalpinges and were damaged beyond repair. Fortunately, the uterus was not affected. We explained to the couple that IVF would be the best solution to their problem. They plan to try becoming pregnant after a few months.

Our centre at Jaslok has been among those conducting pioneering international work in genital TB. In 1997, we published an article on genital TB among Indian women and how it decreases the chances of pregnancy, in the prestigious journal *Fertility and Sterility*. We have continued this work and our current data, on six hundred women afflicted with genital TB, shows that this disease is one of the major factors causing infertility in Indian women. Many women from affluent families look at me with utter disbelief when I make a diagnosis of genital TB. I assure them that the TB bacteria, unlike the doormen of five star hotels, do not respect wealth and social class.

Endometriosis

Imagine the pelvis to be lined by multiple miniature uteri and imagine them menstruating in unison. This is what happens in endometriosis. The tissue that resembles the inner lining of the uterus burrows its way and implants itself in various pelvic organs such as the ovaries, fallopian tubes, the space between the uterus and the intestines, or the uterosacrals—supporting ligaments of the uterus (see Figure 4.10 in insert pages). Rarely, it can affect the urinary bladder, the intestines, and the umbilicus.

Santoshi, now twenty-eight years old, suffered from endometriosis even before she was married. When I conducted an internal examination, I could feel the dense adhesions between her uterus and bowels. Even a light examination made her wince. I suspected that her endometriosis had worsened. My fears were confirmed when I performed a sonography on her. There was endometriosis in both the ovaries (chocolate cysts) and both tubes appeared dilated (hydrosalpinges). After a laparoscopy, I found that the bowels were completely adherent to the fallopian tubes. We drained almost 300 millilitres of chocolate-coloured fluid from both the ovaries, and cut the adhesions to finally free the bowel. Her endometriosis was graded as very severe (stage IV). In view of this, we suggested that she try ICSI. She is currently on medication to keep the endometriosis under control. We plan to perform ICSI soon.

Adhesions following surgery

Surya developed acute appendicitis at the age of twelve. She was operated and had a complicated recovery with fever persisting for more than fifteen days. When she did not conceive at twenty-five after three years of her marriage, Surya figured that something was wrong. On palpating her abdomen, I felt a distinct swelling in the area from where the appendix was removed. An internal bimanual examination revealed a fullness in her vagina. This usually occurs in the presence of a chronic inflammation. When we performed a laparoscopy on her, we found that the bowels were adherent to the tubes on both sides (see Figure 4.11 in insert pages). The past infection in the appendix had spread to the fallopian tubes, particularly the right one, which is usually in close proximity to the appendix. We cleared the adhesions and asked her to try becoming pregnant naturally. She did and recently delivered a healthy boy.

Complications from intrauterine contraceptive devices

Valerie had an intrauterine contraceptive device (IUCD) placed in the uterus after a medical abortion. In a few months, she noticed that her periods became scanty to the point that she hardly bled. When she removed the IUCD, the doctor informed her that she had developed scarring inside the uterus due to an infection that was triggered by the IUCD. The infection had tracked up along the threads of the IUCD and found residence inside the uterus. This scarring was successfully removed under hysteroscopic guidance. After several courses of estrogen therapy, she underwent IVF, which failed. Unfortunately, after four unsuccessful attempts, the couple is now contemplating surrogacy.

Ectopic pregnancy

An ectopic pregnancy can occur in various parts of the fallopian tube, the ovary, the abdomen, and the cervix. In any of these situations, the pregnancy does not usually survive, and requires removal before the foetus grows too large. In some circumstances, the doctor may use a chemotherapeutic agent called methotrexate to dissolve the pregnancy.

If the ectopic pregnancy shows signs of bursting or is too large (see Figure 4.12 in insert pages), then we prefer to perform a laparoscopy to remove the embryo.

Just as Sudha, a gynaecologist, entered the cinema hall, she felt a sharp, shooting pain through her back and on the right side of her abdomen. She had been experiencing cramps over the last five days and had attributed it to her delayed periods. Since she did not want to ruin the evening for her husband, she continued to bear the pain. However, during the intermission she went to the restroom and collapsed. Sudha was rushed to the hospital. An emergency sonography revealed that there was blood in the pelvis.

Her haemoglobin had dropped from a 12 to an 8 because she had lost about 2 litres of blood. She underwent an emergency laparoscopy. Her doctors found that the right fallopian tube had burst and was actively bleeding. It was removed and the bleeding was controlled. Sudha was pregnant but the baby was lodged in the wrong place—her right fallopian tube. Sudha recovered slowly after receiving two bottles of blood transfusion. She visited our centre and after completing blood tests and other investigations, the couple opted for adoption.

The ovaries and their role in fertility

Sometimes the ovaries suffer from either too little or too much in terms of functioning. They can also malfunction in the presence of tumours or infections. Obesity, too, can cause improper functioning of the ovaries and lead to infertility. In fact, it can lead to a vicious cycle of improper ovulation and weight gain.

Problems that can occur in the ovaries

Premature menopause: too little too soon

Fahmida was born in Srinagar and moved to Mumbai after getting married. She was eager to have a baby, and was excited when she missed her period. However, what troubled her was that she had hot flashes and severe dryness in the vagina. Three months into 'the pregnancy' she consulted me for a routine antenatal check. Her sonography results showed that the uterus was small and shrunken. The ovaries, too, could not be visualized. Fahmida had suddenly entered into a state of premature menopause, a condition that afflicts many young Kashmiri women. I conducted many counselling sessions with Fahmida.

The only option for this condition is IVF with donor eggs. The family opted not to undergo further treatment. After seeing many more such cases from Kashmir, we conducted a large study to show the high incidence of premature menopause in Kashmiri women, and have presented this work in international conferences.

When menopause occurs before the age of forty, it is considered to be premature. Premature ovarian failure afflicts a relatively small population of women. This may have a genetic origin. The shortening of a part of, or an absence of the X chromosome can be associated with this condition. Some autoimmune disorders make a woman prone to premature menopause. Women who have undergone multiple surgeries for endometriosis tend to have less number of eggs and can have a diminished ovarian reserve. Removal of one ovary and surgery on the remaining ovary may decrease the number of eggs significantly. Chemotherapy for various forms of cancer can cause menopause, as chemotherapy destroys the eggs.

Who has a diminished ovarian reserve?

As a woman approaches her forties, the number of eggs starts depleting. The cycle becomes anovulatory and the periods get irregular. Blood tests show that the level of FSH is above 8 iu/ml (normal range = 2 to 8 iu/ml). Such a condition may occur at a younger age as well in the presence of endometriosis, or past infection and adhesions.

Caumudi had just celebrated her thirty-second birthday.

Since the age of twenty-seven she had undergone three surgeries for recurrent endometriosis. After the last surgery, she noticed that her periods had become very irregular. I asked her to do an FSH and an Anti-Mullerian hormone (AMH) assay. Unfortunately the FSH was high and the AMH was low, indicating a poor ovarian reserve. The repeated surgeries for endometriosis had depleted her egg reserve and she was heading for premature menopause.

Sometimes diminished ovarian reserve, leading to premature menopause may be due to genetic or chromosomal reasons. Women facing irregular periods or approaching thirty-seven should be on the fast track to having a baby. Those who suffer from endometriosis, or have had repeated surgeries for cysts, are likely to reach menopause at an early age.

Polycystic ovaries

Roopa, currently in her twenties, finds it embarrassing to socialize. She has facial hair, which she waxes once in ten days, is overweight by 15 kilograms, is never sure when she is going to see her next period, and has slightly raised cholesterol levels.

She came to see me, as she plans to get married soon, and wanted to know if it would be easy for her to conceive.

After listening to Roopa's history, I was certain she had polycystic ovaries. I confirmed this when I examined Roopa after a sonography—her ovaries showed the 'necklace' appearance, characteristic of women having polycystic ovary syndrome (PCOS). Her hormones showed an increase in the LH as compared to the FSH, and also an increase in male hormones like testosterone. She also had slightly raised blood sugar levels. I explained to Roopa that she had a metabolic syndrome related to polycystic ovaries. She needed to lose weight through exercise and avoid any food with high carbohydrate content, such as chocolates, cakes, and soft drinks.

I put her on Metformin, which is an insulin-sensitizing agent. Since Roopa's periods were always irregular I added progesterone tablets to regularize her cycle. She promised to see me in three months time after losing about 8 kilograms. When she came to me after three months, she was 7 kilograms lighter than before. She looked happy and more confident.

This is not just Roopa's story. I see a considerable increase in the number of young girls suffering from polycystic ovaries. Various lifestyle related problems such as lack of exercise, eating fast food, and lack of sleep can further aggravate the condition of polycystic ovaries.

What does PCOS mean?

Although there may be a genetic or a familial origin to PCOS, one of the most common causes of PCOS is excessive insulin production by the pancreas. This in turn increases the secretion of LH and testosterone from the ovaries and causes anovulation—when ovulation does not take place. A woman with PCOS may put on weight and may have an excess of insulin and, paradoxically, an excess of sugar and fat in her body. While the estrogen keeps on accumulating in her body, there is a lack of progesterone.

Women with polycystic ovaries have many tiny cysts (Figure 4.13) in the ovaries. These are, essentially, follicles that have not ruptured at the time of ovulation and continue to form, over many period cycles. Consequently,

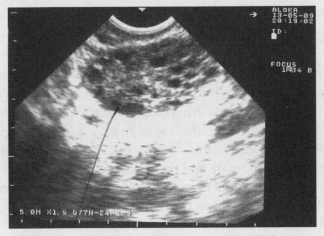

Figure 4.13 Ultrasonographic picture of multiple tiny
cysts in PCOS

the ovaries get bulky and have a pearly white appearance
filled with fluid.

What is masked PCOS?

Occasionally, a woman may not have the signs and
symptoms typical of PCOS. On sonography, the ovaries
may appear dormant, and it would appear that higher
doses of hormones may be required to stimulate the
ovaries. This is because the core of the ovary is very thick
and does not permit visualization of the multiple, tiny,
fluid-filled follicles. Such women are at the risk of ovarian
hyperstimulation, which is a potentially risky condition. In
ovarian hyperstimulation, fluid leaks out of the capillaries
of the body and collects in the lungs and the abdomen.

There may be decreased fluid in circulation leading to
a medical emergency.

Other factors contributing to infertility

Immunological and endocrinological issues

Numerous immunological and endocrinological diseases also contribute to infertility. A malfunction of any of the endocrine glands (thyroid, pituitary, pancreas, and adrenal) can disrupt the reproductive process. Figure 4.14 is a pictorial representation of the endocrine glands important to the male and the female reproductive system. The antibodies in men and women can affect themselves or their partners. These antibodies come in the way of egg and sperm function and fertilization.

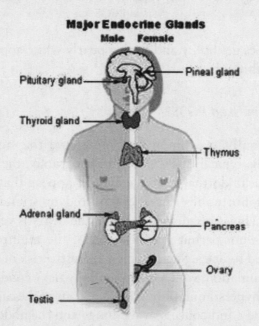

Major Endocrine Glands

Male   Female

Pineal gland

Pituitary gland

Thyroid gland

Thymus

Adrenal gland

Pancreas

Ovary

Testis

Figure 4.14 Some of the important endocrine
glands in the body

A simple but effective cure for infertility lies in the correction of a sluggish thyroid. Men and women living in the sub-Himalayan belt in Jammu and Kashmir, Himachal Pradesh, and Uttar Pradesh, in India, are known to suffer from thyroid hypofunction. The soil and water in this region is deficient in iodine—an essential element required for our well being. In the case of iodine deficiency the thyroid works overtime in order to remain functional. Because of this, it enlarges to form a swelling called a goitre. Adding iodized salt to the diet can correct the thyroid status. You may take this with a pinch of salt but it is a simple cure for endocrine related infertility.

Sudden weight loss or gain
Sudden loss of fat can shut down the pituitary and hypothalamic glands. It can also cause an absence of ovulation.

Manali, thirty years old, is an exercise freak. Her body fat percentage was 8 percent when she came to see me. She weighed 47 kilograms, but wanted to knock off another 3. She managed to lose these, but in the process lost her periods too. She had not had a period for seven months when I first met her. My examination of her revealed that she had small ovaries and her blood work showed a high prolactin level. On our urging, she began to to eat well, the periods resumed. She now plans to have a baby after six months.

Obesity is also associated with infertility. This can be due to increased deposition of fat in the peripheral tissues. Obesity is also associated with other disorders such as thyroid malfunction, insulin resistance, and increase in cholesterol, which in turn have an adverse impact on becoming pregnant.

Scientists at Brigham and Women's Hospital in Boston, USA found that severely obese women are far more likely to have abnormally arranged chromosomes in their eggs as compared to women who are not overweight. This may be due to higher levels of hormones like leptin, which make the chromosomes more fragile.

Stress and its role in fertility

Several studies have shown that stress decreases the count and quality of sperm in men, as well as the number and quality of ova in women. It can also cause early miscarriages.

I recall a couple who had tried several cycles of IVF with me. After their sixth failed attempt at IVF, I asked them if they would consider adopting a baby. Four months after their paperwork was processed, they came to my clinic to show me their bundle of joy. In passing, the lady mentioned that her periods had now become irregular, and that she could be entering menopause. I conducted a sonography and, to her disbelief, I showed her a tiny foetus with a prominent heartbeat cushioned and protected in her womb! After finally giving up the idea of a successful IVF, the couple adopted a baby and got rid of their stress. Their new stress-free situation helped them conceive naturally.

Our centre is recognized as a pioneering international body for its work on stress and reproductive failure. We have consistently shown that stress affects chances of becoming pregnant, and that reducing stress increases the chances of having a baby. We have presented this work in many conferences and published our research in several scientific journals. Twenty-five years ago, we were among the first centres in the world to offer psychological and psychiatric counselling as an integral part of assisted reproduction.

Among the most poignant and tragic stories that I have heard in my practice is that of Bhoomika, a lovely twenty-eight-year-old woman married to a thirty-year-old wealthy businessman. Bhoomika came, accompanied by her sister-in-law, to me in 1992. She had already undergone three IVF cycles by then, in India and abroad. This was the time prior to ICSI and there was little one could do for a couple with male factor infertility. Her husband's sperm count was below five million and I advised donor insemination. I was actually rather surprised that the couple had even undergone three IVF cycles when the odds were so overwhelmingly against them. 'You must understand where I come from, doctor. Donor insemination just cannot be considered. Please do not even mention it to my husband. He'll kill me,' Bhoomika had told me with tears in her eyes. Her sister-in-law nodded sympathetically.

Subsequently, I learnt from both of them that word was out in the family that Bhoomika was infertile and that the family was already considering a divorce and another marriage for her husband. These developments reached Bhoomika via her husband's brother, who would tell his wife, not realizing how close the two sisters-in-law were to each other. The oppressive customs within the family had brought the two women together.

Bhoomika's husband came to see me just once and I was immediately struck by his arrogance. I politely explained to him that there was very little I could do, and that, perhaps, they could wait for other developments in treating male infertility. In the meanwhile, I felt Rajesh could counsel Bhoomika, who was clearly going through clinical depression and was bordering on the suicidal. When I suggested this to Bhoomika's husband, he said to me, 'Why should we see a psychiatrist? There is nothing wrong with her other than her infertility. Do you send all your patients to your husband?' Eventually, he agreed to send Bhoomika but refused to accompany her, as he thought that there was nothing wrong with him.

Bhoomika connected so well with Rajesh that she shared her dark secrets with him and consented that he share them with me. For the past four months, her sister-in-law had arranged liaisons with half a dozen different men, two of them complete strangers, in the hope that Bhoomika gets pregnant and ends her misery. They called it off because one of the men started pursuing Bhoomika and she was terrified. In an attempt to cheer her up, her sister-in-law once joked that this must be more fun than undergoing insemination at a doctor's office. Bhoomika told Rajesh, 'Perhaps you, too, think it was fun. What you should know is that having sex with a man you do not love is worse than death. I have died a hundred deaths with my husband, and it has been worse with strangers. But I am moving on.'

When she filed for divorce, the family tried to placate her with everything including agreeing for donor insemination, but finally consented to a fair financial settlement. Rajesh and I attended Bhoomika's second wedding. She conceived in the third month. Her husband knows her entire story and loves her even more for her honesty, her endurance, and her strength of character.

The past twenty-five years of practice have been like

watching Tolstoy, Shakespeare, Cervantes, Pushkin, Maugham, and Tagore come alive for Rajesh and I. We are truly privileged to witness tales of human endurance and heroism. Treating patients is never a one-way process. Our patients teach us and inspire us too.

5

Treating Male Factor Infertility

- Azoospermia (no sperm)
- Oligospermia (very low sperm count)
- Asthenospermia (low sperm motility)
- Abnormal morphology
- Oligoasthenoteratospermia (low count, motility, and morphology)
- Pre-implantation genetic diagnosis (PGD)

Sushil and Shantamma were seeking infertility treatment. Sushil was hesitant to subject himself to a semen analysis. His argument was that he was fertile as he had already had a thirteen-year-old son from his first marriage. Three years into the second marriage, they were keen to have a baby. It took considerable persuasion to get Sushil to agree to a routine semen analysis. Much to his surprise the result of his report was that Sushil had azoospermia. He had undergone surgery for a hydrocele—swelling of the sac surrounding the testes—three years ago, which had caused blockage of the vas deferens, obstructing the flow of semen.

The best solution for this was intra cytoplasmic sperm injection (ICSI) . At the time of ICSI the sperm were obtained directly from the testes by testicular sperm aspiration (TESA). The couple soon had a baby boy.

Vishwas wanted to see me without his wife, Vibhuti, as he was embarrassed to discuss his situation in her presence. He felt that the volume of his semen was the cause of their infertility. He observed that when they had sex, the volume of his ejaculate was less, and he thought that this reflected on his potency. I assured him that this was not so. I suggested he undergo intrauterine insemination (IUI) to circumvent this problem. Vibhuti conceived in the third cycle of IVF.

Table 5.1 sums up the abnormalities in the semen.

Azoospermia (no sperm)

There are several causes of azoospermia. Either the sperm are not being produced (non-obstructive azoospermia)

Table 5.1: Abnormal Semen: Volume, Colour, Content

Volume

Problem	Causes	Treatment
less volume	frequent ejaculation	no treatment unless the counts are low, in which case abstinence of three days may improve counts.
	chronic infection of the prostate (Prostatitis), vas aplasia blockage of sperm ducts, retrograde ejaculation, drugs such as Finasteride (for prostate enlargement), marijuana, alcohol, advancing age (more than forty-five years)	antibiotics, anti-inflammatory agents PESA/TESA + ICSI TESA with ICSI stop drug abuse —
excessive volume (more than 5 millilitres)	abstinence for a long duration acute infection	frequent ejaculation antibiotics

Colour

Problem	Causes	Treatment
reddish/grey	infection/increased pus cells	antibiotics

Content

Problem	Causes	Treatment
high sugar	diabetes	control of diabetes

or if they are produced, they are unable to be discharged (obstructive azoospermia).

Childhood infection with mumps can lead to destruction of the cells producing sperm and cause azoospermia. Several genetic conditions and chromosomal abnormalities can also result in azoospermia. Some of the common genetic conditions are Y-chromosome microdeletions or abnormalities in the arrangement of chromosomes such as 46 XXY, also known as Klinefelter's syndrome. Germ-cell aplasia or Sertoli-cell only syndrome (SCO) is a rare condition which mostly has a genetic basis causing azoospermia.

Oligospermia (very low sperm counts)

Most of the conditions that cause azoospermia can also cause oligospermia.

Treatment options

1. Medical approach

Men with oligospermia, and low FSH and LH, may be prescribed Clomiphene Citrate in small doses of 25 milligrams per day, for twenty-five days, with a break of five days over three to six cycles. Some men who do not have enough stimulation of the testes with FSH and LH may respond temporarily during which time it is worthwhile to add other treatment options such as IUI and ICSI.

Tablets of Mesterolone, taken over a few months, can improve sperm counts. Testosterone injections do not help and, in fact, may cause azoospermia. Certain dietary and lifestyle changes, such as taking vitamins, minerals such as zinc and manganese, enzymes such as Coenzyme Q, antioxidants such as Arginine, Lycopene, and Carotenoids have been prescribed but these are more helpful to improve the vitality rather than the count of the sperm. The deleterious effect of smoking on the count, motility, and vitality of the sperm is well known. The faster the smoking ceases, the sooner it is possible to have a baby.

2. Surgical approach

Occasionally, there may be blocks in the vas deferens due to past infections such as filariasis, TB, or other infections. These are sometimes amenable to microsurgery. Men who have undergone vasectomy as a method of family planning can resort to reopening of the vas by a microsurgical technique. Varicocele ligation may help if the low count, motility, and poor sperm morphology are due to a varicocele—a condition where varicose veins develop in the spermatic cords.

3. ART approach

Most of the conditions that cause azoospermia can also cause oligospermia. It is important for men with low sperm counts to freeze their semen as biological insurance. Men with low counts may, over the years, develop azoospermia.

If the count is borderline, ranging between 10 million/millilitre and 20 million/millilitre, with satisfactory motility of at least 30 percent, it may be worthwhile to consider IUI before attempting IVF/ICSI. This is more so if the woman is young and the other parameters, such as motility and morphology, are not compromised. After four to five unsuccessful attempts of IUI, we consider IVF/ICSI/IMSI.

Time is of essence with diminishing sperm counts, or if several reports show counts varying between 0.1 million and 10 million per ml.

I was once faced with an unusual situation where three brothers and a cousin had azoospermia. The urologist had diagnosed the condition of obstructive azoospermia due to congenital absence of vas deferens (CAVD). We suggested all of them to conduct ICSI, using sperm obtained from the epididymis, with the technique of percutaneous epididymal sperm aspiration (PESA). Since the cousin's wife was already over forty, they opted for adoption. The other three brothers tried ICSI. Ultimately two of the couples were blessed with children. In both cases, the wives delivered twins. The last couple did not conceive and chose to adopt instead. They too are happy.

Viral Patel was unusually tall. He came to our centre with his wife, Rachna, as they had been childless for over three years. Viral had small testes. We performed a chromosomal analysis, and the results concluded that Viral had Klinefelter's syndrome (see p 75)—a condition best treated by using donor sperm.

On rare occasions, there may be severe oligospermia, in which case ICSI may be conducted. However, the chances of miscarriage with this condition are very high. In order to prevent the baby from having abnormal chromosomes, we can conduct genetic testing of the embryos by pre-implantation genetic diagnosis (PGD), so that those embryos with a normal chromosomal structure, may be transferred. Sperm may occasionally be obtained by TESA, and ICSI may help too. But most of the time, the use of donor sperm may be the only option. Rachna and Viral are now undergoing treatment.

Asthenospermia (low sperm motility)

Low sperm motility is a leading cause of male factor infertility. Low motility may be caused by infection, varicocele, wearing tight underwear, having very hot showers, or may have an unknown cause. Oligospermia and asthenospermia are most prevalent and may suggest problems related to the formation and production of sperm (spermatogenesis). Many factors which contribute to oligospermia can also contribute to low sperm motility.

Treatment options

1. Medical approach

Men with low sperm motility should not wear tight underwear or have hot showers. A significant improvement in sperm motility is observed in some men, when they discontinue these practises. Several antioxidants and supplements such as Vitamin Q, Arginine, Lycopene, Zinc, and Magnesium have been suggested. Tablets of essential fatty acids, such as eicosapentaenoic acid (EPA) and docosahexaenoic acid (DHA), taken over a few months have shown improvement in some men. Vital to the treatment is eliminating smoke in the lungs, heat in the testes, free radicals in the blood, and stress in the mind, and replacing these with oxygen, frequent ejaculation, antioxidants in the blood, and happiness in one's being.

2. Surgical approach

Occasionally, the sperm motility will show an upward swing following the repair of a varicocele. It may then be appropriate to combine the treatment with IUI.

3. ART approach

The laboratory has a significant role to play in the preparation of good quality sperm. Depending on the type of sluggishness of the sperm, the sample is processed with percoll density gradient separation, and swim-up or swim-down techniques (see pp 125–6).

IUI can work if, at least 30 percent of the sperm show forward motility. If the sperm move sluggishly, then the only way is to move on to IVF/ICSI. IVF is usually skipped and ICSI is preferred when there is a low count and motility.

Abnormal morphology

A normal sperm is depicted in Figure 3.2 (see p 28). To pass the quality control check of nature, at least 14 percent have to be of normal shape. This is called passing Kruger's strict criteria test.

Sometimes the tail of the sperm is short, absent, double, bent, curled, or coiled. The neck sometimes gets bent and does not come back to its normal position. The head is oval but, under environmental stress, becomes tapering. With diabetes, the head turns abnormally large and the tail coils up (Figure 5.1).

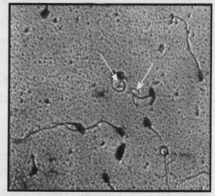

Figure 5.1 Microscopic photograph of sperm showing coiled tails in diabetes

Treatment options

1. Medical approach

Antioxidants may help men with diabetes (who have abnormal sperm morphology). They may gradually show significant improvement in sperm configuration, when their diabetic status improves.

2. Surgical approach

Varicocele surgery may help if this condition accompanies asthenospermia.

3. ART approach

If more than 14 percent of the sperm are of an abnormal shape, ICSI/IMSI (see pp 129–36) offers better chances at pregnancy. IMSI is particularly useful in such conditions as the sperm, to be selected for injection into the egg, is enlarged seven thousand times, ensuring the injection of a normal looking sperm.

Lajvanti and Naresh were trying to have a baby for five years before they consulted me for a problem that had just begun. Naresh had lost interest in sex and had difficulty in maintaining an erection. He had recently taken up a new assignment, which meant longer hours, fast food, sleepless nights, and plenty of air travel. I requested a blood sugar analysis. Naresh was grossly diabetic. His semen analysis showed a large number of abnormal-looking sperm, typical of men with diabetes. He was immediately put on insulin, diet control, and exercise. We are waiting for his sugar level to come down to normal before initiating treatment for infertility. It took almost eight months before we could initiate treatment. They conceived following IUI.

Oligoasthenoteratospermia (low count, motility, and morphology)

If all three factors are present then ICSI/IMSI are the best options. PGD may be offered additionally. In case the treatment does not result in success, donor sperm insemination can be offered.

Pre-implantation genetic diagnosis (PGD)

Repeated failed attempts at ICSI/IMSI

If more than three cycles of ICSI/IMSI have not succeeded, then we may consider PGD. If tests of sperm function, such as sperm apoptosis (see p 240) show that the fertilizing potential is not satisfactory, it may be worthwhile to defer treatment for some time. Treatment can be continued later with antioxidants and/or donor sperm insemination.

Many of the problems associated with male factor infertility may be mitigated through dietary and lifestyle changes—taking vitamins, supplements, and quitting smoking. It may help to alter the frequency of sex. Men faced with severe male factor infertility are offered the ART options of IUI, IVF, ICSI, IMSI, and donor sperm.

The treatment of male infertility has seen dramatic

and rapid advances in the past couple of decades. We have come a long way from the time that infertility was seen, exclusively, as a female problem to today's array of technological interventions for male factor infertility.

6

Treating Female Factor Infertility

- Vaginal conditions
- Cervical conditions
- Uterine conditions
- Pelvic conditions
- Polycystic ovary syndrome (PCOS)
- Premature menopause
- Ovarian cysts
- Immunological factors
- Endocrine factors
- Genetic factors

Urmila had an unduly prolonged labour, which resulted in a forceps delivery. During the procedure, she sustained a tear in her vagina which did not heal perfectly. After the delivery, Urmila and Rakesh stopped having intercourse as she experienced a sudden tightening of the vagina at the time of penetration. Urmila had developed vaginismus due to the scarring. Vaginismus is the involuntary contractions of the muscles surrounding the vagina during sexual intercourse. A minor procedure to remove the scarred tissue helped her recover completely.

Ishwari had considerable guilt as she had had premarital sex with a college friend. She entered into an arranged marriage and found difficulty with intercourse on her wedding night. She needed several sessions of counselling to help her get over her guilt. Soon after, she conceived naturally.

The treatment options for female factor infertility can range from medical and surgical interventions to counselling . Every one of them should be preceded by a detailed patient history, as sometimes the simplest solutions are right before us while we are searching for more complex answers.

Vaginal conditions

Vaginitis due to infections and inflammation

Vaginitis can be caused by bacterial and yeast infections. The most common organism is candida albicans (yeast). Women are more prone to yeast infection just before their period, in the premenopausal phase, and following surgical procedures on the vagina. Vaginal infections can also be transmitted through sexual intercourse.

Tripura had a dull ache in the vagina a few days after sex. This would drag on for a couple of days more and would be accompanied by a light vaginal discharge and itching. It would prevent her from having sex for the next week or so. Her husband would also complain of a burning sensation while urinating. As a result of this, their coital frequency was hardly two or three times a month, and they always seemed to be missing the fertile days. When I examined her, I noticed a thick white discharge, which turned out to be a yeast infection. Both partners were treated with antifungal medication and were soon free of symptoms. However, Tripura's symptoms reappeared after four months, but she was cured with another course of the medicine. This time we were able to treat not just her infection, but the couple's infertility as well since she conceived soon after.

Sometimes a vaginal inflammation is not due to an infection but a thinning of the vaginal lining, because of dryness. This occurs because of decreased circulating estrogen in the body, and is seen frequently in women approaching menopause.

Douching is usually associated with personal hygiene. However, when women douche often, the natural secretions of the vagina dry up, increasing the possibility of acquiring an infection.

Around the time of their menstrual periods, women may experience vaginal inflammation due to acid changes in the vagina. This can be relieved with the help of hydrating gels and probiotic tablets. Occasionally, estrogen replacement may help.

Mechanical obstruction in the vagina, such as a thick hymen, or a vaginal septum can cause pain and discomfort as there is an obstruction at the opening of the vagina, and can even prevent sexual penetration. Ruksar could not imagine how sex could ever be enjoyable. The very act of attempting vaginal penetration made her husband Alim, lose his erection, as she would have severe pain. On examination, we found that her hymen was very thick, and a minor procedure helped to resolve the problem.

Table 6.1 summarizes the causes and the treatment of various vaginal conditions.

Table 6.1: Vaginal Conditions: Causes and Treatment

Problem	Causes	Treatment
vaginitis	• infection with bacteria or yeast	• local/systemic antibiotics and antifungal agents • to improve gavinal flora using probiotic capsules containing lactobacillus
inflammatory	• less circulating estrogen resulting in dryness due to menopause	• estrogen replacement • hydrating gel
	• repeated douching • acidic changes around the menstrual period	• stop douching • hydrating gels • estrogen replacement • probiotic tables
vaginismus	• recent surgery	• anti-inflammatory drugs
	• infection	• local and systemic antibiotics/ antifungal agents

Contd...

Table 6.1: Contd....

Problem	Causes	Treatment
mechanical obstruction	• psychological • thick hymen • vaginal septum	• counselling • hymenectomy • septoplasty

Cervical conditions

The cervix forms the important passage, where the sperm get 'capacitated', that is they obtain the ability to penetrate and fertilize the egg. The cervical mucous plays an important role in facilitating this process. If the mucous is too thick, the sperm get imprisoned and cannot find a way out. Antibodies in the cervical mucous may immobilize the sperm. In the absence of estrogen secretion, or in the presence of infection, cervical mucous is not produced, or it may turn hostile to the sperm.

Cervicitis may be due to an infection or due to inflammation. Bacteria, as well as yeast, can cause cervicitis. This can be treated with antibiotics or antifungal agents. Inflammation of the cervix can be due to cervical antibodies causing hostility to the sperm. Sometimes the inner lining of the cervix can protrude out (eversion) and this can cause discharge and inflammation. This is sometimes treated by cauterizing the exposed part of the cervix, and can be improved with the help of antibiotics. The doctor may suggest IUI if the cervix remains hostile, as this method would bypass the cervix. Table 6.2 summarizes the causes and the treatment of various cervical conditions.

Table 6.2: Cervical Conditions: Causes and Treatment

Problem	Causes	Treatment
cervicitis	infection with bacteria and/or yeast	systemic or local antibiotics and antifungal agents
inflammatory cervicitis	hostility of the cervix due to antibodies	hydrating gels
	eversion of the cervix following intercourse	cauterization or probiotic capsules
increased mucous production where the mucous is clear and watery	hyperestrogenic status during ovarian stimulation	no treatment required
increased mucous production where the mucous is thick and malodorous	fungal and/or bacterial infection	antibiotics and antifungal creams/tablets

Uterine conditions

The uterus is shaped like an inverted pear; thicker at its upper part and tapering towards the cervix. A unicornuate uterus—having only one horn (see Figure 6.1 in insert pages) has decreased volume and hence can cause problems with implantation, resulting in miscarriages. The volume of the uterus can be increased marginally with the use of estrogen and progesterone tablets over a few months. In some situations, surrogacy may be the better option. A T-shaped uterus (see Figure 6.2 in insert pages) has diminished volume in the lower part. It can be associated with a decreased ability to implant, and miscarriages.

A surgical procedure known as lateral metroplasty helps to increase the volume of the uterus and broaden its walls. During a lateral metroplasty, a cautery is used along with a hysteroscope, and slit-like incisions are made in the lateral walls of the uterus thus expanding its volume (see Figure 6.3 in insert pages).

A bicornuate uterus occurs when the two uterine horns remain separated in the foetus and do not fuse (see Figure 6.4 in insert pages). Often a bicornuate uterus may remain asymptomatic but in some cases it can cause infertility and miscarriages. Occasionally, only one of the two horns may develop, and one may remain rudimentary and cause infertility.

Bindu had a history of four miscarriages. She came to me with a diagnosis of a bicornuate uterus. In such a situation, an open surgery is usually performed, to unite the two horns. Dr Neeta Warty performed this procedure via laparoscopy. The partition between the two horns was cut and the two horns were united using sutures. We asked Bindu to not conceive for four months to allow the healing of the uterine wall. Bindu conceived seven months after the surgery. Our work on laparascopic unification of a bicornuate uterus has been presented in several conferences.

A small uterus may cause problems with implantation. If the uterus is small in all dimensions, its size can be improved with estrogen progesterone replacement therapy. In cases of amenorrhoea (absent periods) due to pituitary dysfunction, the uterus responds by increasing its size under the influence of gonadotrophin injections. On the other hand, the uterus may be abnormally enlarged due to adenomyosis. The condition of advanced adenomyosis requires surrogacy, as the chances of conceiving are low and the chances of miscarriages increase.

The passage of the uterus may be blocked by the presence of a septum (see Figure 6.5 in insert pages), which may be complete or partial. A septum can cause infertility by decreasing the blood supply to the uterus or can cause an obstruction to implantation and to the normal growth of a pregnancy, leading to miscarriage.

Sunita and Mahesh were terrified to try and conceive again. Sunita had miscarried seven times. They had stopped having sex lest she got pregnant again. We found a very thick septum in the uterus on examination. We resected this by hysteroscopy. She conceived spontaneously and delivered a healthy baby girl at term.

It is often believed that a retroverted uterus or a backwardly tilted uterus causes infertility and miscarriage. However, if it is not fixed in the retroverted position, it does not impact fertility.

Uterine fibroids

The uterus often contains benign growths known as fibroids. The treatment of fibroids depends upon their size, number, position, rapidity of growth, and the likelihood of their causing infertility. Small fibroids do not interfere with fertility; however, large ones can cause mechanical obstruction. If they have other symptoms such as pressure symptoms and bleeding, those need to be treated along with infertility. Rarely do they turn cancerous.

Large fibroids can reach the size of a watermelon or

even larger. A single, symptomless fibroid can be ignored. Multiple fibroids can increase the bulk of the uterus and contribute to infertility.

Naval who was married for four years and was trying to get pregnant since then, started complaining of severe pressure in the pelvic area. Her examination showed the presence of multiple fibroids. The entire uterus was studded with fibroids, and the uterus itself reached the insertion of the breastbone. She underwent laparoscopic removal of thirty-three fibroids. Three months after the laparoscopy, the uterus had come back to normal shape and size. We are now planning IVF for her.

Submucous fibroids (see p 52) can occupy the entire uterine cavity, causing infertility, along with irregular and heavy bleeding. These may need surgical intervention.

Intramural and subserous fibroids add to the bulkiness of the uterus, and can cause prolonged bleeding and infertility (see Figure 6.6 in insert pages).

Fibroids close to the fallopian tubes can cause mechanical blockage of the tubes. Submucous fibroids can cause occlusion, and intramural fibroids can cause impingement of the uterine cavity. Such fibroids can be removed laparoscopically without damaging other structures.

Unless the fibroids are a direct cause of infertility, or cause other symptoms, they can often be left untreated. More often than not, they are harmless objects rather than the explosives they are hysterically made out to be. Fun fact: the words uterus, hysterical, and hysteroscope share the same Latin root 'hysteros'! In select cases, the gynaecologist may suggest taking injections of Gonadotrophin releasing hormone (GnRH) agonist analogue depot, in order to reduce the size of the fibroids.

When surgical intervention is required, most fibroids can be removed by the laparoscopic approach. Occasionally, a subserous fibroid can undergo torsion, or a twist, resulting in pain, and require urgent removal. I was once woken up late at night by Sharan who had undergone IVF and was three months pregnant. She had felt an excruciating pain and had several bouts of vomiting. We rushed her to the hospital. Her examination revealed that she had a pedunculated fibroid (see p 52) which had got twisted. It was removed laparoscopically with minimal blood loss. She was discharged from the hospital the next day and delivered a baby boy six months later.

A polyp is a benign growth in the uterine cavity. It is made up of uterine glands, which grow into a clump under the action of estrogen, forming a ball-like structure within the uterine cavity (see Figure 6.7 in insert pages). If they occlude the uterine cavity, they may contribute to infertility.

Ritika was trying to get pregnant for four years. Her periods had become very heavy in the past year. She had also noticed spotting in between her periods. A transvaginal sonography revealed a large polyp inside her uterine cavity. This was removed easily by hysteroscopy (see Figure 6.8 in insert pages). She conceived within four months.

Uterine transplant from mother to daughter

This pioneering procedure is the latest in the string of fertility feats that has already produced a pregnancy. In September 2012, Swedish doctors successfully transplanted a uterus from mother to daughter, raising hope for women without wombs who want to carry their own babies.

This procedure gives hope to women who have lost

their fertility due to uterine and cervical diseases such as TB and cancer. However the procedure requires life-long support with anti-rejection medicines.

A Turkish team at Akderiz University have announced in May 2013 the first successful pregnancy after uterine transplantation. Mrs. Derya Sert, a 22 year old woman became the first successful recipient. At the time of reporting in May 2013, the pregnancy was at 6 weeks gestation! Unfortunately, she miscarried at 8 weeks but plans to try again soon.

Pelvic conditions

Some of the common causes of blockage of the fallopian tubes and pelvic adhesions are genital TB, endometriosis, past surgery, and pelvic inflammatory diseases (PID) caused by gonorrhea, chlamydia, and other bacteria.

Genital TB may be present with symptoms of infertility, miscarriage, ectopic pregnancy, irregular bleeding, and decreased menstrual blood flow, or it may be symptomless. Thus, the very first symptom of genital TB may be infertility and one has to be sensitive in discussing this with someone suspected of suffering from it.

The medical treatment of genital TB involves taking a multidrug anti-TB course for eight to nine months along with vitamin supplements. A close watch is kept on the liver, kidney, and retinal function during the treatment. While on the treatment, some women develop fibrosis of the uterine cavity. Hence, it is imperative to do pelvic sonography frequently to assess the uterine cavity and add estrogen tablets to prevent fibrosis. Microsurgery for tubal blockage has virtually no role when the blockage is due to genital TB. This is because the tubes are usually damaged beyond repair and trying to open the tubes can cause the occurrence of an ectopic pregnancy. Surgical intervention may be required when there are severe adhesions between the tubes and the ovaries, causing tubo-ovarian (TO) masses. Severe intestinal adhesions may require surgery.

The fallopian tubes are open at both ends. If their connection to the uterus is blocked, it results in a condition called a cornual block. If the distal end of the tube is blocked, secretions collect within the fallopian tubes. Since the fimbrial part of the tube has thin, distensible walls, the tube continues to bloat like a balloon and is known as a hydrosalpinx (see Figure 6.9 in insert pages). Such a tube is unhealthy and can cause infection, inflammation, and ectopic pregnancy, and needs to be surgically removed. Women suffering from genital TB and having hydrosalpinges are usually advised to have a salpingectomy or delinking (see Figure 6.10 in insert pages) of their tubes prior to doing IVF/ICSI. This improves the chances of conception and prevents the risk of an ectopic pregnancy.

Several studies have pointed out that chances of pregnancy are halved in the presence of hydrosalpinges, and the rates of miscarriages and ectopic pregnancies increase. Besides, the larger the hydrosalpinx, the worse is the prognosis for the pregnancy.

Ipshita's hysterosalpingogram (HSG) showed both tubes filled with pockets of retained fluid following a past infection with genital TB. Her gynaecologist had performed a laparoscopic salpingostomy to open up the fallopian tubes. Ipshita was asked to try conceiving naturally for six months. She conceived in the second month but the pregnancy grew in the left fallopian tube (see Figure 6.11 in insert pages). The incidence of ectopic pregnancy is significantly increased in women suffering from genital TB.

Neeta, who is thirty years old recently consulted me after having suffered from three ectopic pregnancies. Much to my dismay, Neeta refused to have a delinking of the fallopian tubes to prevent a fourth ectopic pregnancy. Neeta did not come back to see me. She consulted someone else who acceded to her demand. Unfortunately, she came back to us with another ectopic pregnancy. She agreed to delink her tubes after the successful termination of the ectopic pregnancy, and became pregnant following IVF.

Sometimes the tubal ectopic pregnancy can be treated by injections of Methotrexate, if the pregnancy is small. However, if the ectopic pregnancy is large, or if the tube is about to rupture, a laparoscopy or laparotomy may be required.

An ectopic pregnancy can rarely implant on the cervix (see Figure 6.12 in insert pages) or the ovary. Both are potentially dangerous conditions and need immediate attention.

Endometriosis (see pp 56–7) is another major pelvic contributor to infertility. Medical, surgical, ART treatment, or a combination of these may be suggested in the presence of infertility.

Since endometriosis is aggravated by stimulation of the ovaries, its cure would necessitate suppressing them. It can be controlled either by creating an environment similar to menopause or to the pregnant state. The use of progesterone is another option.

Medroxyprogesterone is administered over a period of three to six months. The other medication used is GnRH agonist analogue, which creates a menopause-like state. It is used as a depot preparation to be used monthly for three to four injections. This must be supplemented with calcium to prevent osteopenia—decreased calcium in the bones. Birth control pills can be used over three to six months to keep the endometriosis under control.

Sometimes medication alone is not enough to cure endometriosis and surgical intervention may be required. The best surgical approach is by laparoscopy. The adhesions can be dissected, and the cysts drained. The areas of endometriosis are fulgurated (cauterized by an electric current), and the relationship between the ovaries and the tubes is restored. Women with endometriosis complain of severe pain during their periods (dysmenorrhea) and also during intercourse (dysparuenia). A procedure of presacral neurectomy can free the woman of this pain. The nerves giving the pain sensation are arranged in a bundle in front of the tail bone. In this procedure, the pain causing nerve fibres are disconnected from the uterus. The doctor may also perform a simultaneous dilatation of the cervix to relieve the dysmenorrhea.

IVF/ICSI may be indicated, either after medical and surgical treatment, or may be carried out directly, depending on the severity of the disease. Severe endometriosis and surgery on the ovaries may compromise the number of eggs present in the ovary. Hence, women with long-standing endometriosis may produce very few eggs and may have to resort to using donor eggs. We include the procedures of Cumulus Aided Transfer (CAT) and Laser Assisted Hatching (LAH) (see p 136) in these women, in order to improve implantation rates.

Adhesions following surgery

If the adhesions are mild, a laparoscopy and/or a hysteroscopy will help. If the pelvic condition is irreversible, IVF/ICSI can be done directly. Uterine adhesions (see Figure 6.13 in insert pages) can be treated with removal by hysteroscopy. However, sometimes these adhesions may recur and the only recourse then, may be to consider surrogacy.

Polycystic ovary syndrome (PCOS)

As the name suggests, in this condition, the ovaries have multiple tiny cysts, which form because of lack of ovulation, due to an imbalance of the hormones FSH and LH. The ovaries are large and appear pearly white. A sonography will show multiple cysts arranged along the margin of the ovaries, giving it an appearance of a necklace (see Figure 6.14 in insert pages).

Typically, the patient has irregular and heavy periods. There may be other metabolic problems such as diabetes and high cholesterol. Excess of male hormones may result in excessive facial and body hair and acne.

Table 6.3 encapsulates some of the common concerns regarding PCOS:

Table 6.3 Common concerns regarding PCOS

Frequently asked questions	Answer
Is PCOS treatable?	Yes.
Can women with PCOS conceive naturally?	Yes, but they can face difficulty more often than not.

Contd..

Table 6.3 Contd...

Frequently asked questions	Answer
Can women with PCOS have regular periods?	Yes, if they exercise and maintain a healthy diet. They may need medicines such as progesterone.
How is the infertile woman with PCOS treated?	With lifestyle modulation, medication, laparoscopic electrocauterization of the ovarian surface (LEOS)/ART.
What can be done about the rapid weight gain in women with PCOS?	Regular exercise, healthy diet, keeping blood sugar under control, and ensuring regular periods.
What about diabetes and hypertension that usually accompany PCOS?	Women with untreated PCOS are more prone to diabetes and hypertension and hence need to be careful about these as well

PCOS is essentially a condition of excess—extra fat, extra insulin and sugar, extra cholesterol, extra skin pigmentation and skin tags, extra hair, and excess response during ovarian stimulation, resulting in extra eggs. The basic treatment consists of removing all the extras and normalizing the body environment.

First, the fat. It is a storage zone for excessive estrogen, and this in turn perpetuates the vicious cycle of PCOS. Exercise and dieting are recommended. Counting calories helps. Small frequent meals speed up metabolism. Those on a diet may need supplementary essential minerals and vitamins. A brisk walk for over an hour is a good stress and weight buster. It is a good idea to look at the scales every week. My father-in-law, Dr Mahendra Parikh, who is 87 years old and has kept his weight almost the same over the past sixty-five years. He watches the scale regularly. Every time his weight goes up by a kilo, he stops taking the elevator, and walks up the eight floors to his clinic. On the other hand, I am terrified to look at the scale.

Next, the extra insulin and the extra sugar. Women with PCOS have a higher circulating sugar level because their body is not sensitive to the circulating insulin. They are hence called 'insulin resistant'. The additional weight perpetuates this cycle further because increased weight increases insulin resistance. Weight loss decreases insulin resistance and brings down the sugar levels. Sometimes, insulin-sensitizing medication such as Metformin may be indicated. The extra insulin also increases the levels of male hormones produced by the ovaries and the adrenal glands. This leads to extra hair on the face and acne.

Options for hair removal may include bleaching, waxing, depilatories, and laser treatment. Spironolactone tablets decrease hair growth and make hair lighter and finer. However, it can take up to six to eight months to see an improvement. Acne can be tackled with a topical antibiotic cream, a good face wash, and birth control pills, which bring down testosterone levels.

The extra pigmentation of the skin particularly around the nape of the neck (acanthosis nigricans), under the arms and groin, and tags on the face, occur because of extra insulin, which causes increased deposition of the pigment melanin. Weight loss diminishes the pigmentation. Skin-lightening lotions may help. The extra skin tags may require laser treatment.

Now, the big one—excess estrogen and lack of progesterone. This prevents ovulation and results in irregular periods. Ironically, women with PCOS produce eggs in multiples during ovarian stimulation and can suffer from ovarian hyperstimulation, which is a potentially dangerous condition.

Regular exercise helps burn fat and sensitizes the ovaries to insulin, allowing spontaneous ovulation. Sometimes the ovary needs a little push to cross the threshold and ovulate. This can be done with the help of ovulation inducers such as Clomiphene and Letrozole. The challenging cases may need the addition of a steroid such as Dexamethasone, in small doses, to counter the effect of high androgens.

Meera had given up hope of ever having a baby. She had taken nine rounds of Clomiphene in a year's time before she came to see us. She felt bloated, irritable, and experienced extreme mood swings. When I examined her, I noticed that her ovaries had multiple fluid-filled cysts. Women such as Meera, whose ovaries do not respond to this gentle push, may need gonadotropin injections. I prescribed her a course of birth control pills for a month. These brought the ovaries to baseline. We then started by giving her small doses of a purified hormone called recombinant FSH. This is particularly useful in women with PCOS. Having sensitized her ovaries, by shutting them down, we finally saw a lone follicle emerging. She ovulated that month and, fortunately for all of us, she conceived without any further treatment.

In the final phase, Meera required a combination of FSH and LH to ovulate. However, great care has to be taken as these injections can cause lots of follicles to mature leading to ovarian hyperstimulation. Hence, it is of paramount importance to tailor the treatment specifically to meet the needs of individual women. Meera does not want to waste any time for her second baby. She wants to start with the injections the moment she stops breast-feeding.

A surgical technique called laparoscopic electrocauterization of the ovarian surface (LEOS) is used for some women with PCOS (see Figure 6.15 in insert pages). Using a cautery, carrying an electric current, the ovarian surface is drilled with multiple openings. This allows the pent up fluid to escape and results in reducing the testosterone content of the ovary, sensitizing it to the effects of hormones and spontaneous ovulation. IUI, along with ovulation induction, can also be considered.

Premature menopause

Around the age of forty-five, some women may experience irregularity in the periods. The periods may occur every two to three months, then even more sporadically, and finally stop. Menopause may be associated with a lack of libido, weak bones, aches, and depression. Some women may be prone to heart conditions associated with menopause. When menopause occurs before the age of forty it is considered premature, and is also called premature ovarian failure. This afflicts a small population of women and may have a genetic origin. Shortening of a part of, or absence of, the X chromosome can be associated with this condition. Women who carry the mutated gene for fragile X syndrome can also get menopause early. Many autoimmune disorders make a woman prone to premature menopause.

Women who have multiple surgeries done for endometriosis tend to have lesser number of eggs, and can have a diminished ovarian reserve. Removal of one ovary, and surgery on the remaining ovary, may decrease the number of eggs significantly. Chemotherapy for various forms of cancer, particularly ovarian, breast, and blood cancer can induce a state of menopause as the chemotherapy destroys the eggs.

Women who enter early menopause and are desirous of becoming pregnant may need hormone replacement prior to using donor eggs. Calcium and vitamin supplements are essential. It is very important to identify women who are at risk for early menopause. In such women, child bearing must not be delayed. For women already into premature menopause, IVF with donor eggs may be the only option. The gynaecologist would also want to treat other problems such as endometriosis, absence of periods, dryness of vagina, and lack of libido.

In an announcement in October 2013, Japanese scientists have found a way to beat the menopause by waking up dormant follicles, offering new hope to women who run out of eggs early in life. This research shows that women who suffer premature menopause still retain tiny, dormant, 'primordial' follicles which can be awakened. The experimental technique has been tested on a group of infertile women who reached the menopause at around the age of 30. Of the 13 treated women, one has given birth to a healthy baby boy while another is said to be pregnant.

The 'In-Vitro Activation' (IVA) technique involves removing the ovaries, cutting them into small one to two millimetre square cubes, and treating the fragments with special stimulating drugs.

With this treatment on 27 Japanese women, 2 women conceived, one has delivered and one is currently pregnant.

However, this technique is still considered in the research phase.

Ovarian cysts

Most women are terrified when they are told that they have an ovarian cyst, thinking that it could turn cancerous. Ovarian cysts are usually benign (see Figures 6.16 and 6.17 in insert pages).

However, all ovarian cysts should be investigated. Cystic ovaries may become associated with infertility and may fill up with watery or thickened fluid. The fluid may be present in the entire ovary or in some part, or parts, of the ovary. Most often the fluid is clear and the cyst is formed as the hormones from the previous menstrual cycle are not removed from the body. Alternatively, ovulation may have been defective in the previous cycle, preventing the release of the egg from the ovarian capsule. This makes the fluid collect within the ovary. Although such cysts may disappear on their own, sometimes they may persist for a few months. An ovarian cyst can be as small as a pea or as large as an orange. In some situations, it can even be the size of a grapefruit or a football.

The most common type of ovarian cyst is called a functional cyst because it forms when the normal function of ovulation is deranged. There are two types of functional cysts—follicular and corpus luteum cysts. Follicular cysts form when the follicle does not rupture at the time of ovulation. Corpus luteum cysts form when the follicle that held the egg seals off after the egg is released. Both types of cysts are usually symptom-free or can cause mild pain and cramping. They usually disappear in six to eight weeks. While follicular cysts can occur at all ages, they tend to occur closer to menopause.

However, if ovulation induction is planned with tablets or hormonal injections, then birth control pills may be administered in the previous month to suppress these cysts. A large cyst can be drained vaginally. If they are small, they are best left alone.

Endometriomas are ovarian cysts that form as a result of endometriosis. In this condition, endometrial tissue grows in areas outside of the uterus, such as the ovaries. This tissue responds to monthly changes in hormones and continues to grow. Eventually, an endometrioma may form, as the endometrial tissue continues to bleed with each menstrual cycle. These cysts are sometimes called 'chocolate cysts' because they are filled with dark, reddish-brown blood (see Figure 6.18 in insert pages). These can cause severe dysmenorrhea and infertility. Chocolate cysts can be removed by laparoscopy, and very rarely, may need to be surgically removed.

Maniti noticed a strange blackish discharge coming out of her navel. She had observed for a few months, that the discharge coincided with her periods. Maniti's navel felt very sore a few days before her period, and the pain would ease once the periods were over. Maniti suffered from extensive endometriosis. After a laparoscopy, we found extensive endometriosis in the pelvis. Both the ovaries were filled with chocolate cysts. On the inner aspect of the umbilicus, there were multiple deposits of endometriosis, which we cauterized. The umbilicus had to be reconstructed after we removed all the implants of endometriosis. We put Maniti on birth control pills for six months to prevent its recurrence.

Dermoid cysts are sometimes seen during investigation for infertility. They form a type of cell, capable of developing into different kinds of tissue, such as skin, hair, fat, and teeth. Dermoid cysts often are small and may not cause symptoms. If they become large they may cause pain. Sometimes the dermoid cyst may even undergo twisting. When they occur in both ovaries, care has to be taken to conserve as much normal tissue as possible.

Ratna lost one ovary to surgery when she was thirteen years old. She suddenly developed severe abdominal cramping after she came back from football practice. Her condition worsened over two days. Her doctor conducted a sonography examination, which showed a dermoid cyst. The cyst had undergone a twist. On the operation table, the surgeon found that the blood supply to the ovary, had been cut off for over more than a day. He had to perform an oopherectomy. For the next ten years Ratna had no problems. She got married at the age of twenty-three. A few months into the marriage, Ratna was brought into the casualty for she was in extreme pain. When I saw her she complained of severe stomach cramps, vomiting, and high fever over the last four days, for which her family physician had treated her with antispasmodic medication.

Ratna diagnosed her own condition, and told me that she thought that she had a dermoid cyst in the remaining ovary and this had caused the torsion. A sonography confirmed Ratna's fears. She consented to the removal of her ovary if necessary. Fortunately, we could untwist the ovary and remove only the part affected by the dermoid cyst (see Figure 6.19 in insert pages) and Ratna recovered completely. We advised her to undergo IVF as the tubes were full of adhesions. Ratna's run of good luck continued. She conceived right away and soon delivered a healthy baby boy. We continue to monitor her ovary every six months.

About 95 percent of ovarian cysts are benign. Cysts that persist beyond two or three menstrual cycles, may require some form of medical or surgical treatment. Laparoscopy may be required if the cyst is more than 5 centimetres in diameter and does not dissolve following a course of medication.

In cases of recurring functional cysts, birth control pills can be tried for one to two months in order to block ovulation. Cysts which are endometriotic may respond to a course of progesterone tablets—the most common of which is Medroxyprogesterone. Occasionally Danazol, which is related to testosterone may be recommended. Some gynaecologists may prefer to administer a long acting GnRH agonist analogue injection. The effect of all these injections is to create a state similar to menopause. This prevents the endometriosis implants from growing.

If the cyst is large or causing symptoms, laparoscopy or open surgery may be needed. The extent and type of surgery that is needed depends on the size and consistency of the cyst, the symptoms, and the fertility status of the woman. It is always advisable to conserve and preserve as much of the ovarian tissue as possible.

Immunological factors

The reproductive system sometimes comes under immunological attack. Women with immunological infertility may have antibodies to the thyroid, ovaries, adrenal glands, and the pancreas. They may also show increased number of Natural Killer (NK) cells in the uterine lining, and secrete Tumour Necrosis Factor alpha (TNFα), which is toxic to the embryos. Treatment calls for immunomodulation using oral steroids, such as Prednisolone, infusions of immunoglobulins (IVIG) at regular intervals. Lymphocyte Immunization Therapy (LIT) using paternal leucocytes injected under the female partner's skin have been tried with limited success.

Endocrine factors

A sluggish thyroid can cause delayed periods and disturbances in ovulation. Correction with thyroid replacement can reverse the infertile condition. Obesity and diabetes have a strong link. Women with PCOS can exhibit both. A reasonable diet and exercise regime, and insulin sensitizing agents are helpful. A benign tumour of the pituitary (Prolactinoma) causes an elevation of prolactin. This can disrupt the menstrual and reproductive cycle and is easily treated with medication.

Genetic factors

Preimplantataion genetic diagnosis (PGD) (see pp 133–35) may be suggested in conditions where there is an abnormal arrangement of chromosomes. Some genetic conditions such as Turner's syndrome (see p 167–68) are not amenable to IVF and may require the use of donor eggs.

Thus, the treatment of the female factor is varied; from simple do-it-at-home procedures to more complex surgical interventions. The importance of studying the patient's detailed history, paying adequate attention to all her symptoms, studying her past records meticulously, and tailoring the treatment to her specific needs, cannot be over emphasized. As a general rule, it is important to bring the environment to as natural a state as possible before offering definitive treatment. Today's medical and technological innovations make female factor infertility resolvable most of the times.

7

Stimulating the Ovaries

- The suppression and stimulation phases
- Ovarian hyperstimulation syndrome (OHSS)
- Luteal support

The processes of IUI, IVF, and ICSI are planned in a manner that is as similar to nature as possible. In order to produce a good number of high quality eggs, we administer hormonal tablets or injections. While tablets stimulate the production of FSH and LH, which in turn trigger ovulation, injections contain the same FSH and LH found in the body and hence directly bring about ovulation.

For women who do not ovulate on their own, tablets of Clomiphene Citrate and Letrozole are used. If these do not work, injections are considered. Ironically, Clomiphene is an anti-estrogenic substance and Letrozole's main use has been for the treatment of breast cancer. Both these drugs are useful when there are problems with ovulation—in women with PCOS and in conjunction with IVF. Rarely are tablets combined with hormonal injections at the time of IVF/ICSI.

The advantages of Clomiphene and Letrozole therapy lie in the simplicity of administration, low incidence of side effects, and low cost. Clomiphene should not be used for more than three consecutive months in a row, without taking a month's break, as its prolonged use can have a contraceptive effect due to its anti-estrogen properties. Studies have reported very few Clomiphene-induced pregnancies in women over the age of forty, and hence for older women, Gonadotropin-releasing hormone (GnRH) injections are the first choice. Clomiphene Citrate is usually started on day five of the period, with a starting dose of 50 milligrams daily for five days. If ovulation does not occur, then the dose can be stepped up to 100 milligrams per day. The upper limit of the dose is 200 milligrams per day. Letrozole is an anti-estrogenic, anticancer agent and its use has recently been extended to trigger ovulation. It is usually given as a dose of 2.5 milligrams daily from day two to day six of the period.

The development of follicles can be tracked by sonography. Since both these drugs may thin down the uterine lining and cause hostility of the cervical mucous, it may be worthwhile to combine the use of these drugs with IUI in order to bypass the cervix.

Women with resistant PCOS may not respond to oral medication and may need to combine hormone injections with tablets, or switch to injections alone.

The initial attempts at IVF were done in a natural cycle without stimulating the ovaries. This was a tedious process because the doctors had to determine the correct time to retrieve the egg. This had to be timed according to the surge of the hormone LH. Since the LH surge occurs thirty-six to forty-eight hours prior to ovulation, patients had to monitor LH in the urine several times a day, so as not to miss the point in time when the surge occurred. As the science of ART developed, ovarian stimulation was considered using gonadotrophins (LH and FSH) obtained from the urine of volunteers.

In the initial days, a pharmaceutical company, located in Switzerland, would collect urine from nuns. This urine would be collected by the gallons and then sent for purification. Over the years, the process of obtaining GnRHs from urine has been refined. Today, recombinant techniques are used to get highly purified gonadotrophins. In this technology, subunits of the FSH and LH hormones are allowed to multiply on cell lines obtained from the ovaries of hamsters. This process produces FSH and LH in their purest form.

In order to acquire good quality oocytes, we may

suggest an initial suppression of the ovaries followed by their stimulation.

The suppression and stimulation phases

Ovarian suppression can be done with tablets or injections. Birth control pills are given in the month prior to the stimulation phase, for eighteen to thirty days. Alternately, Gonadotropin releasing hormones (GnRH) agonist analogues—they contain molecules such as leuprolide, buserelin, nafarelin, goserelin, deslorelin, and triptorelin—are started from the twenty-first day of the previous cycle or from the first day of the period. The hormone injections are started once adequate suppression is achieved. We know if the ovaries are adequately suppressed by an ultrasound scan and by the estrogen values in the blood. These should be less than 30 units.

If birth control pills have been used for suppression, then we use GnRH antagonist injections (Gonadotropin releasing hormone antagonists contain the drugs Ganirelix or Cetrotide) around the sixth day of the hormonal stimulation, to keep the LH under check and prevent premature ovulation. Inappropriate rise of LH and progesterone during ovarian stimulation can adversely affect the quality of ova. Thus, it is important to keep these hormones in check. If GnRH agonists have been used for suppression, these will be continued at a smaller dose during the ovarian stimulation.

There are three different types of injections used for ovarian suppression and stimulation. The first group of hormonal injections includes the GnRH agonists and GnRH antagonists, which contain the drugs Ganirelix or

Cetrorelix. These two types of drugs suppress the LH surge and the ovulation, till the follicles are mature.

The second group of hormones is human menopausal gonadotropins (HMG), FSH, and LH. The purpose of this group of drugs is to stimulate the ovaries to produce multiple follicles, which will contain the oocytes.

The third group of hormones includes human chorionic gonadotropin (HCG). The purpose of this group of drugs is to cause the final maturation of the eggs.

To summarize, we suppress the ovaries, then stimulate them to produce many eggs, and then ensure that they are all of good quality. With the knowledge of different types of hormones we can now proceed to discuss the different stimulation protocols. At the stimulation phase, the decision as to which protocol will work best, is based on the individual's ovarian volume, presence of PCOS, past IVF cycle response, and baseline hormones. Thus, protocols have to be tailored to the individual patient and not the other way around.

The long protocol

Suppression of the ovaries is done with GnRH agonists starting from the mid-luteal phase, around a week prior to the next expected period. The suppression generally takes ten to fourteen days. Sometimes the GnRH agonist analogue is started from day one of the period. FSH and/or HMG is started after ovarian suppression, which usually occurs once the periods begin. There is a reduction in the dose of the agonist once the FSH/HMG is started.

The response to the HMG/FSH is monitored with serial transvaginal ultrasonography and blood levels of the hormones estradiol (E_2), LH, and progesterone (P_4) during the later part of the stimulation. The dose of HMG/FSH is adjusted according to the response. The follicles grow at the rate of 1 to 2 millimetres every day. One's aim is to produce eight to ten good quality follicles. Stimulation is continued till two to three follicles grow to the size of 17 to 18 millimetres. This generally takes about nine to eleven days (see Figure 7.1 in insert pages).

HCG injection, or the trigger injection, is then administered to bring about the final maturation. Egg retrieval is done thirty-four to thirty-six hours after the HCG trigger. The egg retrieval process is short and painless with mild anaesthesia. It is done under ultrasound guidance.

The antagonist protocol

The antagonist protocol is relatively new and more patient-friendly. It entails taking birth control pills in the cycle prior to starting ovarian stimulation. Once the period begins, we start the hormone injections of FSH and/or HMG. By the sixth day of the ovarian stimulation, the antagonist is added. This prevents the LH and progesterone from surging or rising, and ensures good quality and quantity of eggs. Once the follicles mature, the HCG trigger dose is given, and is monitored with ultrasound and blood tests for estrogen, progesterone, and LH.

Microdose and flare protocols

There are protocols that are helpful for women who are poor responders to standard protocols, or who tend to produce very few eggs. In such cases, instead of suppressing the ovaries, the GnRH agonist analogue is used to create a flare response of the ovaries. The GnRH analogue causes a flare in the FSH and LH stimulated by the pituitary, before causing its suppression. This phenomenon is utilized to push the ovaries to recruit follicles in the first few days of the period, by starting the analogue on day one or two of the period. In the flare protocol, GnRH agonist is given only for the first three days, along with the ovarian stimulation, and then stopped while continuing the ovarian stimulation. FSH or HMG is started from the third day of the menstrual cycle and is monitored like other protocols. In the microdose protocol, a GnRH agonist analogue is given in microdoses on the day that the ovarian stimulation begins. FSH or HMG is started from day one of the menstrual cycle. Both are continued till the HCG injection.

The stop GnRH agonist protocol

Suppression is done with a GnRH agonist analogue from the mid-luteal phase—around a week prior to the next expected period—but usually at a lower dose. This is particularly helpful in women who get oversuppressed with the long protocol. The agonist is completely stopped after the woman gets her period; FSH and/or HMG is started. Monitoring is similar to the other protocols. The LH suppressing capacity is not as complete but the risk of premature LH surge is low.

Natural cycle protocol

There are some women who prefer not to take hormonal injections for personal, philosophical, or financial reasons.

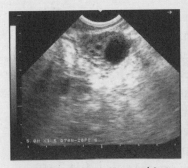

Figure 7.2 A sonographic image of a single follicle being monitored in the natural cycle

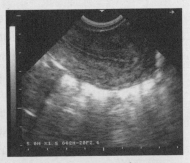

Figure 7.3 A sonographic image of a uterine lining primed with estrogen. A triple line is seen.

We have created a special protocol called the natural cycle protocol where no hormonal injections are administered and the cycle is monitored (Figure 7.2) closely, as it progresses naturally. It costs less than half of the other protocols, though the results are not as good (18 percent versus 45 percent).

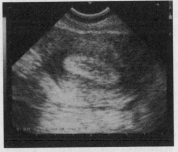

Figure 7.4 A sonographic image of a uterine lining that has been primed with estrogen and progesterone for implantation of the embryos.

Whatever stimulation protocol is used, the ultimate aim is to acquire good quality embryos with the ability to implant in a well prepared uterine environment.

Ovarian hyperstimulation syndrome (OHSS)

This condition occurs when the ovaries are extra sensitive to the hormone injections used for ovulation induction.

Women with PCOS are more prone to this condition.

During ovulation induction, the ovary develops multiple follicles (see Figure 7.5 in insert pages) and many eggs are obtained at the time of egg retrieval. After ovulation, the ovaries enlarge and are painfully tender. There may be breathlessness and fluid collection in the abdomen.

The condition can be seen in three stages—mild, moderate (see Figures 7.6 and 7.7 in insert pages) and severe. In the mild stage, symptomatic relief suffices. A woman having moderate hyperstimulation is given intravenous fluids, pain medication, high protein diet, and can be observed for a few days with or without hospitalization. Women having severe hyperstimulation need hospital admission and critical care. Besides receiving intravenous fluids and albumin supplements, the extra fluid in the abdomen may need drainage. Their intake and outflow of fluid is strictly monitored.

OHSS is a self-limiting condition and usually resolves within eight to ten days. Women who hyperstimulate tend to be pregnant. The risk of hyperstimulation is significantly cut down with proper follicular monitoring, dose adjustment of hormones, and use of antagonists instead of agonists.

Nishita had developed hyperstimulation in every cycle of IVF. She had had four cycles, admitted in the ICU once, had embryos transferred in only one cycle, and in the other three cycles the embryos were frozen. When she consulted me, the condition she put forth to me was that she would undergo one more cycle of IVF, provided she did not hyperstimulate. After she was explained the physiology behind OHSS, she seemed more relaxed and ready for the next cycle. My assistant, Dr Sujatha Reddy, was assigned the task of strict monitoring during ovulation induction. She ensured that Nishita did not hyperstimulate and conceived in that cycle.

Luteal support

All stimulated cycles need to be supplemented with progesterone and HCG injections in order to keep the ovaries and the uterine lining in phase (Figures 7.3 and 7.4). Estradiol may be added in the luteal phase, if the uterine lining appears thin. Some of the problems that can occur during ovarian stimulation are ovarian hyperstimulation, inadequate recruitment of follicles, and a uterine lining that does not respond well. Some of these situations may prompt us to omit the current cycle and plan the stimulation again.

Types of progesterone supplementation

Progesterone can be given in the luteal phase either as injection of pure progesterone, as vaginal and rectal pessaries or vaginal gel. There is no difference in results in case of vaginal route or intramuscular route of progesterone.

A phase III clinical trial is ongoing in 2013 and is conducted by a pharmaceutical company called TEVA looking at the use of a progesterone vaginal ring called milprosa which is injected once a week in the vagina. Results for pregnancy rates are encouraging.

8

Getting Pregnant in the Laboratory

- Intrauterine insemination (IUI)
- In vitro fertilization (IVF)
- Intra cytoplasmic sperm injection (ICSI)
- Percutaneous epididymal sperm aspiration (PESA), testicular sperm aspiration (TESA), and testicular sperm extraction (TESE)
- Pre-implantation genetic diagnosis (PGD)
- Intracytoplasmic morphologically selected sperm injection (IMSI)
- Laser Assisted Hatching (LAH)
- Early Embryo Viability Assessment (EEVA)
- An ideal IVF laboratory

The andrology and embryology laboratories where many 'test-tube procedures' take place, play a vital role in the treatment of both male and female factor infertility.

This chapter takes the reader from the simple procedures such as IUI, IVF to more complex ones such as ICSI, PGD, CAT, and the intracytoplasmic morphologically selected sperm injection (IMSI).

Intrauterine insemination (IUI)

Artificial insemination is scientifically called intrauterine insemination. It involves the placement of sperm prepared in the laboratory, directly into the uterus. IUI is useful when there is unexplained infertility, or when donor sperm is used, or in conditions of male infertility where the count is mildly decreased and the sperm motility is at least 30 percent. This procedure is not useful when there is a severe male factor infertility. It is useful when combined with stimulation of the ovaries, in conditions where there is no ovulation—such as with PCOS, luteal dysfunction, and mild endometriosis. In these conditions, it is worthwhile to consider IUI rather than IVF as a first option, as the cost of IUI is 10 percent of the cost of IVF/ ICSI. IUI is not recommended when the fallopian tubes are blocked or are partially open.

Sperm processing for IUI

The purpose of IUI is to place active and motile sperm as close to the oocyte as possible. In order to do that, the best sperm are selected from the semen sample, which is collected in a sterile container, in the privacy of an isolated room free of noise and disturbance. The procedure starts after allowing the ejaculated semen sample to liquefy for about fifteen minutes after collection. About 1 millilitre of the semen is placed in a sterile test tube to which a highly purified liquid culture medium is added. The mixture is then centrifuged. This helps rid all the debris, leaving behind only the sperm and other accompanying cells. The sperm gather into a tiny pellet at the bottom of the tube. The pellet is shaken up to loosen the sperm that are clumped together, and gently overlaid with a fluid medium (see Figure 8.1 in insert pages).

The procedure utilizes the swimming ability of the sperm. Those that can swim the fastest, come to the top of the fluid medium and are gently siphoned out and placed in another tube, in which fresh fluid medium has been added. A tiny drop of this sample is placed under the microscope to see how many motile sperm have swum up through the liquid medium. The sperm thus obtained, free from debris and bacteria, are energetic and improve the success rate of IUI.

Sometimes a swim-down technique is used. This uses percoll or ficoll media of two different concentrations (see Figure 8.2 in insert pages). The sperm are trapped in these two layers and have to swim downward to the bottom of the tube, from which they are gently siphoned and further purified by culturing them in liquid medium.

In both techniques, the fittest sperm swim through and are prepared for insemination.

Semen cryopreservation and banking for IUI

In cases of azoospermia, where ICSI is not an option, one could consider the use of donor sperm. A good sperm bank ensures that sperm donors, and donor semen, have undergone stringent evaluation. The donors are tested for HIV, Hepatitis B and C, and VDRL. Besides, the semen quality is ensured by utilizing semen with sperm counts greater than 50 million/millilitre, with more than 50 percent motility, and predominant normal morphology.

In vitro fertilization (IVF)

As we have seen, the journey of the egg and the sperm is not smooth. There are many uphill and downhill tasks that they have to perform. Besides, both can encounter obstacles which may not be surmountable or may injure them. If they survive, they may be deformed or incapacitated. If they do meet, their union may not be fruitful. For those men and women whose gametes cannot take the treaded path, there is the option of IVF. In IVF, although the women's eggs are fertilized outside the body, the process of fertilization mimics that of nature. The development of the oocyte follows the cycle as it would occur naturally. A major difference is that the procedure of ovarian stimulation produces more than one egg. The oocytes are collected, under mild anaesthesia, through the vagina, using transvaginal sonography guided procedures. As soon as the oocytes (Figure 8.3) are obtained, they are isolated by the embryologist (see Figure 8.4 in insert

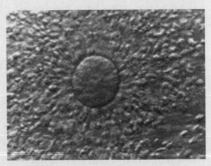

Figure 8.3 A mature oocyte

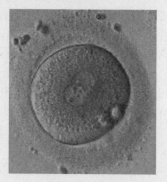 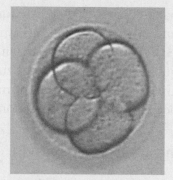

Figure 8.6 A microscopic
photograph of the two
pronuclei

Figure 8.7 A microscopic
photograph of a four-celled
embryo at Day 2

pages) and placed in the warmth and comfort of the carbon-dioxide incubator (see Figure 8.5 in insert pages) which is tuned to maintain the conditions found inside a woman's fallopian tubes.

Semen is processed in order to obtain the healthiest sperm. The procedure of obtaining healthy sperm is very similar to that of obtaining sperm by IUI processing.

The eggs and sperm are incubated together. The next day, the oocyte is checked for fertilization. If fertilization takes place, two tiny circles in close proximity are visible under the microscope. These are called the pronuclei (Figure 8.6) and carry the male and female genetic material. Within eighteen hours of the IVF procedure, these will fuse and initiate the division of a one-celled embryo into two. The cell division progresses quickly so that the two cells become four (Figure 8.7), then eight (Figure 8.8), then sixteen (Figure 8.9), and finally form a ball of more than hundred tightly arranged cells—the blastocyst (Figure 8.10). The blastocyst stimulates the lining of the uterus,

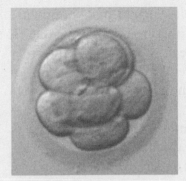

Figure 8.8 A microscopic photograph of an eight-celled embryo at Day 3

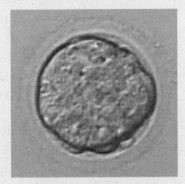

Figure 8.9 A microscopic photograph of a sixteen-celled embryo at Day 4

resulting in processes called villi, growing out of the embryo. These will anchor the embryo, firmly, to the uterine lining. Embryo transfer is usually carried out between Day 2 and Day 5 of embryo development.

IVF is ideal for women with tubal blockage, pelvic adhesions, previous tubal sterilization not amenable to tubal reversal, and some cases of endometriosis.

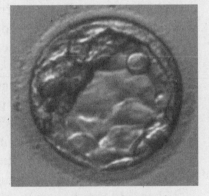

Figure 8.10 A microscopic photograph of a blastocyst

Intra cytoplasmic sperm injection (ICSI)

ICSI has completely revolutionized the treatment of male factor infertility. Before this procedure was discovered, males with a sperm count of less than 5 million/millilitre had virtually no chance of fathering a baby. With ICSI, one needs only one viable healthy sperm. Yet the story of ICSI, like that of most scientific discoveries, is full of twists and turns, and chance findings combined with astute observations and analysis.

In 1992, Gianpiero Palermo—a scientist working in Dr André van Steirteghem's laboratory in Brussels—was placing sperm around the egg underneath the zona when, accidentally, he punctured the cytoplasm with the pipette. He thought it was a disaster. One sperm went inside the egg. Dr Palermo concluded that this egg would not survive the procedure, and he put a question mark on the petri dish containing this egg. But the surprising result was that, that was the only egg that fertilized. It was finally transferred to the patient, and this became the first ICSI baby.

A new procedure had been discovered. The procedure was replicated numerous times. The data was analysed and published as a research paper. The rest is history. Professor André van Steirteghem and Gianpiero Palermo became instant medical celebrities. Professor Steirteghem is internationally known as the father of ICSI, or as my American colleagues refer to him, 'Mr ICSI himself!'

I must add that he carries his fame lightly, and like all truly great scientists, he is humble and eager to teach and learn. I had the good fortune of being trained in ICSI by Professor Steirteghem himself, when he and his charming wife, the internationally renowned geneticist, Professor Ingbar Liebars, visited our centre and our home in 1994. Rajesh took him around to see the city and they paid a visit to Rajesh's alma mater, St Xavier's College.

I am eternally indebted to Professor Steirteghem, for

ours is the first centre in Southeast Asia to have an ICSI baby—Luv Singh who is now nineteen years old (see Figure 8.11 in insert pages). The entire procedure of ICSI is done on the warm platform of a microscope. The movements in the micromanipulation system are controlled by joysticks (see Figure 8.12 in insert pages), similar to those for kids playing on a Playstation. The oocyte is prepared by removing its outer coat of cells called the cumulus complex. The oocyte is then held gently by a glass micropipette, using mild suction (see Figure 8.13 in insert pages). This pipette is twenty times thinner than human hair. The processed sperm are deposited in a substance called polyvinylpyrrolidone (PVP). This slows down the movement of the sperm, facilitating the embryologist to pick up motile, healthy-looking sperm from the many present.

Once the sperm is isolated, the sharp injection pipette (sixty times thinner than human hair) is used as a sword to cut off the tail of the sperm. This serves two functions. It immobilizes the sperm so that it does not wiggle inside the egg and damage it. Secondly, it exposes the covering of the sperm. This is required to activate the ovum. Once tail-less, it is picked up by the same micropipette, which is advanced towards the waiting egg. The egg is no larger than the tip of a pin, but under magnification it looks like the sun. The pipette punctures the zona (see Figure 8.14 in insert pages) in one quick move and enters the egg, where it releases the sperm (see Figure 8.15 in insert pages). The microinjected egg is returned to the warmth of the incubator. About sixteen hours later, a check is conducted for fertilization. The fertilized egg is then allowed to grow in a controlled environment.

ICSI is ideally suited for cases of very low sperm count or zero count, sperm with little or no motility, and many sperm with abnormal shapes. ICSI benefits women who are advanced in age, those with endometriosis, immunological complications, and unexplained infertility. If IVF has failed in a previous cycle or if less number of eggs have been fertilized with IVF previously, ICSI becomes the suitable option.

Percutaneous epididymal sperm aspiration (PESA), testicular sperm aspiration (TESA), and testicular sperm extraction (TESE)

ICSI revolutionized treatment for men with very low sperm count. This treatment has also opened doors for men who produce sperm but have an obstruction to their release (obstructive azoospermia). This can be due to the blockage of the sperm tubes or vas aplasia (absence of the vas), or surgical vas blockage following a family planning operation, or because the number of sperm produced are so few that none reach the ejaculate (non-obstructive azoospermia).

In the situation of obstructive azoospermia, sperm can be retrieved by PESA. TESA and TESE are preferred in cases of non-obstructive azoospermia (see Figure 8.16).

The procedure of PESA

The genital area is sterilized with an antiseptic solution. The procedure is made painless with the help of local anaesthesia. The epididymis is palpated and isolated. Fluid from the epididymis is aspirated using a fine needle.

A tiny drop of this fluid is checked under the microscope for the presence of sperm. If adequate sperm are obtained the procedure of ICSI is completed.

The procedure of TESA/TESE

The procedure is made painless with the help of local anaesthesia. Under sterile conditions, the scrotum is isolated and the testes are palpated and held in position. A fine needle with tubing attached to it, is inserted into the substance of the testis. Gentle suction is applied and the needle is withdrawn. This teases out few sperm tubules, which are handed over to the embryologist. The sperm are teased out under magnification. If sperm are not seen, then the urologist repeats the procedure until an adequate number of sperm are obtained. After the procedure of ICSI is completed, the remaining testicular tissue is frozen for future use.

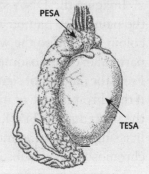

Pregnancy rates from ejaculated, testicular, or epididymal sperm are similar. However, the incidence of miscarriage is slightly higher when testicular sperm is used. This may be because men with non-obstructive azoospermia are more likely to have genetic problems in their chromosomes.

Figure 8.16 Diagrammatic representation of PESA and TESA

Pre-implantation genetic diagnosis (PGD)

This is a technique used to select genetically normal embryos. The procedure involves ICSI. Following this, a microsurgical operation is performed on the eight-celled embryo in order to extract a single blastomere. Using a laser, an opening is made in the zona (see Figure 8.17 in insert pages). A single cell is gently removed (see Figure 8.18 in insert pages) using a PGD pipette. At this stage, the cells are totipotent—every cell of the embryo can form all parts of the body. Therefore, the removal of one or two cells does not hinder the development of the baby. The cell (see Figure 8.19 in insert pages) is carefully fixed on a microscope slide and then analysed by the FISH technique (see Figure 8.20 in insert pages).

The geneticist will put this cell through an overnight procedure called hybridization—a procedure that zips open the DNA strands and attaches coloured probes—perform fluorescence in situ hybridization (FISH), and identify the chromosomes of interest.

Imagine the DNA strands to be a wall, and the probe the paint. The painter (the geneticist) applies a particular colour of paint to the wall and gets a signal identifying the particular chromosome (see Figure 8.21 in insert pages). From the number of signals emitted, the geneticist will know if the chromosome of interest is normal or abnormal. With the procedure of FISH, five chromosomes can be checked in a single step using multicolour probes. A few additional chromosomes can subsequently be checked on the same cell.

Six or seven chromosomes responsible for abnormalities are checked. Some of the common anomalies that can be checked are Trisomy 21 (Down's syndrome), Trisomy 18 (Edward's syndrome), Monosomy X (45 X or Turner's syndrome), and 47 XXY (Klinefelter's syndrome).

PGD is used for couples with repeated early miscarriages, severe male factor infertility, repeated failed IVF/ICSI attempts, presence of chromosomal problems in the parents, and in some X-linked genetic conditions such as haemophilia. We are now in the process of developing the technique of PGD for single-gene disorders such as thalassemia. Our centre was the first to start the facilities for PGD in India in 1999. We plan to offer a more advanced technique called Array CGH (Comparative Genomic Hybridization) for PGD shortly.

DNA sequencing - the next step

Only about 30 percent of IVF embryos result in a baby. The loss is primarily due to DNA abnormalities. Each cell of the embryo has 3 feet of DNA. In order to test this DNA in a traditional way, it would take weeks and cost several thousand dollars.

However, recent advances have made this genetic analysis possible in just several hours by the technique of next generation sequencing (NGS). The first baby Conner Levy was born in May 2013 due to efforts of scientists at Oxford University. It is estimated that this technique will improve IVF success rates by 50 percent.

Intracytoplasmic morphologically selected sperm injection (IMSI)

This technique has added a new dimension to the procedure of ICSI. Normally ICSI is carried out at a magnification that is twentyfold. The IMSI procedure uses a specialized lens, which enlarges the sperm seven thousand times. This makes isolation of normal-looking sperm simpler. IMSI is particularly useful when there is severe male factor infertility, with a large proportion of abnormal-looking sperm, repeatedly failed IVF procedures and repeated miscarriages.

Imaan and Gulab had three cycles of ICSI with us. The embryos showed fragmentation in all the cycles. Ninety-five percent of the sperm showed abnormalities. We performed IMSI in the fourth cycle. The embryos turned up much better, with minimal fragmentation. We also acquired enough embryos for transfer, and could also freeze four of them. Imaan did not conceive the first time but did on her second attempt, when we transferred the frozen embryos.

Laser Assisted Hatching (LAH)

Prior to implantation, the embryo has to hatch out of its protective shell known as the zona pellucida. If this process is not completed properly, implantation will fail and a pregnancy will not occur. In older women, the zona pellucida is thick, jeopardizing the hatching process. Laser Assisted Hatching (LAH) uses a diode laser beam. This is focussed on the zona pellucida making a small opening of 30 microns to facilitate embryo hatching (see Figure 8.17 in insert pages). This technique is particularly useful in cases where the embryo has a thick zona and also if previous cycles have failed.

Our centre was the first in India to have a successful pregnancy using LAH in 1999.

Early Embryo Viability Assessment (EEVA)

The technique of Early Embryo Viability Assessment (EEVA) uses time-lapse imaging to monitor embryos while they are incubated. It then uses computer software to select those embryos that are at a low risk of chromosomal defects. In this technology the embryos are not removed from the incubator for checking their growth as the incubator is equipped with a camera.

Eva, is the first baby in the world to be conceived via this technique carried out by scientists in Scotland.

An ideal IVF laboratory

The IVF laboratory, where the embryos are cultured, should be of the highest standards. The air within the laboratory has to be pure, free of airborne micro-organisms, spores, mold, paint, and chemical particles. Current research shows that indoor air environment has a direct impact on IVF success. A good embryology laboratory is fitted with a high efficiency particulate air (HEPA) filtration system, for getting rid of particulate matter, and a CODA tower (named after two scientists, Jacques Cohen and Brian Dale) to get rid of volatile substances. A good laboratory must have an adequate number of well-trained personnel who are capable of gentle handling of the eggs, sperm, and embryos. The equipment needs to be duplicated so that the breakdown of any one piece of equipment does not have a detrimental effect on the working of the laboratory.

A daily check has to be carried out on the liquid culture media, and log books of the day-to-day functioning of all instruments and equipment need to be maintained. Prior to deciding on a laboratory procedure, all records of the couple should be thoroughly studied. Take for example the case of Vibhuti and Ramesh. When they came to see me, Vibhuti brought four files with her. All of them were chronologically arranged. It took me over two hours to go through the papers. At the end of this inspection, I found that Vibhuti had undergone twelve cycles of IUI, two laparoscopies, and one laparotomy, while Ramesh had undergone varicocele surgery. I also discovered that Vibhuti's tubes were blocked and several attempts had been made to open them. After surgery, the couple had been told that her tubes had been partially opened. It was obvious that Vibhuti could not conceive with IUI as her tubes were damaged. I advised her to undergo IVF, after taking adequate leave from work. Happily, Vibhuti is the mother of a healthy baby boy.

9

Freezing for Fertility

- Sperm freezing
- Embryo freezing
- Oocyte freezing
- Ovarian tissue freezing

The somewhat hesitant science of ART of the 1970s has evolved into the advanced version that it is today. This has facilitated enhanced pregnancy rates. As techniques undergo refinement, the process becomes less wasteful, and we salvage and preserve sperm, oocytes, embryos, and ovarian and testicular tissue.

Sperm freezing

Semen freezing has been practised for over 60 years, in the veterinary field. It has been used in humans since 1953. The ejaculated semen sample is allowed to liquefy at room temperature under sterile conditions. A fluid medium is added, volume for volume, to the liquefied semen to protect it during freezing. Small vials are used for storage. These are labelled, exposed to liquid nitrogen vapours, and then plunged into liquid nitrogen canisters (Figure 9.1).

Freezing semen has several uses

1. The process of ART requires the use of sperm at regular intervals. Freezing sperm helps if the male partner

Figure 9.1 Cryogenic containers housing frozen sperm in liquid nitrogen

is unable to give a semen sample on the day of the procedures.

2. Multiple samples can be harvested from men suffering from oligospermia, so that there is never a shortage of sperm when required.

3. It helps in the quarantining of donor sperm. After six months, if the repeat blood tests for VDRL, HIV, Hepatitis B and C are negative, it is then used to fertilize ova.

4. It is necessary for preservation of extra-testicular sperm tissue/sperm following TESA or PESA.

5. It is useful prior to chemotherapy for various cancers, particularly that of the testes. Chemotherapy arrests sperm production and hence sperm freezing serves as a biological insurance.

World record broken for birth through cryopreserved sperm.

In August 2012, the existing world record of 28 years for a successful live birth through cryopreserved sperm was broken when a baby was born from the frozen sperm of a Japanese American war hero. The sperm had been frozen 41 years ago.

Ratnamala and Abhay wanted to have a baby quickly, as Abhay had male factor infertility. His counts were a cause of concern as many reports showed them to vary between zero and 0.1 million/millilitre. On the day of the ICSI, he could not produce any sperm. However, his back-up frozen semen sample was used to perform ICSI on twenty oocytes. In that cycle, Ratnamala did not show a good endometrial lining. So we decided to freeze the fourteen embryos that were formed. During the next cycle, we transferred three good quality thawed embryos. Figures 9.2 and 9.3 illustrate the stages of a thawed embryo. And there was great news after fourteen days! Nine months later they had a healthy son.

Three months prior to his marriage Rashesh came to see us. Over the past few weeks, he had a dull aching pain in the groin region. He had initially ignored it. However, when it persisted he consulted his general physician who immediatcly referred him to a urologist. Rashesh was diagnosed to have a seminoma, a form of testicular cancer that requires the removal of the testes followed by chemotherapy. The couple consulted me beforc the surgery. They were relieved when I suggested freezing multiple samples of semen as insurance against the chemotherapy. Rashesh recovered well. Luckily for the couple, Rashesh and Veerbala conceived in their first attempt at ICSI with frozen sperm. They plan to attempt a second baby with the cryopreserved sample.

Embryo freezing

Due to controlled ovarian stimulation, usually several mature oocytes are produced. Optimally, only two or three embryos are transferred. The remaining embryos are frozen for use at a later date. There are two methods of freezing them, and the embryos are stored in liquid nitrogen in both procedures. The two procedures are:
1.   slow freezing
2.   vitrification

1. The process of slow freezing takes upto five hours. A computer program allows the freezing to proceed

slowly, till a temperature of minus 180°C is reached.

2. Vitrification is the preferred method of freezing. It is quick, economical, and does not require a computerized system. We have a 40 to 45 percent pregnancy rate using frozen embryos by the vitrification technique.

In a case dating back to 1981, one of three embryos was implanted and two were preserved for future use for an American couple that was seeking treatment in Australia. The wife miscarried and soon after they both died in an air crash without a will. The man had a son by a previous marriage and the estate of the couple was worth a million dollars. This raised the issue of the distribution of their wealth and whether the frozen embryos had a 'right' to be implanted into a surrogate mother and to inherit a part of their wealth thereafter. The State of Victoria passed legislation which did not permit this, and in fact suggested that the embryos be implanted in a surrogate and the children thereafter be placed for adoption without any inheritance rights, as the embryos were created using donor sperm!

Who can benefit from embryo freezing?

a. Women undergoing IVF/ICSI who have produced multiple good quality embryos. The ovulation stimulation for IVF/ICSI results in multiple embryos. Since only two or three embryos are transferred into the uterus, the surplus embryos can be frozen for future use.

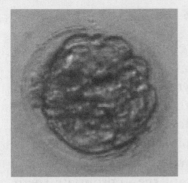 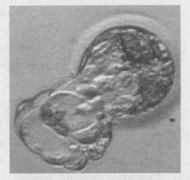

Figure 9.2 A freshly thawed embryo

Figure 9.3 A hatching blastocyst stage embryo twenty-four hours after thaw

b. Women who have been recently diagnosed with breast cancer or ovarian cancer, may have the option of embryo freezing, provided the tumours are not estrogen dependant.

c. Embryos may be frozen for use by couples wanting to preserve them for subsequent use. Research studies have demonstrated that babies born out of frozen embryos are as healthy as those born without freezing.

Oocyte freezing

It is worthwhile for women planning to defer childbearing, to consider freezing their eggs. During freezing, the water from the oocyte has to be removed. If the water is retained, it can form ice crystals and damage the oocyte permanently. Hence, oocyte freezing is not a perfect science yet. In our programme we use the vitrification method for oocyte freezing.

Who can benefit from oocyte freezing?

1. Women who want to defer childbearing for a few years.
2. Women undergoing chemotherapy for breast and ovarian cancer. The oocytes may be harvested and frozen prior to the chemotherapy.
3. Oocyte freezing can be done on the day of the egg retrieval, if the semen sample is not available due to the absence or performance anxiety of the male partner.
4. Oocytes can be frozen until the appropriate sperm sample is available for ICSI. A paper published by Noyes and Group (RBM Online, February 2009), followed nine hundred babies born from oocyte freezing. There was no increased incidence of any abnormalities.

Just a word of advice, I see women in their late 30s and early 40s who want to freeze their eggs. They should bear in mind that at the age of 30 the chances of success with IVF are 45 to 50 percent, at age 40 they 15 percent or less and between 42 to 44, 3 percent or less. Hence the earlier one freezes one's eggs, the more the likelihood of a pregnancy.

Ovarian tissue freezing

In some situations, it may not be possible to have enough time for egg or embryo freezing, particularly in women who need to start chemotherapy. In such cases, thin slices of ovarian tissue from the rim of the ovary, are obtained by laparoscopy. These slices are then frozen. Several reports have shown the successful recovery of hormonal functions following the retransplantation of the ovarian tissue.

The University of Southern Denmark, in Odense, recently reported a successful spontaneous pregnancy after such a transplant. Doctors had frozen tissues from the ovaries of Ms Stinne Holm Bergholdt, after it was discovered that she had cancer. After she recovered, the frozen ovarian tissue was thawed and transplanted back in her body. She underwent IVF and conceived. After a few years, she decided to have another baby and went back to her doctor to plan her treatment. She discovered then that she was naturally pregnant!

Sometimes the ovary may be reimplanted underneath the patient's forearm for the purposes of delaying menopausal symptoms. Many such developments, enhancing fertility, will emerge as the science of ART advances. With rapid scientific advances, the future is indeed exciting and full of optimism for those desirous of becoming pregnant through ART.

So far 20 successful pregnancies using frozen ovarian tissue have been reported all over the world.

10

A Squirrel on Marine Drive

I love late night walks on Marine Drive with Rajesh as that is our time together. We get a chance to talk about our children, our friends, our values, bounce off ideas, and in the process, lose some calories. On one of these walks about nine years ago, I suddenly realized that I was walking alone. I turned back, only to see Rajesh down on his knees near one of the trees on the pavement. He was as excited as a child, marvelling at a squirrel, eating a nut at the base of the tree. 'An Indian palm squirrel is not indigenous to the city,' he mumbled and then said, 'Must be someone's lost pet.'

Rajesh went on to talk about how squirrels conserve food and then continued on 'the incredible wisdom and bounty of nature' (a favourite phrase of his). We started discussing how nature can be used to conserve energy and that one must not waste anything in life. At some point in the conversation, we started talking about nurturing the embryos in a safer and a better way to contribute towards better implantation. I told Rajesh about the work that one of my PhD students was doing on cumulus cells. Rajesh suggested that I try using these cumulus cells to nurture the embryos in a petri dish and extend their use in the uterus. It was here, one evening on Marine Drive, while observing a stray squirrel that the concept of cumulus aided transfer (CAT) was born.

The cumulus cells surround the oocyte prior to ovulation. They are important for providing nutrition and promote the growth and maturation of the oocyte. In fact they are a treasure of growth factors, adhesion-producing substances, and substances called interleukins and cytokines that participate in the 'conversation' that occurs between the egg and the uterus in order to promote implantation.

During the IVF and ICSI procedures, these cells are displaced from the egg and discarded. We decided to culture these cells, to see if they could help the embryos to develop better in the laboratory. As these cumulus cells proliferate, they form layers of expanding cells called feeder or helper cells because they help the embryos to receive nutrition. The embryos are then transferred to dishes containing cumulus co-cultured cells and allowed to grow over two to four days (see Figure 10.1, 10.2, and 10.3 in insert pages). At the time of transfer, the embryos are transferred to the uterus along with these co-cultured cumulus cells.

We discovered a sudden jump in the success rate of women becoming pregnant. To curb our initial excitement, we decided to replicate this on a larger scale.

We selected 517 women who were undergoing ICSI and divided them into two groups. Group A had a total of 267 women who had undergone embryo transfer with CAT. The remaining 250 women in group B had undergone embryo transfer without CAT. Women in both groups were matched for age and had an equal number of embryos transferred on day three. The pregnancy rate was 47.6 percent in the 267 women who had undergone the CAT procedure, and 34 percent in the 250 women who had not undergone it. We also noticed that women in the CAT group had a higher rate of twins than in the other group. We realized that we were onto something important.

I telephoned Rajesh excitedly while he was in a meeting in Boston, to share the great news with him. 'Firuza, I am about to give a lecture! What are you calling the procedure?' he asked. 'Cumulus co-culture and cumulus aided embryo transfer; COCAET,' I replied. 'You need a better name,' he responded. 'What is the difference?' I asked. 'Let's call it cumulus aided transfer or just CAT. A rose *can* smell sweeter by its name. Gotta go,' he said and hung up just as I heard them call his name. Today, I get patients from all over the world and they just want 'CAT'!

The article we wrote was accepted in the internationally acclaimed journal *Fertility and Sterility,* and was featured on the cover (October 2006, volume 86 No. 4, pp 839–47). Five years later, they decided to start an Indian edition, the only other edition outside the US. Indian ART had arrived on the international scene and I was invited to be its editor-in-chief. When I thanked Rajesh he added with customary grace, 'Well, let's not forget the squirrel.'

We've never seen another squirrel on Marine Drive nor has anyone else we've talked to.

To get back to the cumulus cells. They continue to secrete growth factors and cytokines within the uterine cavity, helping improve the embryo quality. Since they produce integrins—glue-like substances—they may make the embryo sticky and help with the implantation. They produce progesterone, which primes the uterine lining, making it more conducive to implantation. The cumulus cells also secrete an antioxidant called Glutathione, which scavenges harmful substances surrounding the embryo.

Since we introduced this technique to complement and enhance success with ART, we have seen better success, particularly in older women, those with less number of embryos, and those who had previous unsuccessful IVF/ICSI cycles. The CAT procedure utilizes the mother's own cells and hence does not pose any danger. This procedure can be safely used for all women undergoing IVF/ICSI. However, it should not be used where women show auto-antibodies, such as antinuclear antibodies (ANA), antimicrosomial antibodies (AMA), antithyroid antibodies (ATA), and antiovarian antibodies (AOA). Women exhibiting lupus antibodies should not undergo this procedure as the antibodies may be present in the cumulus cells and attack the embryo.

We were advised to patent the technique. However, Rajesh and I have our own views on intellectual property rights, so we put it up on the internet for all to use instead. It is offered in centres across the world today. At a recently held international conference, I was introduced as the CAT woman. In my defense, I told them that although I have nothing against Batman, it is actually the Joker whom I find more interesting!

Over the past nine years, we have seen an increase in implantation and pregnancy rates at our centre, using this technique and have delivered over 2,000 babies. The bounty and wisdom of nature is truly limitless.

11

Bonus Issues: Multiple Pregnancies

- Incidence of identical and fraternal twins
- Complications of multiple pregnancies
- Preventing the occurrence of multiple pregnancies in ART
- Management of multiple pregnancies

Arti was delighted when she heard that her IVF cycle was successful in the first attempt. We had transferred three embryos into Arti's uterus at the time of ICSI, as she was thirty-eight years old and there was male factor infertility. When we told her that her beta human chorionic gonadotropin hormone (β hCG)—a hormone that is secreted by the placenta and testing for which in the blood can detect a pregnancy even before missing a period—value was high and that it looked like she was carrying twins (Figure 11.1), she was a bit nervous. This is what Arti had to say, 'Although I am happy today, I don't know how I will cope if both babies cry at the same time, if they are both hungry at the same time, and if they both need a diaper change at the same time!' Of the three embryos that were transferred, two implanted resulting in fraternal twins. Arti and her husband are thoroughly enjoying bringing up the babies.

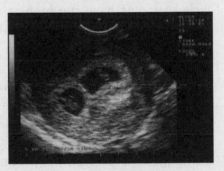

Figure 11.1 An ultrasonographic picture of Arti's IVF twins

Incidence of identical and fraternal twins

In nature, the chances of multiple pregnancies are governed by Hellin's Law. Accordingly, the rate of twins is 1 out of 80 pregnancies, triplets—1 out of 6,400 pregnancies, and quadruplets—1 out of 5,12,000 pregnancies. For math buffs it would be 80, 80^2, and 80^3 respectively.

W. Somerset Maugham is one of our favourite writers.

He almost became a gynaecologist before opting to become a writer. At one of his parties in the Villa Mauresque, he narrated the following joke. After a woman had triplets she told a friend, 'the doctor tells me that it happens only once in 1,67,000 times.' 'Goodness,' he replied, 'how did you find time to do anything else?'

While the incidence of monozygotic or identical, twins remains constant worldwide, the incidence of dizygotic or fraternal twins varies. Identical twins are a result of the splitting of a single fertilized egg into two or more embryos, while fraternal twins result from multiple eggs being fertilized with individual sperm in the same menstrual cycle. Africans have the highest rate of twinning, while Asians have the lowest. During IVF/ICSI, the chances of multiple pregnancies are as high as 25 percent, because more than one embryo is usually placed into the uterus.

Within the next year, two of Arti's friends came to our centre requesting IVF twins! Both were counselled, and it turned out that they neither needed twins nor IVF.

Complications of multiple pregnancies

Although many couples are relieved at the thought of completing their family when they conceive twins, they need to be aware of the risks associated with multiple pregnancies, particularly the risk of maternal and foetal complications. Many of these risks are easy to handle. However, some of them can cause significant distress.

Excessive nausea, vomiting, and anaemia

Women with multiple pregnancies may experience excessive nausea and vomiting, more mechanical pressure in the abdomen as the pregnancy progresses, and may also become anaemic. Nature invariably chooses to conserve the baby over the mother and hence the mother's iron reserves are depleted in favour of the babies. The drama of the mother's sacrifice is not just a Bollywood fantasy!

High blood pressure, diabetes, and hydramnios

Later in the pregnancy, women with multiple pregnancies are at a risk of developing high blood pressure and diabetes. Since the placenta is large, or there may even be two placental sites, extra fluid may surround the babies for their protection. This can cause a condition called hydramnios. Due to the extra fluid, the chances of premature delivery increase. Rarely, the placenta may separate during the third trimester, which can cause bleeding requiring hospitalization and even early delivery of the baby.

Prematurity

A more serious complication of multiple pregnancies is prematurity. Babies of multiple births are usually small for their gestational age. Premature babies require incubators and care in an ICU setting. The lungs of premature babies are immature and they may develop respiratory distress. It is important to allow these babies to deliver with minimal trauma. Hence, the doctor may prefer to deliver twins and triplets by caesarean section.

Other complications

Retinopathy and brain haemorrhage of the baby are some other complications that may arise. The delivery must be conducted in a hospital setting with excellent intensive care facilities. A paediatrician, trained in high-risk pregnancies, will make the outcome of such pregnancies favourable, thus preventing disability. Furthermore, babies born at preterm need extensive care in the first few months of delivery.

The incredible couple, Farah Khan and Shirish Kunder, being fully aware of these risks took the decision to go ahead with triplets (see pp 265–75). With faith in God, herself, and me, Farah bravely went ahead with her multiple pregnancies, all along shooting *Om Shanti Om*, judging TV reality shows, choreographing dances and fashion shows, and not being late for a single medical appointment! Someday I will tell Diva, Anya, and Czar—the lovely babies born out of ART and super human determination and courage—the story of their coming to this world. Bollywood would be hard pressed to match the heroism!

Preventing the occurrence of multiple pregnancies in ART

There are several ways in which the incidence of multiple pregnancies can be brought down. Today, the trend all over the world is to put in less number of embryos. In some western countries only one good quality embryo is transferred. This ensures a single pregnancy, but also brings down the pregnancy rate. This may be acceptable in some countries where the cost of the IVF cycles is borne by their government. Many countries with a negative birth rate offer up to four IVF cycles free of cost, and hence couples may accept single embryo transfers. In our country, since the couples themselves bear the cost, they often want the best possible chances. Hence, we often transfer two to three embryos.

Vitrification is the instantaneous super cooling of a liquid, resulting in a swift transition, which assures that all biological processes stop instantaneously. This technique of freezing extra embryos helps the embryos recover well after the thaw. The required number of embryos are placed into the woman's uterus, while the others are frozen, bringing down the chances of multiple pregnancies.

For women who are pregnant with triplets or more, the doctor may suggest foetal reduction. First trimester foetal reduction can be carried out both by transabdominal or transvaginal sonography. Every procedure carries a risk. There is a small possibility that other foetuses will miscarry, but the procedure reduces the overall risk to the remaining foetus or foetuses and to the mother.

The American Society for Reproductive Medicine (ASRM) have issued guidelines in 2013 on the number of embryos to be transferred. The number depends on the age of the woman, her past IVF history and the quality of embryos. The guidelines ensure that the risk of multiple pregnancies is minimized without compromising the pregnancy rates.

Management of multiple pregnancies

Women carrying multiple pregnancies need thorough supervision at all times. Supplementation of the pregnancy with increased nutrients helps to reduce the incidence of anaemia. Frequent antenatal visits help detect various complications at the earliest, so that timely management is possible.

Antenatal administration of corticosteroids, which are immunosuppresants, has resulted in a decrease in the incidence of the two most significant complications of twin pregnancies—respiratory distress syndrome and intraventricular haemorrhage. The delivery should be conducted in a hospital with facilities for intensive care for the babies with adequate skilled personnel. The couple and the doctor must weigh the advantages and disadvantages of multiple pregnancies, and then decide what the best possible outcome should be. With proper care, healthy babies can be delivered and bring double and, sometimes, triple the joy.

12

Repeated Miscarriages:
Losses of Lives Unborn

- Factors that contribute towards miscarriages
- The good news

A miscarriage results in considerable emotional turmoil. This is more so when the conception has occurred after years of efforts in becoming pregnant. It has been estimated that in nature about 50 percent of implanted embryos are lost even before the period is missed. Another 12 to 15 percent of pregnancies are lost within the first twelve weeks of pregnancy. Those who have had one miscarriage, need not despair, as the chances of a viable birth after one miscarriage are approximately 76 percent. After two or three miscarriages, the chances of a live birth are 70 and 65 percent respectively. When one has experienced four miscarriages, the chances of a live birth are approximately 60 percent. So the future is not too bleak.

Spontaneous abortion is the scientific name for a miscarriage. Several studies have shown that the most common cause of miscarriages is the production of genetically abnormal embryos. These are responsible for approximately 50 percent of first trimester pregnancy losses.

Recurrent spontaneous abortion (RSA) or recurrent miscarriage has been defined as the occurrence of three or more clinically recognized pregnancy losses, before twenty weeks of pregnancy. However, doctors usually start investigating possible factors once a woman has had two miscarriages.

Factors that contribute towards miscarriages

Age

Rachna had just turned forty-three, and she and her husband, Amar, were in a state of despair. They had had a late marriage and had started planning for a baby only after she turned thirty-nine. Between thirty-nine and forty-one she had three miscarriages. I opined that her miscarriages were age related and had ruled out other causes. At forty-one they decided to stop trying to have a baby. Rachna missed her period and did not give it a second thought because she attributed it to the onset of menopause. When she started spotting and then bleeding heavily, she called me saying, 'Doctor, I don't feel normal. I have the same nausea that I used to get when I was pregnant. Her examination revealed that she was indeed pregnant. A sonography confirmed that the baby was of ten weeks. However, examination for nuchal thickness (NT) showed a thickened neck fold—suggestive of Down's syndrome in the baby. A blood screening revealed a higher risk for Down's syndrome. A few days after the scan she had a spontaneous miscarriage.

After thirty-five, the risk of miscarriage increases. After age forty, more than 33 percent of normal pregnancies will result in miscarriage, and this risk continues to increase as the woman ages. This is attributed to the ageing egg. As the woman ages, degenerative changes occur in the meiotic spindle—the store house of genetic material in the egg. That is why women over forty are more prone to having babies with Down's syndrome.

Hence, it is vital that one should not delay childbearing indefinitely. A woman's fertility peaks at twenty-four and starts declining by thirty-seven. In spite of all the daily pressures, couples should plan their first child before the woman crosses thirty.

Genetic and chromosomal abnormalities

We have 46 chromosomes in pairs in most cells of our body except in the sperm and oocytes, which have a single set of 23 chromosomes. When the sperm and oocyte fuse, the baby has 46 chromosomes again. If any one chromosome of a pair fails to separate during cell division, the child will have 47 chromosomes instead of 46. This is called aneuploidy, and can cause birth defects. Generally, the defects are so severe that the foetus does not survive, resulting in a miscarriage. This is nature's way of ensuring the birth of healthy children.

Of the chromosomal abnormalities, the majority are trisomies, such as in Trisomy 21. When any one chromosome is extra it is called Trisomy where as dropping of a chromosome is called Monosomy. If one of the X chromosomes are deleted, it is called Monosomy X or 45XO, commonly called Turner's syndrome. In triploidy, all the chromosomes are tripled, eg. 69XXX or 69 XXY. In tetraploidy, the chromosomes are quadrupled—92 XXXX/92 XXYY—are present.

Although chromosomal errors are the cause of the majority of miscarriages, they are not usually caused by an inherited trait from the mother or father. Less than 5 percent of couples tested will have an inherited genetic cause of such chromosomal defects. Thus the vast majority occur by chance and may not repeat in the future.

Trisomy 21, also known as Down's syndrome or mongolism, is a condition in which the children have low IQ and characteristic facial features. Another common trisomy is that of Chromosome 18 or Edward's syndrome (Figure 12.1) characterized by club feet and developmental delay. Trisomy 13 or Patau syndrome causes cleft lip, cleft palate, and many other congenital malformations. Trisomies 16 and 22 are other common aneuploidies found in miscarriages, although other chromosomes can be involved.

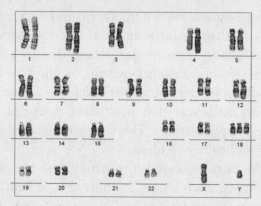

Figure 12.1 Karyotyping reveals Trisomy 18

The most common type of monosomy is Turner's syndrome, where one X chromosome is absent. In this condition, the girl may have small or absent ovaries and a short stature. This is generally picked up on ultrasonography (USG) as a cystic hygroma or swelling around the neck. Monosomy of other chromosomes results in early abortions. Hence, it is important to check if there is a chromosomal cause for spontaneous abortions, especially if other causes such as hormonal imbalance, clotting factor abnormalities, or specific antibodies have not been identified.

Sometimes there may be an extra sex chromosome (X chromosome) resulting in a karyotype of 47XXY or Klinefelter's syndrome (Figure 12.2) in males. These males are infertile due to azoospermia and they develop breasts (gynaecomastia) at puberty. Some young children with this condition are known to have autistic features. When women have an extra X chromosome, the karyotype is 47XXX. Such women may have irregular periods and infertility.

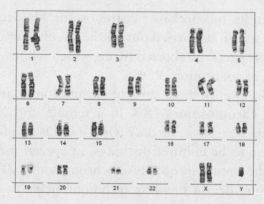

Figure 12.2 Karyotyping reveals Klinefelter's syndrome 47XXY

Triploidy is yet another common cause of miscarriages. Here, an entire set of 23 chromosomes is extra, resulting in a total of 69 chromosomes. This condition can also manifest as a molar pregnancy, where the villi of the placenta are swollen. Besides numerical abnormalities in the number of chromosomes, there are many structural abnormalities in the shape of the chromosomes, such as translocations, inversions, duplications, and deletions. Chromosome analysis or karyotyping of apparently normal couples can detect certain hidden abnormalities called balanced translocations. This means that although the DNA is intact, because of which there is no obvious defect, all the chromosomes are not in matching pairs. There is a rearrangement between two pairs of chromosomes, where a segment has been interchanged. If the child inherits only one of the two rearranged chromosomes, it results in an unbalanced translocation causing severe abnormalities, which are not compatible with survival. If the rearrangement is very small, a child with a low IQ could be born. Karyotyping and FISH are the most common genetic tests to check for chromosome abnormalities. These tests can be carried out on the couple, but it is also necessary to test the aborted tissue, which is known as the product of conception (POC).

All the twenty-three pairs of chromosomes, including the sex chromosomes (XX in a female and XY in a male), are clearly visible only when a cell is dividing. The cells have to be cultured for days, in special incubators to get the optimum quality of chromosomes. The high resolution Giemsa banding technique helps to pick up more aberrations, as the chromosomes are thin and long, with many dark and light bands. The chromosomes are arranged in pairs, where the bands are matched to form a karyotype and checked for abnormalities.

FISH is a procedure used to detect some common chromosome abnormalities rapidly. A karyotype report usually takes fourteen to twenty-one days, whereas FISH results are available in twenty-four to thirty-six hours. The procedure uses a reagent, which paints a chromosome a particular colour. This can be seen as a brightly coloured dot by using a specialized microscope.

Considerable expertise is required to pick up small chromosomal rearrangements. Balanced translocations can be inherited, so several blood relatives could be carriers without knowing it, and they have a risk of getting a child with a birth defect. Hence, genetic counselling is crucial, because a detailed pedigree analysis can help to identify other relatives at risk, who may also need genetic testing at the chromosomal or DNA level.

PGD by FISH is carried out at our centre for the detection of aneuploidies and translocations. PGD is an additional step in the ICSI procedure, where one cell is biopsied on day three, after the oocyte retrieval, and tested for certain chromosome abnormalities. Only normal embryos are transferred after the test.

All genetic abnormalities cannot be detected by karyotyping. Certain chromosome abnormalities called microdeletions, such as DiGeorge syndrome (DGS), which causes congenital heart defects, are too small to be visible under the microscope and can only be detected by FISH.

Single-gene disorders cannot be detected by chromosome analysis as these defects occur in the DNA (see Figure 12.3 in insert pages). Specific DNA-based molecular diagnostic tests have to be carried out, and the affected child, or foetus, also needs to be tested to detect the mutation. Therefore, it is important to extract and store the DNA of the aborted foetus or of children suspected to have a genetic disorder. This will enable a proper diagnosis in subsequent pregnancies.

There are different patterns of inheritance of single-gene disorders. These can be determined by obtaining a detailed family history during genetic counselling, and determining the risk of recurrence.

In autosomal recessive conditions, both the apparently normal parents carry a mutation of the same disease on one chromosome of a pair, while the other chromosome carries the normal gene. The normal gene overrides the effect of the abnormal gene, so the parents look normal. If the child inherits the chromosome with the mutated gene from both parents, there is no normal gene to mask the effect of the abnormality, and therefore, such children are affected with the disorder. In a pregnancy where both the parents are carriers, there is a 25 percent chance that the child will be affected with the disorder. When a marriage takes place between blood relatives such as cousins, there is a greater chance that the same abnormal gene, running silently in the family, is present in both the husband and wife, hence a genetic disease can manifest strongly in the children of such couples.

Autosomal dominant conditions are generally passed on from an affected parent to the child, and the risk of recurrence is 50 percent. X-linked recessive disorders affect males, while females are carriers, since they have two X chromosomes, one of which is normal. In such conditions, there is a 50 percent chance that males will be affected and females will be carriers. Genetic studies can help couples with recurrent miscarriages, to find ways of bypassing the causative factors.

Malti and Vijay had lost two pregnancies, both in the first trimester. When they consulted me, I asked for both their karyotypes. Malti had a Robertsonian translocation. In Robertsonian translocation, a part of one chromosome is transferred to another. This is abnormal. We advised them to undergo PGD to help us select those embryos which did not have the translocation. Out of four eggs, two fertilized. One was normal and subsequently transferred. This resulted in a healthy pregnancy. Malti and Vijay can now fulfil their dream. In fact this is the first report of a successful pregnancy for Robertsonian translocation using PGD in India, and was published as a cover article (see Figure 12.4 in insert pages) in the *Journal of Prenatal Diagnosis & Therapy* (January–June 2010). Malti recently delivered a healthy girl. We have had more such pregnancies since then.

A mutation of a gene called MTHFR gene, prevents the utilization of folic acid in the body, thereby causing miscarriages. Folic acid is very important for the growth of the embryo and the foetus. Its deficiency can cause miscarriages.

Endocrine disorders, particularly diabetes and hypothyroidism

Hyperthyroidism as well as hypothyroidism can cause miscarriages. Rarely, high levels of prolactin can cause imperfect implantation. Lack of, or decreased levels of progesterone could also be responsible for a miscarriage. One of the common reasons for an early miscarriage is the decreased level of progesterone in the body after ovulation. This is known as a luteal phase defect and can occur in women with polycystic ovaries (see pp. 61–3), older women, women who have undergone ovarian stimulation with hormones, and those with diminished ovarian function.

Correction of these endocrinal disorders with medication, dramatically reduces the incidence of miscarriages in these patients.

Anatomic defects of the genital system

The developing foetus has two separate compartments of the uterus, cervix and vagina. As the baby develops, these two compartments break down and unite. If they don't, it can result in various defects such as unicornuate, bicornuate (see Figure 12.5 in insert pages), septate uterus (see Figure 12.6 in insert pages), T-shaped uterus (see Figure 12.7 in insert pages), and double cervix. These can cause miscarriages. The presence of synechiae or adhesions within the uterus can cause a weak implantation with less blood supply to the baby, which can result in a miscarriage.

Many of the defects such as septate and bicornuate uterus are correctable. Earlier these problems required open surgery. Today, with the advent of laparoscopy and hysteroscopy, such defects can be treated by keyhole surgery. However, not all women with bicornuate and septate uterus would require surgical intervention. Some defects, such as unicornuate uterus, may not have a surgical solution, as the volume of the uterus is very small and it may not have the ability to carry a child. Surrogacy can be recommended in this situation.

Infections

The uterus is rich in its blood supply. Occasionally a uterine infection can cause the bacteria to spread throughout the uterine cavity resulting in scarring. Scarring can also occur following a medical termination of pregnancy (see Figure 6.13 in insert pages). Fibrotic bands result from damage to the inside of the uterus and can diminish the blood supply, causing an inability to hold on to the pregnancy. High fever and infections such as hepatitis and malaria can cause the pregnancy to abort. An infection can occasionally develop after an intrauterine procedure, such as embryo reduction, chorion villi biopsy, or amniocentesis. Hence, these procedures should be always considered judiciously.

All procedures during pregnancy should be done with complete aseptic precautions. In case of a suspected infection, suitable antibiotics need to be given. Often the patient needs hospitalization and vigilant care. A hysteroscopic procedure followed by a few months of estrogen replacement therapy is generally helpful.

Growths in the uterus

Fibroids can cause pressure on the growing pregnancy. Fibroids can also cut off the blood supply of the growing pregnancy. Adenomyosis is a condition of generalized enlargement of the uterus. If significant adenomyosis occurs, the uterus loses its elasticity and stretchability causing a miscarriage. Adenomyosis is not a curable condition. Chances of pregnancy continuing till term are rare. Women with adenomyosis of significant dimensions, should consider the option of adoption or surrogacy. Fibroids that cause pressure on the uterus or prevent the blood from reaching the baby need to be removed. Once sonography is carried out, one would know if the fibroids are the cause of the miscarriage. We usually remove fibroids laparoscopically. Open surgery for fibroids is a rarity in my practice.

Floppiness of the cervix (incompetent cervix)

Rosie would check her underwear several times in the day to look out for tell-tale signs of an impending miscarriage. She had conceived spontaneously four times over and aborted painlessly in the sixth month of every pregnancy. By the beginning of the third month, she was a nervous wreck. A slight tug on the pelvis, or a back cramp, caused her so much distress that she developed severe acidity. Rosie suffered from the condition of an incompetent cervix.

In this condition, the uterus opens up without notice and the baby slips out. The entire process is like a relatively painless, mini labour. After Rosie completed twelve weeks, we took a stitch encircling the cervix, known as cervical cerclage, in order to strengthen it. With the help of medicines to relax the uterus, Rosie crossed thirty-six weeks and delivered a healthy 6 pound baby vaginally. One of the tragedies of obstetrics is the silent opening of an incompetent cervix. This usually occurs without warning signs at around five to six months of pregnancy; at a time when the baby is well formed but not mature enough to survive in the outside world.

A simple procedure of tying a purse string suture around the cervix, along with medicines to relax the uterus, can help an incompetent cervix. This stitch, called Shirodkar's stitch, was designed by Dr V. N. Shirodkar—a stalwart obstetrician and gynaecologist in 1955.

Immunological conditions

Antibodies are designed to fight off infection in the human body. With certain autoimmune disorders, antibodies fight off the developing pregnancy, as if it were a foreign body or infection. The presence of ANAs, AMAs, ATAs, AOAs, anticardiolipin antibodies (ACA), and anti-phospholipid antibodies can interrupt the blood supply to the baby. Some antibodies can disrupt the formation of eggs, and can even disrupt implantation. Antiphospholipid syndrome (APS) is an autoimmune disorder, diagnosed by blood tests that detect levels of ACA and lupus anticoagulant.

A recent study published in the scientific journal *Human Reproduction*, showed that the presence of natural killer cells can harm the growing pregnancy, or may even prevent implantation. These antibodies usually cause early miscarriages. Antibodies, such as ACA, can cause blood clots that clog the blood supply to the placenta, resulting in foetal demise.

A successful pregnancy occurs when the mother's immune system does not treat the foetus like a foreign body. Sometimes similarity in maternal and paternal human leukocyte antigens (HLA) can cause the mother's body to reject the baby.

Autoimmunity caused by antibodies can be treated with the help of steroids and immunoglobulins (IVIG) given intravenously. In case there are tiny clots which disrupt the placenta, aspirin and/or heparin therapy is recommended. These therapies should be carried out under the strict supervision of a doctor. Rejection due to sharing of HLA, can be treated by giving IVIG or by injecting the mother with lymphocytes (white blood cells) obtained from the father.

Male factor

There is some evidence that defects in the sperm may cause miscarriages. DNA damage is also responsible for miscarriages. Earlier, it was believed that it was only older women who were susceptible to miscarriages, but scientific data has shown that older men can also cause miscarriages in their wives.

Stress

We recently published a chapter in the book, *Pregnancy at Risk*, on the role of stress factors in early pregnancy loss. The first trimester, which is considered as the period of greatest stress, has the highest rate of pregnancy loss. Several stress-related hormones have a direct detrimental impact on placental hormone secretions and thus contribute towards miscarriages. Destressing strategies, and psychologically healthy coping mechanisms should be emphasized to enhance psychological well being and diminish reproductive loss. Sometimes, antidepressant medications are indicated.

Unknown causes

It may not always be possible to determine the cause of a miscarriage even after extensive testing. Besides, it is possible to have different causes for each miscarriage.

The good news

When cardiac activity is seen at six weeks of gestation by ultrasound, over 75 percent of these pregnancies will result in a live birth. Women often deliver healthy babies in spite of one or more miscarriages. With genetic analysis and counselling, as well as vigilant antenatal care, we can prevent many miscarriages and ensure the birth of healthy babies.

13

Are ART Babies Normal?

- Will my baby be normal?
- Risk of birth defects in IVF babies
- Factors associated with birth defects
- Are IVF children more intelligent?
- Is IVF linked to childhood cancer?
- The risk of autism and mental retardation
- Can abnormalities be detected during pregnancy?
- The double marker, triple marker, quadruple marker and the NACE test
- What is amniocentesis?
- Chorionic villus sampling (CVS)
- Prevention of abnormalities
- The importance of being realistic

Will my baby be normal?

Louise Brown is a unique woman. Born on July 25, 1978, Louise is the world's first test tube baby, and in January 2007 she delivered her own baby naturally. In October 2010, Robert Edwards, one of the two doctors responsible for Louise's birth received the long overdue Nobel Prize for Medicine. In the intervening period, more than four million babies have been born by various techniques of ART. However, the question that couples undergoing ART are most likely to ask is, 'Will my baby be normal?'

A review of cumulative data indicates that IVF babies are as normal as naturally conceived babies. (See p. 182)

In general, the data regarding the outcome of children born after IVF, either with or without the use of ICSI, has been reassuring. The problem with these studies remains the identification of an appropriate control group with which to compare the children conceived by advanced fertility techniques. Although the vast majority of studies do not show a significantly increased risk of anomalies in children conceived after IVF, these studies have not looked at the rate of congenital anomalies in children conceived naturally to parents who suffered infertility, and at those conceived naturally to parents without infertility. Comparisons with these groups of patients would more accurately answer our question as to whether IVF/ICSI babies are more at a risk of having abnormalities.

Risk of birth defects in IVF babies

The risk of birth defects in the general population is usually around 2 to 3 percent of all births. A recent study from

Finland showed the rate of defects, in IVF babies, to be 4.3 percent. This may be due, in part, to the age of the mother, and the higher rate of multiple births seen in IVF cycles.

To find out if the fears of having developmental abnormalities in babies born through ART were valid, Dr Alastair Sutcliffe, a London-based paediatrician, and his collaborators studied the development of 541 ICSI children, 440 IVF children and compared them with 542 normally conceived children, and followed them up to the age of five. This study was carried out in five countries. These researchers compared health at birth and obstetrical complications, birth defects, physical growth, mental development, psychological profile, social development, and family relationships.

No significant differences were found in birth weight, growth, total IQ, motor development, and behaviour problems or in the parental stress levels between the children conceived with infertility treatments and those conceived naturally. Hospital admission rates were slightly higher for ICSI and IVF babies, although the rate of medical illnesses across the three groups was similar. It was also found that ICSI mothers and fathers were more committed to their role as parents than others.

All the children were tested on various developmental markers. At the age of five, the ICSI and IVF babies were doing just as well as the naturally conceived babies in many areas, such as height and weight, verbal performance, overall IQ, and motor development. The only negative aspect was the finding that there was a slightly higher rate of bodily malformations among the IVF and ICSI children. The authors of the study explained this on the basis that the age of mothers undergoing ART was higher and that couples with infertility may have genetic problems integral to their infertility, which can be passed on to their children.

Factors associated with birth defects

Many known factors are associated with an increased incidence of congenital anomalies. Researchers suggest that the problem lies not so much with the IVF process but, unfortunately, with the patients who require IVF/ICSI to conceive.

The use of ICSI to fertilize eggs has been linked with a higher incidence of sex chromosome abnormalities in the male offspring. Currently, this is thought to be due to the transmission of chromosome abnormalities from the father, rather than an effect of the ICSI. This is because sex chromosome abnormalities are seen in the sperm of men with severe male factor infertility. In other words, were these men to father children naturally, the same genetic anomalies would be seen in their male children. But then again, were they able to father children without ICSI, they would not need to undergo the treatment in the first place.

Angelman syndrome, in which the child has mental retardation and inability to speak, is one of the genetic disorders that is very rarely associated with IVF babies. Another is Beckwith-Wiedemann syndrome, which is characterized by a 15 percent risk of childhood cancers of the kidney, liver, or muscle. The other possible abnormalities could be a large tongue, abdominal wall defects, and low levels of blood sugar in infancy. These disorders are rare. Angelman syndrome occurs once in about every ten thousand children, and Beckwith-Wiedemann occurs once in thirteen thousand children.

Data over the years shows that IVF children may rarely have defects in the heart valves. They may develop cleft palate, kidney problems, and a rare form of eye cancer known as retinoblastoma—common among children born by IVF in the Netherlands. Most of these are correctable by surgery by the age of five, and the children go on to be normal and healthy.

Margaret Allinson, spokesperson for the European Society for Human Reproduction and Embryology (ESHRE), commented that the risk of malformations is 6 percent for ICSI babies, 4.5 percent for IVF babies, and 2.5 percent for naturally conceived babies. The general consensus among practitioners of ART was that these results should reassure patients undergoing IVF and ICSI.

Are IVF children more intelligent?

A study by Belgian psychologist Lize Leunens, from the Free University in Brussels, compared 151 ICSI children with another group of 151 naturally conceived children, and showed that the ICSI children had higher IQ than those conceived naturally. The most likely explanation for the finding is that mothers of ICSI children might provide more stimulation, and spend more time interacting with their children.

Is IVF linked to childhood cancer?

A large UK study carried out by Dr Carrie Williams and researchers at the Institute of Child Health looked at 1,06,381 children born through ART between 1992 and

2008. They concluded that there is no increased risk of cancer in IVF children.

The risk of autism and mental retardation

A Swedish study that evaluated more than 2.5 million children was recently published in JAMA (Journal of the American Medical Association). The study looked at the neurodevelopment of IVF children. Sven Sandin & colleagues looked at this data and studied the offsprings born between 1982 and 2007. They looked at whether these children were born through IVF, ICSI, fresh or frozen embryos. Of these 2.5 million children, about 30,000 (1.2 percent) were born following an IVF procedure. The findings were both reassuring and worrisome. The reassuring part was that IVF treatment was not associated with autistic disorder. The worrisome part was that there was a small but statistically increased risk of mental retardation in those children who were born following ICSI. However, this risk vanished when the researchers looked at another risk factor - multiple pregnancy. This means that if the child was born following ICSI and was a singleton, the risk was much less than the risk if the child was from a multiple pregnancy. Also, if the child was born prematurely, there was more risk. The researchers also showed that the risk of mental retardation increased if the sperm were obtained surgically (as with TESA and PESA) rather than from ejaculated sperm.

The scientific explanation that is given is that couples who use ICSI already have problematic sperm to begin with as happens with men with male factor infertility.

Can abnormalities be detected during pregnancy?

Using high resolution sonography and a battery of blood tests, it is possible to pick up a majority of abnormalities in the foetus. The sonologist will have to pay special attention to the anatomy of the baby. If the thickness of the fold of skin over the baby's neck, or Nuchal Translucency (NT), is increased, special tests are conducted to rule out Down's syndrome. The sonologist will also look at the flow of blood in a blood vessel called the ductus. By twelve to fifteen weeks, a foetal echocardiogram will confirm the presence of Down's syndrome.

This testing is particularly useful if the mother is more than thirty-four years old. An evaluation of the stomach, the limb length, and the brain will throw light on any subtle defects. Defects in the spinal cord, the digestive system, and the kidneys can be detected sonographically. A 3D sonography is helpful in picking up a significant number of defects. First trimester blood screening tests, and a second trimester triple screening tests are both very sensitive tests to screen for neural tube disorders, Edward's and Down's syndromes.

The double marker, triple marker, quadruple marker and the NACE test

First trimester screening for foetal chromosomal disease is carried out using the maternal serological markers, pregnancy-associated plasma protein-A (PAPP-A), and BhCG in combination with the ultrasound marker for NT. It is a fairly accurate screening test for Down's syndrome and neural tube defects.

The triple screen or triple marker test is performed between the sixteenth and twentieth week of pregnancy. This test should be offered to all pregnant women. The triple screen looks at the levels of alpha fetoprotein (AFP), BhCG, and estriol.

Additionally, information regarding the mother's age, weight, ethnicity, and gestation of pregnancy is noted, in order to interpret the results of the triple and quadruple marker test. In addition to the triple screening, the quadruple marker test also looks at the levels of inhibin A—a hormone produced by the placenta. An elevated level of inhibin A indicates an increased risk of having a baby with Down's syndrome.

During the second trimester, the levels of AFP and unconjugated estriol increase, whereas that of BhCG decreases, and the amount of inhibin A stays relatively constant. AFP is produced by the foetus and then crosses into the mother's blood. A foetus with a neural tube defect has an opening in its spine or head that allows an increased amount of AFP to pass into the mother's blood. Sometimes the increased AFP may also arise from multiple gestation, foetal reduction, foetal demise, miscalculation of gestational age, an abdominal wall defect, or an unknown reason. In pregnancies where the foetus has Down's syndrome or Edward's syndrome, the results of the triple or quadruple marker screen tend to show decreased levels of AFP and unconjugated estriol, and increased levels of BhCG and inhibin A.

If the triple and quadruple screenings are positive (see Figure 13.1 in insert pages), we suggest a detailed sonography and an amniocentesis to check for chromosomal abnormalities in the baby.

However, it is important to remember that a triple test is a screening and not a diagnostic test. This test only acts as a warning that a mother is at a possible risk of carrying a baby with a genetic disorder. The triple screen test is known to have a high percentage of false positive results. Abnormal test results warrant additional testing for making a diagnosis. A more conservative approach involves performing a second triple screen, followed by a high definition ultrasound. If the testing still reveals abnormal results, a more invasive procedure such as amniocentesis may be performed.

The Non-Invasive Analysis for Chromosomal Examination (NACE) test is done around the twelfth week of pregnancy. It is less invasive than amniocentesis since it only involves the mother's blood sample. The test uses genomic analysis with massive sequencing and can detect the three most common chromosomal abnormalities: Trisomies 21, 18 and 13. It can also detect defects in sex chromosomes such as those seen in Turner's Syndrome 45XO and Klinefelter's Syndrome 47XXY. The NACE test has a very high detection level even when there is a low concentration of fetal blood in the maternal blood.

What is amniocentesis?

A baby is cushioned in the womb safely, as it is surrounded by amniotic fluid—a fluid secreted by the kidneys. The amniotic fluid contains many skin cells that have been shed from the baby's skin. These cells can be used to diagnose many abnormalities such as Down's syndrome, Edward's syndrome, and Turner's syndrome.

During amniocentesis, a local anaesthetic is injected

through the skin. Using a fine needle, the sonologist removes about 10 millilitres of amniotic fluid, which is then tested in the laboratory. FISH gives the results in twenty-four to thirty-six hours. This shortens the parents' anxiety time. Karyotyping of the fluid takes twenty-one days. Figure 13.2 in insert pages is a photograph of a normal male karyotype and FISH as compared to a photograph of an abnormal karyotype and FISH (see Figure 13.3 in insert pages).

Chorionic villus sampling (CVS)

Chorionic villus sampling (CVS) is a prenatal diagnostic procedure, used to determine chromosomal or genetic disorders in the foetus. The test is usually performed at ten to twelve weeks of pregnancy, and involves taking a tiny bit of placental tissue from the uterus and sending it for genetic testing. CVS is done either through the cervix (transcervical) or through the abdomen (transabdominal). Both techniques are safe when performed by an expert.

The transcervical procedure is carried out by inserting a thin plastic tube through the cervix, in order to reach the placenta using ultrasound guidance. A small sample of placental tissue (chorionic villus tissue) is removed.

The transabdominal procedure is performed by inserting a needle through the abdomen and uterus, into the placenta under ultrasound guidance. A small amount of tissue is drawn into the syringe. The sample obtained by either technique is then sent to the genetics laboratory. Both the procedures are relatively pain-free, and can be performed under local anaesthesia. The doctor needs to maintain extreme asepsis while conducting the procedure.

There is a 0.5 percent chance of miscarriage following these procedures.

Some of the conditions that can be detected by prenatal screening are: neural tube defects, Down's syndrome, Tay-Sachs disease (TSD), sickle-cell anaemia, thalassemia, cystic fibrosis, fragile X syndrome, Angelman syndrome, and Duchenne muscular dystrophy. Some of these genetic conditions are lethal.

Prevention of abnormalities

We strongly recommend folic acid to all pregnant women and those planning a pregnancy, because adequate intake of folic acid is important for the normal neurological development of the child. For older women undergoing IVF/ICSI, we can perform the technique of PGD to reduce the risk of having an abnormal baby. This technique is very useful and can increase the chances of a successful IVF.

The importance of being realistic

Whenever a technique has been associated or even suggested to be associated with a problem, it is important to look at that association to see if it is real. IVF babies are looked at and scrutinized much more carefully than naturally conceived babies. Just the process of studying babies conceived through ART in more detail can reveal problems which might otherwise be ignored in the general population.

My mentor, Dr Alan DeCherney—Chief of the Reproductive Biology and Medicine Branch at NICHD, Washington, and past editor-in-chief of *Fertility and Sterility*, says that patients aren't deterred when they hear about some of these studies. This may be because of the strong desire to have a baby as well as the low risk of abnormalities.

As with any medical procedure, it is important that patients understand what the treatment entails, and the risks involved. Our ethical code of practice states that clinicians must inform patients about the possible side effects and risks of treatment, including any risks for the child. At Jaslok, this is our basic commitment to those who entrust themselves to our care.

14

Roads Less Taken: Other Options

- Guidelines for considering other options
- Donor sperm
- Donor eggs
- Donor embryos
- Surrogacy
- Adoption
- Keeping a time frame—however, failed IVF does not always mean no baby
- Checklist before giving up
- Strategies for moving on

Sunila and Rishab, aged forty and forty-three, had undergone six cycles of IVF. They were now at crossroads regarding further treatment. Sunila wanted to try it one last time. Rishab came to me for advice. They had both put their careers on hold, giving up their hectic jobs, in order to devote their full attention to IVF. I had a long counselling session with them. I explained to them that the chances of conceiving with their own eggs and sperm were significantly diminished if a pregnancy did not occur after six attempts. Sunila and Rishab then decided to try donor eggs. Sunila conceived twins in the first cycle.

Priscilla and Noren had undergone seven cycles of IUI in the United States. Noren's semen report showed severe oligospermia. They decided against using donor sperm and took a call to try ICSI once. The embryos did not look healthy. I advised them that the sperm factor may prevent successful IVF. Priscilla did not conceive. The couple opted for adoption. Each year they send me photographs of the beautiful daughter they adopted from India.

On the other hand, there is Vaishali and Suresh's story. On their second meeting with a gynaecologist, Vaishali was told that she did not have a chance at becoming a mother. Suresh had spent sleepless nights consoling Vaishali. When they saw me, their tests revealed that Vaishali had an infantile uterus, due to her condition of hypogonadotropic hypogonadism. In this condition, the pituitary gland does not secrete the hormones FSH and LH, which are required to stimulate the ovaries. This is a very treatable condition. We started her on gonadotropins and her ovaries responded to the stimulation. When ovulation was imminent, we performed an IUI. Vaishali got pregnant and delivered a healthy baby girl.

There are several options available for those who do not succeed with IVF/ICSI using their own sperm and ova. These include the use of donor sperm, donor ova or donor embryos. In addition, there are the options of surrogacy and adoption.

Guidelines for considering other options

Here are some guidelines for those who would like to know when to consider options other than ART:

1. If a woman is under thirty-eight, and her partner has normal semen parameters, they should try IVF/ICSI up to six times. Beyond that, there are diminishing returns.

2. If the female partner is between thirty-eight to forty-two, with normal FSH and AMH, and the male partner has normal semen parameters, they should try conceiving with her own eggs for three cycles. After that, the couple should consider donor eggs, particularly if the quality of eggs and embryos is suboptimal.

3. Women with low AMH and a rising or high FSH should consider donor eggs.

4. If the sperm function tests show poor sperm function repeatedly, and the embryo quality at the time of ICSI is poor, a couple may want to consider PGD along with ICSI. If poor quality or genetically abnormal embryos are consistently produced, the couple may consider the use of donor sperm.

5. If the uterine lining does not grow well (beyond 7 millimetres), and if the woman has suffered from genital TB, the chances of having a successful intrauterine pregnancy are low. The couple may want to consider surrogacy or adoption.

6. The couple should always ensure that a thorough discussion is had with their doctor. One should never hesitate in taking a second opinion.

'Giving up' is a very difficult decision facing a couple that has not succeeded with ART. There are several situations—financial, social, family pressures, relationship problems, mental as well as physical exhaustion—which result in a couple wanting to give up trying for a baby.

Donor sperm

Donor sperm can be considered, in case the male partner has azoospermia, due to a condition called Sertoli cell only syndrome. When the FSH value of the male partner is more than twice the normal range, the chances of obtaining sperm by techniques of TESA are decreased. Before agreeing to donor sperm, we may suggest doing a trial TESA. In this situation, the urologist will extract tiny bits of tissue containing the seminiferous tubules from the testes under local anaesthesia. The embryologist will then check for testicular sperm under the microscope. In the event that sperm are found, these will be frozen for use at the time of ICSI.

There are other compelling reasons to use donor sperm. Some of these are hereditary genetic defects in the male and Rh incompatibility. Rh incompatibility is a mismatch condition that occurs during pregnancy if a woman has Rh-negative blood and her baby has Rh-positive blood. We quarantine the semen sample for six months, in order to ensure that the sample used at the time of IUI or ICSI is free of HIV and other sexually transmitted diseases. On the day of the procedure, the semen sample is removed from the cryocontainer. It is then processed for donor use.

Donor eggs

If the quality and quantity of eggs that are produced are not sufficient for a reasonable chance of success, one may consider using donor eggs. ICMR has laid down several guidelines for the use of donor eggs which I have helped draft.

This is how our programme works: The donors are young (between the ages of twenty-five and thirty-two) and married. They are in stable relationships and have their own children. They are educated. They undergo physical and psychological screening and are selected if they are physically and mentally fit. The following blood tests are done for the donors:

1. Thyroid-stimulating hormone (TSH),
2. Prolactin,
3. ATA, AMA,
4. Blood sugar fasting and two hours post lunch,
5. Karyotyping,
6. HIV,
7. Hepatitis B and C,
8. VDRL,
9. Hb Electrophoresis, and
10. Rubella IgG and IgM.

The husband's blood is tested for HIV, hepatitis B and C, and VDRL. We ask for a photograph of the couple in order to match the profile to that of the donor. The donor receives hormone injections, and the recipient is given tablets of estrogen and progesterone to develop the uterine lining. The cycles are then matched closely so that the recipient's lining is ready to receive the embryos (donor eggs fertilized with the husband's sperm). The recipient gets hormonal support after the embryo transfer. We transfer up to three embryos. Extra embryos are frozen. Success rates at our clinic are between 45 to 55 percent for donor eggs.

Donor embryos

We might ask the couple to consider embryo donation if we find that there is a male and female factor. Some of these conditions include genetic disorders, premature ovarian failure, and cases in which the woman is a carrier of a recessive autosomal disorder. There are situations in which the couple cannot adopt for several reasons. In those circumstances, accepting embryo donation and embryo adoption becomes a viable option.

Meenakshi and Surinder recently lost a baby in the fourth month of pregnancy. The karyotyping of the baby revealed Down's syndrome. Hence, Meenakshi had to undergo a medical termination of pregnancy. Not wanting to go through the trauma of losing another baby, they opted for embryo donation. They could not consider adoption as it was not acceptable to the extended family. Being healthy, Meenakshi conceived in the very first attempt.

Surrogacy

Surrogacy is an arrangement between a woman and a couple, or an individual, to carry and deliver a baby. Women or couples who choose surrogacy, often do so because they are unable to conceive due to medical or other reasons. In gestational surrogacy, the embryo of the genetic parents is transferred into the surrogate through the technique of IVF/ICSI.

Vandana wept tears of happiness when she picked up her newborn baby. She had not experienced the baby's first kick in her abdomen nor had she gained any weight. Hers was a long and sad story but one with a happy ending. Vandana was born without a uterus but had normal ovaries. She met Prashant at her cousin's wedding. When she explained to him that she could never be a mother, Prashant was even more determined to marry her. I was relieved after examining Vandana, as both her ovaries were functioning well. I explained to them the concept of surrogacy and how it works in India. They could not wait to start. Vandana produced enough eggs so that some embryos could be frozen. Luckily for the couple, the surrogate lady conceived in the first attempt.

Surrogacy, as a treatment for some types of infertility, is well established in India. Some of the common reasons why the doctor may suggest surrogacy are the presence of multiple fibroids which destroy the shape of the uterus, previous genital TB where the lining of the uterus is too weak to allow the embryo to implant, repeated miscarriages due to a uterine factor, the presence of Rh isoimmunization, and severe maternal diseases such as high blood pressure, renal transplant, or diabetes.

The Indian government has ensured that many single men and women can avail of this method. This is what Zohar and Guy (Picture 14.1), who have recently been blessed with twins through surrogacy, have to say about our surrogacy programme: 'There are not enough words to describe our appreciation and gratitude to you for the joy you have entered into our life. We were blessed to get your superb, professional, medical treatment, and human attitude. You will always be part of our family!'

Picture 14.1 Guy, Zohar, Yarden, and Arbel

This is how our surrogacy programme at Jaslok works.

The surrogates are married, in a stable partnership and have children of their own. They are between the ages of twenty-five and thirty-five. They undergo physical and psychological examination. They are selected only if they are physically and mentally fit.

The following blood tests are routinely carried out:

1. Haemoglobin, complete blood count
2. Hb electrophoresis
3. TSH, prolactin, ATA, AMA
4. Blood sugar, fasting and two hours post lunch
5. HIV, Hepatitis B and C
6. Rubella IgG and IgM
7. Liver and renal function tests

Sometimes couples ask for other tests to be done. If the request is appropriate we carry out those additional tests. The surrogate also undergoes a pelvic sonography, to evaluate the uterine lining, uterus, and pelvic organs. The uterine lining is scanned at various intervals in the cycle, to make sure that the lining is receptive for implantation.

Typically, the surrogate comes from an economically middle class background and stays with her family in Mumbai. The surrogate signs a contract, including a celibacy agreement. At this point in time, the commissioning parents would also sign a legal contract. The surrogate receives medication to match the periods of the biological mother. In case one is carrying frozen embryos or using donor eggs, then cycling is done accordingly. The cycling is either with oral estrogen and progesterone, or with hormone injections, to develop the lining, in case the lining does not respond well to tablets. The transfer is carried out when the uterine lining is ready. Luteal phase support is with injections or tablets.

The pregnancy test is conducted fourteen days after transfer. If the test is positive, it is repeated every fourth day till the βhcg values cross 20,000 iu. The first scan is done about five weeks after transfer. During this time, the surrogate continues to receive folic acid, other protein supplements, and hormonal support.

An important sonographic evaluation is conducted at ten to eleven weeks of gestation, to look for soft markers for any foetal abnormality, including a nuchal fold scan. In the first trimester, a double marker screening is also conducted.

Antenatal blood tests include:
1. Hb, CBC
2. VDRL
3. HIV/Hepatitis B and C
4. Blood sugar, fasting and two hours post lunch
5. Urine examination

The surrogate is provided with supplements of iron and calcium, once the twelfth week of pregnancy begins, and also given fruits and protein supplements. At seventeen weeks, a triple screen is carried out to check for Down's syndrome and neurological abnormalities, along with a level-III sonography, which is a detailed and advanced sonography where major organs of the body are visualized. During this period, the surrogate continues to have routine checkups by our team. A coordinator visits the surrogate's household to confirm her state of hygiene and compliance with medicines. Once she crosses twenty weeks, she is seen every two weeks. A repeat sonography is done at twenty-four, twenty-eight, and thirty-two weeks. At thirty-four weeks, a detailed colour doppler and biophysical profile is conducted. A close watch is kept on the pregnancy, with weekly visits after the thirty-fourth week. Most deliver vaginally but a caesarean section may be planned in case of any obstetric indication. The delivery is carried out by the obstetrician and gynaecologist from our team. The baby is kept under observation in the paediatric unit. When all legal formalities are completed, the commissioning parents can receive the baby—the same day as the delivery if the baby is completely fit. Not many people know that the talented and well-known cartoonist Hemant Morparia is also a brilliant radiologist. He is a close friend of Rajesh's and mine from medical school. Here is a Mother's Day cartoon (Picture 14.2) that he gifted me. It became very popular when it was published in a prominent newspaper.

Picture 14.2 Hemant Morparia's Mother's Day cartoon

Adoption

Many Indian families consider adopting their siblings' children. This is something that can have social and psychological repercussions in later life, and has to be considered carefully. Sachin and Mairaj had an inter-caste marriage. Due to social pressures, they decided to migrate to Australia. Mairaj conceived accidentally but they were not ready for a child. Sachin's brother Avinash and his wife Seema had been infertile for the last eighteen years. Sachin offered to give the baby to his brother in adoption. Mairaj was heartbroken but had no choice in the matter. Four years later when Sachin and Mairaj had enough savings, they decided to have a family. They discovered that Sachin had severe oligospermia and in spite of three attempts at ICSI in Australia, they were childless. They tried to readopt their biological child but that was very traumatic for all concerned. They have now decided to adopt from an Indian agency once they return to India.

Adoption is a very gratifying way to start a new period in one's life. When I suggested adoption to Ashish and Mehul, it was with a sense of relief that they both agreed. They wanted to adopt a girl. Arihant, their first-born had muscular dystrophy—a condition which usually affects male children. Ashish's only hesitation was whether she would be able to love her adopted girl as much as she loved Arihant. I put them in touch with a leading adoption agency in Mumbai. Within six months, Ahilya found a place in their hearts and home. Arihant is as excited as his parents, and has already passed on most of his toys to her.

'Adoption is not about finding children for families, it's about finding families for children,' says Joyce Maguire Pavao, founder of the Adoption Resource Center, Cambridge, USA. 'It is a process that our society developed so that children can grow in a loving environment. Every child has a right to grow in healthy surroundings. Adoption is a legal procedure that makes the birth child of one man and woman into the legal child of other adults.'

Basic rules of adoption

Before both partners decide to adopt a baby, they should realize that it is a time-consuming process that requires a fair amount of paperwork to be completed. Of course, the satisfaction and fulfilment of a baby in one's arms is worth the wait. Fortunately, the Indian government has made the process easier from 2010 onwards.

All adoptions are regulated by the Central Adoption Resource Agency (CARA). It sets out the eligibility conditions, processing steps, documentation, costs, court process, foster care conditions, issuance of the birth certificate, and post-adoption follow up. It is mandatory for adoption agencies, placing children in adoption, to follow the CARA guidelines. It is important to go through a reputed agency so that there are no legal complications.

Keeping a time frame— however, failed IVF does not always mean no baby

Often my patients ask me, 'When should I give up?' I often guide them through a time frame. It is good to look at the calendar, and give oneself the date after which you may consider other options of having a child.

One must remember that IVF does not work for everybody. What follows may be difficult for some to read and one may even skip it thinking that it is irrelevant for someone who is keen on having a baby. I would urge the reader to go through this chapter carefully so that there is a realistic awareness of what IVF can and cannot do.

Checklist before giving up

1. The doctor should be asked to summarize the treatment that has been carried out. The causes of failure should be enumerated. The doctor should be asked if the infertility is an irreversible condition.
2. Is there a financial crunch? Infertility treatment is expensive. If that is the only reason, then one should consider taking a break from treatment and making one's financial position stronger. The doctor should be able to work out a concessional rate in some situations.
3. Is there a strain in the marital relationship? Some couples find the entire process of trying for a baby through ART tiring, unnatural, and may even think that sexual

intimacy is futile. I once treated a couple who came to me with a three-year calendar of the dates on which they had had sex. A pattern emerged as I was looking at the dates. The circled dates were about two to three in a month, and around ovulation time. The husband was resentful of this kind of programmed sex and the couple argued very often. I advised them to put treatment on hold for a while, till they sorted out their personal problems.

4. Is there a sense of resentment towards oneself, one's spouse as well as the doctor? ART treatment can be quite intrusive on the woman's body and personal space. Each cycle consists of injections, blood tests, sonography scans, and the suspense on day fourteen of the treatment. It is important that one does not lower one's self esteem. One must understand that this is not a personal failure; it is the treatment that has failed.

5. Consider using donor eggs, donor sperm, or surrogacy. To succeed with IVF, we need five satisfactory parameters—good eggs, good sperm, good embryos, a good uterine lining, and calm minds. If a couple is unsure, it may be worthwhile to take a break from the treatment in order to assess the situation.

Strategies for moving on

Aparna and Atul wanted to have their own baby. They were unwilling to consider egg or sperm donation, surrogacy, embryo donation, or adoption. 'If it is not our own baby we would be happy enjoying life without children,' Aparna had said. Yet, when I told Aparna that we had come to the end of the road and, as much as I wanted her to be my patient, there was not much I could do for her, she broke down. She said, 'Doctor, you are my only hope. Please don't abandon me.' It is one of the few times that I have had tears in front of a patient. I found her plea emotionally difficult to handle. Moments such as this remind me of my own vulnerability as a human being. Aparna had added, 'Today, it feels like my unborn child has died. A child that I did not breastfeed, a child that I did not caress, to whom I did not tell a bed-time story, and who did not play a prank on my neighbour. A child whose report card I will never see. A child who will not be present at my funeral!' Aparna needed time to grieve, and so did I. She and Atul went through several sessions of counselling. Aparna started working again, joined a gym, and still drops by to say hello. But she has moved on.

When Rajesh heard their story, he immediately had me remove a picture of him and our three children from my office. He felt that we should be sensitive to the feelings of those who are childless, and not display our happy family photographs in contrast to their childless state.

If one has to accept not having a baby, one must do things that give meaning to life. There are many ways of keeping one's life full and happy. There are simple things such as going for a film, catching up with friends and relatives, joining a gym, swimming, meditation and yoga, learning to play a musical instrument, starting a job and a career, and spending more quality time with one's spouse. Sometimes counselling may be required to close this chapter of your life and start a fresh one. One should remember that life has a lot of good things in store for everybody. Life is indeed beautiful! With or without children.

15

Myths and Facts about ART

1. Myth: Eating spicy food causes anovulation, low sperm count, miscarriage, and premature delivery.
   Fact: Eating spicy food only occasionally disturbs the gastrointestinal system and sometimes causes heartburn.
2. Myth: Seven to eight days of abstinence are required before a semen analysis, or before giving a sample for IVF/ICSI/sperm freezing.
   Fact: Increased days of abstinence can in fact decrease the sperm motility. Two to four days of abstinence are adequate for a good semen sample.
3. Myth: Masturbation causes impotency and low sperm count.
   Fact: Masturbation should not be associated with guilt. It does not have an impact on fertility.
4. Myth: The chances of pregnancy are reduced if the ejaculated semen comes out of the vagina after intercourse.
   Fact: Ejaculated semen liquefies after a few minutes in the vagina and some of it can come out. This does not decrease the chances of pregnancy.
5. Myth: The sexual position determines the gender of the baby.
   Fact: No sexual position has any effect on the gender of the baby. There may be other compelling reasons though, for some variation.
6. Myth: Having sex daily increases the chances of pregnancy.
   Fact: Daily sex does not increase the chances of pregnancy and may, in fact, decrease the sperm count on the day of ovulation.

7. Myth: PCOS goes away after having a baby.

   Fact: PCOS is a condition that has a genetic basis. It does not go away by itself. Treatment needs to be continued.

8. Myth: A retroverted uterus causes infertility.

   Fact: A retroverted uterus is present in about 30 percent of women. As long as it is not fixed in the retroverted position, it does not impact fertility.

9. Myth: IVF is completely unnatural.

   Fact: IVF mimics nature and the seven steps of fertilization. The culture medium, incubator, and processes are made as close to nature as possible.

10. Myth: IVF results only in girls.

    Fact: IVF does not change the demography or percentage of girls over boys.

11. Myth: IVF results in weight gain.

    Fact: The hormones may cause water retention but do not lead to weight gain by accumulation of fat. Of course if pregnancy occurs, weight gain ensues!

12. Myth: IVF increases the risk of cancer, particularly of the breast and ovaries.

    Fact: There are several scientific studies that have shown no increased risk of cancer after IVF.

13. Myth: Complete bed rest is required for all patients following IVF.

    Fact: Women can, and should, live a normal life after doing IVF. Recent studies have shown no increase in pregnancy rates in the group of women who took bed rest after IVF as compared to those who did not.

14. Myth: Housework and cooking are prohibited after IVF.

    Fact: Housework, cooking, bending, sleeping on the

stomach, and mild exercise such as walking, are all usually permitted after IVF.

15.   Myth: Taking progesterone injections after IVF is better than vaginal pessaries of progesterone.

Fact: Progesterone injections are painful. They do not have any advantage over vaginal pessaries of progesterone.

16. Myth: This is a comprehensive list of the myths associated with ART.

Fact: No such list can be complete. The reader is welcome to expand this list. Contributors will be acknowledged in the next edition.

17. Myth: Readers will be paid for their contribution.

Fact: Unless one writes Harry Potter novels, authors and publishers earn very little from books!

16

Complementary and Alternative Therapies

- Acupuncture
- Acupressure
- Yoga
- Traditional Chinese Medicine (TCM)
- Mind and body courses
- Homeopathy
- Ayurveda
- Naturopathy
- Nutritional therapy
- Music therapy
- Faith and prayer

There are many complementary and alternative medical therapies (CAM) being used in infertility treatment. These include a variety of healing approaches and therapies taken from around the world, that have historically not been included in conventional western medicine. Although alternative medicine may not provide answers to everything, it may play a role in enhancing the success of infertility treatments. However, I would like to emphasize that I have no research experience with any of these.

Acupuncture

Acupuncture is an ancient Chinese technique, commonly used for migraines, back, neck, and shoulder pain. It has also been tried for infertility. In this technique, needles are placed in several strategic points (Figure 16.1), on the meridians of the body, to improve the blood flow to the reproductive organs. The energy flow is directed towards the reproductive system to improve health and get maximum benefit.

The immediate possible effect of acupuncture is to relax the uterus around the time of embryo transfer.

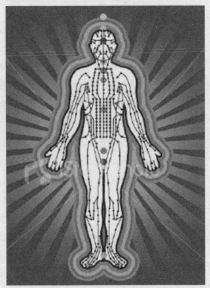

Figure 16.1 Strategic points on the body can cause expulsion of the body meridians that are used for acupuncture

Some studies have shown that uterine contractions transferred embryos. Acupuncture can reduce these contractions, and hence may improve the chances of pregnancy.

Acupuncture is also believed to help reduce stress and promote overall well being and good health. There are claims that acupuncture used during IVF will improve the response to medication, help eggs get healthier, and improve pregnancy rates. Many women with specific problems, such as high FSH levels, or multiple miscarriages have tried acupuncture. However, there is a lack of adequate trials to back these claims.

Cristabelle had several cycles of IUI and IVF. Her problem was that she produced very few ova, and also had inadequate development of the uterine lining. She approached a therapist for acupuncture and had undergone several sessions of therapy. She did not reveal this to me when she came for her sonography. I noticed that she had a very good follicle developing and that the uterine lining seemed to have less inflammation than it normally did. I told her, that this was the first time that I felt that her lining looked receptive. We planned for an IUI in that cycle. It was only after she came with her blood report showing a positive pregnancy test did she reveal to me that she had taken several sessions of acupuncture. I was excited and happy for Cristabelle. I recommended the same therapist to some other patients in similar situations, who inquired about acupuncture, but unfortunately it did not work for them.

Acupressure

Acupressure uses physical pressure rather than needle punctures to treat different energy points, and is based on the same principle as acupuncture, except that it employs pressure, instead of penetration of the skin. It is based on ancient eastern healing techniques. In traditional thought, it works by balancing the energy in the body. Practitioners of acupressure feel that manipulating certain points in the body has a calming effect on the nervous system. As stress has been linked to infertility and lack of success with ART treatment, simple stress relief brought on by acupressure may help improve chances of IVF success. Those practising acupressure on a regular basis, suggest that patients feel calm and energized. This may also keep hormones properly balanced and regulated.

My dear friend Hanifa Bilakhia has used acupressure on me when I have had aches and pains while trekking in the Canadian Rockies. It has worked like magic. I wish I could say that unequivocally about its role in fertility treatments.

Yoga

Yoga is an ancient system of exercise and relaxation. Originating in India, yoga enjoys popularity all over the world, as a way of staying in shape and connecting with the inner self. It is a gentle form of exercise that can reduce stress. Many women undergoing infertility treatment feel calm and a sense of control while doing yoga. It is believed to control negative thought, which might arise from hormonal imbalance. Practitioners of yoga feel that certain poses or asanas help with infertility by opening up the pelvis and hip joints, increasing blood flow to the pelvis, and rebalancing hormones.

Shirshasana or head stand (see Figure 16.2 in insert

pages), Sarvangasana or shoulder stand (see Figure 16.3 in insert pages), Chakrasana or the wheel pose (see Figure 16.4 in insert pages), and Titliasana or the butterfly pose (see Figure 16.5 in insert pages), are the recommended asanas for fertility enhancement. Kapalbhati and Anulom Vilom are breathing techniques suggested for improving the immune system. Gentler forms of yoga such as hatha yoga, ashtanga yoga, and couple's yoga, are practised by couples with fertility problems. Yoga practised with a partner can be a wonderful way to shift focus away from the 'trying to conceive' stress that clouds relationships. This is not to say that yoga is an instant fertility potion or that it works for everyone. It gives you an hour or so of quiet time with yourself. It helps to keep one peaceful during the struggle with infertility.

Since I practise yoga myself, I have recommended it to several patients. We looked at eight women who performed immunity strengthening asanas such as Shirshasana, Sarvangasana, Bhujangasana (see Figure 16.6 in insert pages), Paschimottanasana (see Figure 16.7 in insert pages), and Dhanurasana, over a period of eight to nine months. During this period none of the women took any other immunity modifying medication. We observed a small decrease in the antibody levels of three women. However, the number of women in this study is too small to comment on the utility of yoga. Several large multi-centred trials are needed to authenticate its benefits in fertility management.

Meanwhile, under the guidance of my guru, Pandit Sukhpal Arya (that's him in the photographs), I meditate daily. However, I occasionally cheat on something that he does not encourage—drinking tea. On days when I am busy at work, he is kind enough to come over to the hospital and continue my lessons between surgeries. Needless to add, I encourage all patients to practise yoga.

Traditional Chinese Medicine (TCM)

The benefits of traditional Chinese medicine (TCM) in the treatment of infertility, have been written about in early Chinese medical literature, dating back to the 11th century AD. These therapies have been claimed to assist in regulating the menstrual cycle and invigorating the sperm and the eggs.

TCM sees the person as an integral mind/body organism. Ginseng is the most commonly used Chinese herb. Other herbs used in infertility treatment are maca, red clover leaves, nettle leaves, raspberry leaves, damiana, and false unicorn root. It is claimed that the person practising TCM derives general health benefits and balancing of the endocrine system from specific acupuncture and herbal regimes. TCM also discusses the role of herbs that increase the vitality of women over forty, thus affecting the quality of the eggs.

Mind and body courses

Infertility is not always the result of physical illness or dysfunction. Sometimes, lifestyle factors can play an important role in determining a couple's fertility. Mental health is of particular concern when it comes to fertility. Many couples struggle with severe stress, depression, and emotional concerns as they deal with fertility issues. Mind and body courses offer therapies that reduce stress and encourage relaxation. These include guided imagery, creative visualization, meditation, prayer, hypnotherapy, and emotional counselling.

At our centre, we have been offering psychological evaluation and counselling sessions for the past twenty-five years, and have published several research papers looking at coping mechanisms, as well as other aspects of the impact of stress on fertility. We consider our mind-body work to be one of the unique aspects of our programme.

Homeopathy

Practitioners of homeopathy claim that it can greatly assist both male and female infertility treatments and stimulate conception. Some of the medicines prescribed are Ovarium Compositum, Thyrodeia Compositum, Traumeel, Silica Aurum, Phosphorus, Sepia 6c, and Sabina 6c.

Ayurveda

Ayurveda has its roots in Indian medicine dating back to at least four thousand years. Ayurveda treatments for infertility often target factors such as stress, diet, and exposure to toxins. The foods recommended as a part of an ayurvedic diet include organic fruits and vegetables, broccoli, milk, dates, mango, cumin, and turmeric. Shatavari, or asparagus root, is one of the most important ayurvedic herbs used for female rejuvenation.

Naturopathy

A healthy balanced diet, regular moderate exercise, and a positive attitude are essential for general health.

Naturopathy treatment for infertility includes improving nutrition of both partners, hot and cold splashes of water on the genital area to stimulate local circulation, avoiding alcohol and cigarettes, and getting enough rest.

Nutritional therapy

A balanced diet is essential for the body to function properly. Supplements help to improve fertility. The supplements most important in enhancing fertility in men are Vitamin C, D, E, Zinc, L—arginine, and coenzyme Q. Women benefit from the addition of folic acid, B complex vitamins, Vitamin D, Vitamin E, and coenzyme Q. There are several scientific reports on the benefits of Dehydroepiandrosterone (DHEA) in improving the number and quality of oocytes.

I must confess that my knowledge on the complementary therapies is restricted. At the same time, at our centre we keep an open mind on all possible options. Our mission is to help couples become pregnant, and towards that end, all inputs are welcome. I continue to be a student of various disciplines of medicine and hence my life is full of curiosity, wonder and excitement. Also, I know that modern medicine is not the panacea it is often made out to be.

Music therapy

Spanish scientists at Barcelona played a range of music after injecting eggs with sperm. They subjected 500 eggs to music and 500 did not receive any musical inputs. The eggs that had music played to them had a 5 percent higher rate of fertilization. It is believed that the vibrations from the music create a flow of nutrients and also help in removal of toxic materials surrounding the eggs.

Faith and prayer

Benudevi and her husband Shomnath came to see me at Jaslok after undertaking a bus, car, and train journey, that lasted close to ninety hours. Benudevi unfurled a piece of paper that she had folded away in a tight knot in her pallu. It was a newspaper cutting in Hindi that talked about the procedure of CAT, which we had developed. This is what Benudevi said, 'This is the journey of our lives. We came here as two people. We will not leave Bombay till we go back as three. We want you to do this procedure for us.' What could I say? I only had a prayer on my lips, imploring God to help me fulfil their wish.

They had limited resources, no place to stay, just enough money for two meals a day, but they had lots of faith and determination. My kind and generous friends, Rohiqa and Cyrus Mistry, on hearing their story, paid for their medicines, laboratory tests, and stay in the city. Luckily for Benudevi and her husband, but more so for me, my prayers were granted. Every year during Navratri, Benudevi calls me to give me the progress report of her twins who were born during the auspicious festival of Navratri!

On the other hand, there is the case of Damayanti. Married into wealth, Damayanti has everyone at her beck and call. She is pretty as a picture, manicures her nails twice a week, changes her handbags every day, and her IVF doctor every time her cycle fails. When she came to me, Damayanti demanded to be seen right away, while I was taking a lunch break. Her husband joined her after ten minutes of her coming into my room, was interrupted by five phone calls, quizzed me on things he had read on the internet, and assured me that expenses were not an issue. They only wanted the best. Within forty-five minutes, they had two arguments between themselves. I counselled them regarding their stress levels and asked them to defer their IVF treatment till they were more relaxed. In the meantime, I asked them to take counselling sessions. They did not agree to the sessions and laughed cynically. I apologized to them for my refusal to get involved in their case. They planned to undergo IVF in the USA. I hoped they would succeed. Unfortunately, they did not and I was told by their referring friend that subsequently they separated.

I am a firm believer in the power of prayer. Research studies have shown the healing power of prayer. A famous study conducted by Dr Randolph Byrd—a San Francisco cardiologist in 1986—studied four hundred patients who had chronic cardiac illness. Patients in the first group had many people praying for them whereas no prayer group was assigned to the second group. The first group recovered faster than the second.

As I write this book, I realize that this book is supposed to enunciate treatment options for becoming pregnant. Then again, it is from the point of view of its author and, in that position, I humbly submit that I believe in prayer, enough to pray daily for my patients' well being. I once elucidated my concept of God and prayer in response to a request from the *Sunday Times*. I reproduce it here as self disclosure. The reader is of course free to accept, reject, or modify it.

As a devout Zoroastrian, I try to live by our prophet's adage of 'good thoughts, good words and good deeds.' I have learnt the profound truth of this guiding principle.

Good thoughts are important for filling ourselves with positive energy. Good words make our interactions with the world pleasant. Good actions, such as work and charity, are what make our time on earth worthwhile.

I begin my day with prayers to God, thanking Him for all the happiness my family and I have been blessed with. I know that God listens to all our prayers. That is the foundation of my spirituality.

My husband Rajesh is the most secular human being I have come across. Curiously, we started discussing religion and spirituality on one of our first evenings together, when we were teenagers. Over thirty-five years of close friendship and twenty-five years of marriage, that discussion still continues.

Our three children, Swappy, Manu, and Nikki, and our numerous friends have over the years often contributed towards these conversations. Rajesh has an in-depth knowledge of the major religions. We dwell not just on the similarities between religions, but on their differences as well. We believe that these differences should not only be respected but celebrated as well. Hence, as a family, we celebrate all festivals. Our friends tease me saying that Parsis just need any excuse for celebration!

We are often puzzled, and sometimes amused, at the arrogance of some of our fellow humans. Sometimes, on account of wealth, or knowledge, or power, some humans behave as though they were God themselves. Ordinarily, this would be amusing, were it not to have tragic consequences on the lives of others. We thank God for granting us humility and pray for His guidance in ensuring that we never become arrogant.

Rajesh believes that God has a great, and sometimes naughty, sense of humour. He believes that God creates megalomaniacs, who go about strutting their wealth and power, for His own amusement as well as for ours. Sometimes when I try to coax Rajesh into sneaking out for a film, he says, 'Life is such an ongoing spectacle full of entertainment, let's enjoy it instead!'

Secularism permits us to live in harmony and we should celebrate our similarities as well as our differences. Besides, we should treasure the sanctity of every moment and show gratitude to God.

Among my most prized possessions, is a handwritten note I received from Mother Teresa seventeen years ago, regarding a couple I was treating. When I showed it to Rajesh (who has had a Jesuit education) he was stunned. He asked incredulously, 'Do you realize the significance of this note? The Catholic Church does not approve of assisted reproduction. The Mother has transcended religion into spirituality in writing to you. This is what makes her a saint and not just another nun.' He cautioned me that no one—absolutely no one else—could see the note until years after she reached heaven.

I can now see her smiling benevolently. This is the first time that I have mentioned it.

17

Fertility Testing

- Fertility tests for men
- Fertility tests for women

Prior to requesting any investigations for infertility, a detailed medical history, appraisal of all prior tests, and a thorough medical examination of both the partners is essential. During the initial consultation, we take into consideration, the age of the couple, previous medical history, the number of years that they have been trying to conceive, past surgeries or history of ART, significant male factor and female factor causes, and all previous investigations. Thereafter, we may recommend different types of tests depending on these parameters. Table 17.1 enumerates the fertility tests.

Table 17.1: Different types of tests for men and women

Tests for men	Tests for women
Blood hormone levels	Blood hormone levels
Blood sugar levels	Blood sugar levels
Karyotyping	Vaginal sonography
Semen analysis	Hystersalpingogram
Sperm apoptosis	Hysteroscopy
Sperm FISH	Laparoscopy
Scrotal ultrasound	Endometrial biopsy
Trans-rectal ultrasound	CT scan and MRI
Testicular biopsy	

Fertility tests for men

Tabaha and Anton visited us from Ethiopia. They had been married for ten years. Tabaha had a thick file filled with reports, but while going through the file I did not find a single semen analysis on record. When I asked for the report I was told that it was against their religion to produce a semen sample. It was only when I pleaded helplessness, did Anton produce a sample in which there were no sperm. He had obstructive azoospermia due to congenital absence of the vas deferens (CAVD). A man born with CAVD typically produces sufficient quantities of sperm, but the sperm never reach their intended destination. Tabaha conceived with ICSI and PESA in the very first cycle.

When a couple is unable to have children, it is usually the female partner who first gets investigated for infertility, as infertility is traditionally perceived as a woman's problem. I have often come across couples who have gone through all possible female fertility tests, but a test as simple as semen analysis, which is less invasive and inexpensive, has been neglected.

Semen analysis is an important indicator of the male's fertility status. Abstinence of three days is recommended prior to semen collection. The normal volume of the semen in an ejaculate should be between 2 to 5 millilitres. A semen report will also show the consistency and the colour of the semen sample. It is important to note whether fructose is present. Fructose is a sugar which gives energy and vitality to the millions of sperm present in the ejaculate. The laboratory also reports on the time for semen liquification and if there is any infection in the semen. Besides sperm, the semen also contains immature sperm forms, called spermatogonia, spermatids, and a few white blood cells. It is important to use proper staining techniques to distinguish between immature sperm and white blood cells. The three main parameters of importance are: the count of mature sperm in million per millilitre, the type of motility, and the percentage of normal forms (see Figure 17.16).

Sperm count

Since sperm counts may vary, from a few million to more than a hundred million per millilitre, it is best to classify the count as per the WHO criteria where normal counts are above 20 million per millilitre. Many studies have shown declining sperm counts over the last few decades. A count of less than 20 million per millilitre may

Figure 17.1 The Makler Chamber

need medical intervention. A specially devised counting chamber, called the Makler Chamber, gives an accurate and easy way to take the count (Figure 17.1). Counting the number of sperm present in ten squares on the Makler Chamber, gives us the sperm count in million per millilitre.

Sperm motility

Sperm are the only cells in the body that move. This motility is due to microtubules within the sperm's tail, which propel the sperm forward. An electron microscopic photograph shows the normal and abnormal arrangement of the microtubules (Figure 17.2 and 17.3).

Over 50 percent of the sperm are expected to be motile in a normal semen analysis. According to the WHO criteria sperm motility is graded as:

Grade A: Fast forward motility in a linear pattern (25 percent or greater).

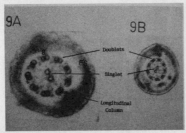

Figure 17.2 An electron microscopic photograph showing normal arrangement of the microtubules of the sperm tail

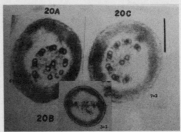

Figure 17.3 An electron microscopic photograph showing abnormal arrangement of the microtubules of the sperm tail
Courtesy Dr Arun Chitale

Grade B: Slower motility with a deviation from the linear pattern (25 percent or greater).

Grade C: Sluggish motility with minimal forward movement.

Grade D: No motility.

Recently, WHO has recommended that sperm should be categorized as progressively motile, non-progressively motile, and immotile (instead of grades A, B, C, or D). A simple system for grading motility, that distinguishes sperm with progressive or non-progressive motility, from those that are immotile, is recommended. The motility of each spermatozoon is graded as follows:

1. *Progressive motility (PR)*: Spermatozoa moving actively, either linearly or in a large circle, regardless of speed.
2. *Non-progressive motility (NP)*: All other patterns of motility with an absence of progression—swimming

in small circles, the flagellar force hardly displacing the head, or when only a flagellar beat can be observed.

3. *Immotility (IM)*: No movement.

Sperm morphology

A mature sperm consists of a head, neck, and tail (Figure 17.4). A normal semen sample should have at least 14 percent of sperm with a normal shape (Kruger's strict criteria test).

Abnormal sperm may have large heads (Figure 17.5), no acrosome (Figure 17.6), tapering heads (Figure 17.7), double heads (Figure 17.8), and absent heads (Figure 17.9).

Figure 17.4 A sperm with normal morphology

Figure 17.5 A sperm with a large head

Figure 17.6 A sperm with an absent acrosome

Figure 17.7 A sperm with a tapering head

17.8 A sperm with a double head

Figure 17.9 A sperm with an absent head

The sperm neck may be short, bent (Figure 17.10), or have extra material called cytoplasmic droplets (Figure 17.11). The sperm tail may be short (Figure 17.12), coiled (Figure 17.13), bent, double (Figure 17.14), or triple-tailed (Figure 17.15).

Figure 17.10 A sperm with a bent neck

Figure 17.11 A sperm with cytoplasmic droplets

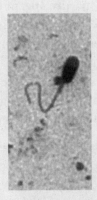

Figure 17.12 A sperm with a short tail

Figure 17.13 Sperm with coiled tails

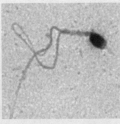

Figure 17.14 A sperm with double tails

Figure 17.15 A sperm with triple tails

JASLOK HOSPITAL

DEPARTMENT OF ASSISTED REPRODUCTION & GENETICS

SEMEN ANALYSIS – WHO 2010 CRITERIA

Date :14/2/2014

Name   : **Mr.** XYZ   Age : 34   Yrs.

H/O   : **Mrs.** ABC

Ref. By Dr.   : **Dr.** rpv

Days Abstinence :   3

Time of Collection : 8.05 a.m.   Time of Examination : 8.20 a.m.

MANUAL AND PHYSICAL EXAMINATION

Volume   : 3.5   ml   Colour   :   White

Viscosity   : Normal   Liquification Time :   15   Min.

CHEMICAL EXAMINATION

pH   8.0   Fructose   Present

DATA SUMMARY		WHO Reference Values
Sperm concentration (Mill/ml)	32	15 (Mill/ml)
Total number (Mill/Ejaculate)	112	39 (Mill/Ejaculate)
Motility %	30	40 %

VELOCITY   TYPE

Progressively motile (PR) %	15	32 %
Non-progressively motile (NP) %	15	
Immotile (IM) %	70	

Figure 17.16 A semen report showing Asthenospermia

		MORPHOLOGY			WHO Reference Values	
Normal Spermatozoa	:	9	%		4	%

HEAD				**MIDPIECE**			
Acrosome Deficient	:	18	%	Thick neck	:	4	%
Acrosome Absent	:	10	%	Bent neck	:	2	%
Large	:	3	%	Cytoplasmic Droplet	:	1	%
Small	:	5	%	Kinked neck	:		%
Pin	:	4	%	**TAIL**			
Amorphous	:	20	%	Short	:		%
Tapering	:		%	Long	:		%
Pyriform	:	4	%	Coiled	:		%
Round	:	6	%	More than one	:	1	%
Double	:		%				
PostAcrosome Elongation	:	13	%				

IMMATURE FORMS

Immature Forms	:	0.2	Million/ml.

CELLS

Pus Cells	:	A few
Epithelial Cells	:	A few
Red Blood Cells	:	Absent
Bacteria :		Absent

Backup Freezing : [--------------]

Figure 17.16 conted...

Please note that our laboratory follows the new WHO criteria 2010 :-

- The velocity type is no longer expressed as Rapid (A), Medium (B), Slow (C), and Static (D).

- The Type A (Progressively motile) of new WHO criteria 2010 corresponds to the sum of Rapid (A) and Medium (B) of WHO criteria 1999.

- The normal counts as expressed by the WHO criteria 2010, are more than 15 Mill/ml with total concentration of 39 Mill/ Ejaculate.

- The normal morphology as per the WHO criteria 2010, is 4% or more normal forms .

TABLE:- Distribution of values, lower reference limits and their 95% C1 for semen parameters from fertile men whose partners had time-to-pregnancy of 12 months or less.

	N	Centiles										
		2.5	(95% Cl)	5	(95% Cl)	10	25	50	75	90	95	97.5
Semen volume (ml)	1941	1.2	(1.0-1.3)	1.5	(1.4-1.7)	2	2.7	3.7	4.8	6	6.8	7.6
Sperm concentration (Mill/ml)	1859	9	(8-11)	15	(12-16)	22	41	73	116	169	213	259
Total number (Mill/Ejaculate)	1859	23	(18-29)	39	(33-46)	69	142	255	422	647	802	928
Total motility (PR+NP,%)	1781	34	(33-37)	40	(38-42)	45	53	61	69	75	78	81
Progressive motility (PR, %)	1780	28	(25-29)	32	(31-34)	39	47	55	62	69	72	75
Normal forms (%)	1851	3	(2.0-3.0)	4	(3.0-4.0)	5.5	9	15	24.5	36	44	48
Vitality (%)	428	53	(48-56)	58	(55-63)	64	72	79	84	88	91	92

*PR, progressive motility (Grade a+b); NP, non-progressive motility (Grade c)
The values are for unweighed raw data. For a two-sided distribution the 2.5th and 97.5th centiles provide the reference limits; for a one-sided distribution the fifth centile provides the lower reference limit.

Ref :- Cooper T. G. , Noonan E., et al. World Health Organization reference values for human semen characteristics. Human Reproduction Update. 2010 : 16(3) ; 231-245

Comments : Asthenospermia.

DR. FIRUZA R. PARIKH, MD.
Director,
Dept. of Assisted Reproduction & Genetics

Figure 17.16 conted...

Sperm apoptosis test

The DNA, which is the genetic material of the spermatozoa, resides in the nucleus of the sperm head. If there is excessive breakage of the DNA, the fertilizing potential of the sperm is compromised. Sperm DNA breakage can be evaluated by the sperm apoptosis test. Apoptotic sperm are those that are dying, and stain green with a florescent dye, whereas those facing impending death stain bluish green (see Figure 17.17 in insert pages) and the non-apoptotic sperm stain blue (see Figure 17.18 in insert pages). A semen sample is considered highly fertile if there are less than 13 percent sperm with apoptosis. On the other hand, if more than 40 percent of sperm are apoptotic, it is suggestive of poor fertilizing potential.

The sperm FISH test

The sperm cell is haploid, that is it contains half the number of chromosomes. Men with male factor infertility may show sperm with aneuploidy—an abnormal number of chromosomes. This may contribute to infertility and repeated miscarriages. The percentage of aneuploidy in sperm should not be more than 3 percent. Normal and abnormal FISH signals are seen in Figures 17.19 and 17.20 in the insert pages. In the FISH test (see p 170), only one bright spot for every chromosome should be seen. If the man is a carrier for a translocation, the sperm FISH test is helpful to determine the percentage of sperm that are affected, prior to carrying out ICSI with PGD.

Sperm in 3D

Researchers from Italy and Belgium have combined microscopy and holography to create videos of moving sperm in 3D in order to obtain data on sperm motility. Professor Di Caprio, the lead author of the study showed that this technique of digital holographic microscopy helps to identify the fertility potential of sperm.

Karyotyping

Males have twenty-three pairs of chromosomes. The sex chromosomes are depicted as X and Y. Chromosomes are microscopic ribbon-like structures containing DNA which is the genetic material. When there is male factor infertility, it is worthwhile to look for a genetic basis. Karyotyping of the blood (see p 169-70) will give the complete genetic picture.

The chromosome pattern of 47 XXY (Klinefelter's syndrome) is associated with severe oligospermia or azoospermia. In this condition, the male partner has one extra X chromosome. Generally, this may be suspected when breast development, or gynaecomastia (enlarged breasts), is noticed after puberty. Secondary sexual characters such as growth of a beard, moustache, and size of the sex organs are compromised. Sometimes young children with speech and behaviour problems may also show this chromosome abnormality. Often, this condition is detected only when a married couple undergoes investigations for infertility. It is possible for such males to father children with a combination of techniques such as TESA and ICSI. This technique is also used in males with XY/XXY mosaicism, where the abnormality is not so severe.

Some males with azoospermia have a normal karyotype. They should be investigated for microdeletions on the Y chromosome (when very tiny segments of the Y chromosome are deleted, some of the genes responsible for male fertility also get deleted resulting in oligospermia or azoospermia), by special DNA techniques such as multiplex Polymerase Chain Reaction (PCR). This is a molecular biology technique which multiplies DNA several million times, allowing analysis of very minute amounts of DNA. These deletions are too small to be visible under the microscope by karyotyping. If sperm from a male with Y chromosome microdeletions are used for ICSI, the sons will inherit the same infertility problem. This is explained to the couple, so they can make an informed decision. In such cases, PGD can help select female embryos for transfer, as the daughters do not inherit the father's Y chromosome.

Another genetic cause of male infertility is CAVD (See p. 36). CAVD is generally found in males who are carriers of cystic fibrosis—a respiratory disease.

A man diagnosed with CAVD, who does not show signs of cystic fibrosis, should consult a clinician, as he may have a milder form of the disease. In case both partners are silent carriers of cystic fibrosis, there is a 25 percent chance in every pregnancy, that their child will be affected with the disorder. It is advisable to check the couple for cystic fibrosis mutations by molecular genetic testing, so that prenatal diagnosis can be offered at eleven weeks gestation.

Blood hormone levels

In males, FSH is essential for sperm production, and LH is necessary for production of male hormones. Less production of FSH and LH by the pituitary gland will result in decreased sperm formation, decreased libido, slow development of secondary sexual characters, and scanty hair on the face and body. High FSH and LH are seen in men with severe oligospermia or azoospermia. Low levels of testosterone may cause lack of libido and may be associated with low levels of FSH and LH.

Blood sugar levels

One out of every sixth Indian is diabetic. A glucose tolerance test is very helpful in the presence of low sperm counts, erectile problems, and repeated miscarriages in the female partner.

Scrotal ultrasound

An ultrasound examination of the scrotum and testes is particularly helpful when the volume of the testes is decreased. The presence of a varicocele (enlarged veins surrounding the spermatic chord) can be picked up by looking at the blood flow through the veins.

Trans-rectal ultrasound

This test is helpful to confirm the absence of ejaculatory ducts in conditions of obstructive azoospermia.

Testicular biopsy

When the cause of severe oligospermia or azoospermia is not clear, and when the FSH and LH are normal or borderline high, a testicular biopsy may indicate the presence of sperm in the testes. The procedure is conducted under local anaesthesia and tiny pieces of testicular tissue are obtained. In Sertoli cell only syndrome, and hypospermatogenesis, occasional sperm may be obtained which can be frozen for future use.

Fertility tests for women

Kamakshi burst out angrily, 'Doctor, the problem is with my husband and not with me. Why do I have to do all these tests?' I had asked her to do blood tests to check her levels of reproductive hormones, before planning an ICSI cycle. The reports showed that Kamakshi's prolactin value was borderline high. I explained to her that prolactin is a stress hormone and can show mildly elevated levels in the presence of stress. This is what she said, 'Nobody understands me or what I am going through. All my in-laws ask is when I am going to give them a grandchild. They never ask me if I am well or even if I have eaten anything. My husband is too busy making money to give me his time.' It took a few counselling sessions with the family to calm all of them and thereby get Kamakshi's prolactin levels within normal parameters.

A woman going through infertility treatment is put through a lot of tribulations. Hence, it is very important to diagnose the reasons for infertility, and treat them appropriately before planning treatment. The non-invasive tests should be given priority over invasive ones.

Blood tests

Blood tests for women aim at checking basic reproductive hormones such as TSH, prolactin, FSH, and LH—all of which play important roles in conception. Occasionally, some more specific tests are indicated. Women with PCOS have insulin resistance. Hence, a blood test to check the level of insulin, at the time of fasting, and again after having ingested a glucose solution, would establish normal processing of glucose. Testing of cortisol and dehydroepiandrosterone sulphate (DHEAS) is indicated if problems with the adrenal glands are suspected. Anti-Mullerian hormone (AMH) testing is done when the ovaries do not produce enough eggs.

It is important to conduct the tests during the appropriate time of the menstrual cycle for accurate results. For instance FSH, LH, and AMH should ideally be tested around day two of the cycle, while cortisol and prolactin should be tested in the early morning hours. Prolactin is a stress hormone and can have elevated levels in those working night shifts, flight attendants, and women taking antidepressants and other psychiatric drugs. Prolactin is also found in higher quantities in women who have high TSH due to thyroid dysfunction.

The best way to perform the FSH test is between day one and day three of the menstrual period. When the ovary has very few follicles left, the pituitary secretes more FSH to goad the ovary into functioning.

Remember that different laboratories have different cut off values for FSH. Therefore, one laboratory's high value may be a normal value for another laboratory. Also the FSH test has poor sensitivity. Hence, a woman with a smaller ovarian volume and a normal FSH may still have less chances of conceiving.

Anti-Mullerian hormone and fertility

AMH is expressed by the granulosa cells of the ovary in the reproductive age, and controls the formation of primary follicles. AMH levels reflect on the ovarian reserve, that is the number of tiny primodial follicles present in the ovary. Therefore, a woman with PCOS will have a high AMH level (4.5 or more) and a woman close to menopause will have a low AMH level (less than 2.0). AMH does not reflect the quality of the eggs. AMH is not dependant on the day of the cycle and hence can be done any time.

At the age of thirty-five, Deepali's day two FSH level was 11 and AMH level 0.29. When she came to me with these reports she said, 'My neighbour conceived her fourth child at the age of forty-two, and you are saying that there is very little chance of me having my own children? Doctor, this is not fair!' I explained to Deepali that there are certain factors that we keep in mind when we counsel couples regarding their chances of having their own baby through ART. We counselled Deepali to consider using donor eggs. She has recently adopted a beautiful baby girl.

Diminished ovarian reserve

One of the best indicators of the performance of the ovary, is its volume and the number of baseline follicles that can be counted by sonography, in both the ovaries during the periods. Ovarian reserve tells us about the quantity of eggs and not of their quality. We have to interpret the results of

AMH, FSH, and ovarian reserve in conjunction. Women with high FSH, low AMH, and less number of antral follicles may want to consider the use of donor eggs.

Behroze came to me with the complaint of a milky discharge from her breasts. She had been diagnosed to have high prolactin levels and was put on medication to correct it. After reviewing her file, I noticed that she was not asked to do the TSH test. We got her TSH tested to confirm what I had suspected. Her high prolactin level was triggered due to her high TSH level. A high TSH level upsets the mechanism of the secretion of prolactin. Behroze's breast discharge stopped when we corrected her thyroid dysfunction.

Vanita was planning an IVF cycle when she developed a milky discharge from her breasts. Her blood tests showed that she had high prolactin levels. On investigating her medical history, we found out that she was on antidepressants, which had caused the rise of prolactin in her body. We waited until the medication could be tapered off.

Nalini wanted an urgent appointment to see me, because she was told that she was menopausal and would never conceive. This prognosis was based on a recent FSH level that was done during the middle of her cycle—when it is bound to be elevated. It took a lot of reassurance from me and two more normal tests of FSH, to calm her down. Hence, it is crucial to undergo the tests on the right day of the menstrual cycle.

Many women in their reproductive age forget to take care of their nutrition and do not include calcium in their diet. Lack of calcium can cause the bones to become brittle and more prone to fracture, due to the conditions of osteopenia and osteoporosis. Calcium is important during pregnancy and lactation, as the woman's calcium reserve gets transferred to the baby, causing a lack of calcium unless it is replenished. I find it useful to include a test for serum calcium.

In cases of unexplained infertility and repeated miscarriages, we may ask for antibody testing. These include the panel for AMA, ATA, ANA, and AOA. Table 17.2 enumerates the various blood tests that help us in investigating female factor infertility.

A simple yet useful test that is frequently overlooked, is the Haemoglobin Electrophoresis Test. This test rules out the presence of life threatening disorders such as thalassemia and sickle cell anaemia, which can be passed on to the baby. I once counselled a couple who had undergone IVF at another clinic. They had conceived but after three months of the baby's birth, they discovered that the child suffered from thalassemia major. This was because both the parents were thalassemia minor and had not been tested before embarking on IVF. Unfortunately for them, the baby got the genes for thalassemia from both the parents and developed thalassemia major.

Women who have a history of repeated miscarriages need more extensive testing. We include a panel of tests labelled as thrombophilia profile, lupus anticoagulant testing Factor V Leiden, prothrombin, and MTHFR mutation analysis. This panel checks the clotting mechanism in women. Some women miscarry frequently because they produce tiny clots around the site of implantation and the placenta.

Infections with toxoplasmosis, rubella, cytomegalovirus, and herpes can cause early or second trimester miscarriages. Testing for infection with these organisms is called TORCH testing. These can also cause congenital brain

Table 17.2: Blood tests for investigating female factor infertility

Name of the test	Purpose of the test	Suspected condition	Cycle day/ time
TSH	Thyroid function	Hypothy roidism, Grave's disease	Morning any day fasting
Prolactin	Pituitary function	Hyperpro-lactinemia	Morning fasting
FSH	Pituitary, ovarian, testicular function	Absence of ovulation testicular dysfunction	Day two morning fasting
LH	Pituitary, ovarian, testicular function	Absence of ovulation, PCOS testicular dysfunction	Day two morning fasting
Insulin	Pancreas function, peripheral resistance to insulin	PCOS, diabetes	Fasting and two hours after lunch or glucose water
Cortisol hormone	Adrenal function	PCOS, hirsuitism	Early morning fasting
DHEAS	Adrenal function	PCOS, hirsuitism	Morning fasting
Serum calcium	Bone metabolism	Osteopor-osis and osteopenia	No fasting required
Antibody testing	Immune compart-ment	High ATA, AMA, AOA, ANA, Anti adrenal antibody	No fasting required

and heart abnormalities in babies who survive. Genital TB is known to cause repeated miscarriages and repeated ectopic pregnancies. TORCH testing and tests for TB are very essential, before allowing a woman who has aborted several times to plan a pregnancy.

Jahanavi and Milind were married for six years. In that period, she had miscarried eight times. In one of her visits, she said to me, 'I conceive even when we take precaution but as soon as I reach the eighth week, doctors do not find a heartbeat in the baby. Now we are even scared to have sex.'

After the regular check up, I asked her to do another panel of tests, which included karyotyping. The results showed that Jahanvi had translocation of chromosomes. The only options for them were donor eggs, adoption, or PGD. The couple opted for adoption. Table 17.3 enumerates the various blood tests that help us investigate the causes of repeated miscarriages.

Table 17.3: Tests Recommended for Repeated Miscarriages

Name of the test	Purpose of the test	Suspected condition	Cycle day/ time
Thrombo-philia profile	Clotting factors	Miscarriages, bad obstetric history	Any day Any time
Karyotyping	Chromosome abnormalities	Miscarriages, bad obstretric history	Any day Any time
TORCH panel	Toxoplasma, rubella, cytomegal-ovirus, herpes	Miscarriages, bad obstetric history	Any day Any time

Name of the test	Purpose of the test	Suspected condition	Cycle day/ time
TB testing	TB infection	Ectopic pregnancy	Any day Any time
Blood sugar	Diabetes	Repeated mid trimester and late trimester loss	Any day Fasting

Vaginal Sonography

The diagnosis of the cause of infertility is usually established with a good medical history. However, a thorough clinical examination adds considerable information to the diagnosis. During the first visit, an internal examination of the pelvis should be conducted to determine the health of the vagina, cervix, and uterus. Sometimes the defects of the vagina, such as a vaginal septum, can be picked up during an internal examination. Abdominal sonography has its limitations and transvaginal scanning is preferred.

An add-on to the internal examination, is the transvaginal ultrasound scan. This gives additional information regarding the uterus, cervix, ovaries, and to some extent, the fallopian tubes. One can get a good idea about the shape, size, and position of the uterus. An instrument with good resolution would pick up fibroids, display their size and shape, their proximity to the uterine lining, and other minute details such as the thinness or thickness of the uterine lining. The ovarian size, the number of growing follicles, and conditions such as polycystic ovaries, endometriosis, chocolate cysts, and benign and malignant growths of the ovaries, can be detected.

Normally, the fallopian tubes are not visualized on a vaginal ultrasound. However, tubes that are inflamed or have hydrosalpinges can be demarcated necessitating further investigation. In some conditions, sonography with colour doppler is conducted. A colour doppler sonography looks at the blood flow to an organ. Depending on the amount and type of blood flow, the presence or absence of disease can be determined. The doppler may reveal less blood supply to the uterine lining or the ovaries. It can also help differentiate between benign and malignant tumours.

Hysterosalpingogram (HSG)

The hysterosalpingogram is an X-ray, which outlines the uterus and the fallopian tubes. It demonstrates whether the tubes are open or not, and also indicates the shape of the uterus after a dye is injected through the cervix. During the HSG, the fallopian tubes appear like wavy, fluffy outlines, with the dye escaping from the openings of the tubes. If the tubes are damaged, the dye may not be seen coming through the tubes, or may be seen just partially entering the tubes. Sometimes the dye is trapped within the tubes, and these appear like balloon-shaped structures. This condition of hydrosalpinges (see Figure 17.21 in insert pages) is caused by the blockage of the outer ends of the fallopian tubes and is commonly seen in patients with genital TB and, sometimes, endometriosis. In conditions of adhesions between the tubes and other pelvic organs (peritubal adhesions), the dye appears to be trapped in multiple pockets.

Laparoscopy

Women with long standing infertility need a thorough check up of the pelvic organs, necessitating a laparoscopy. In this procedure, a telescopic instrument is inserted into the pelvic cavity through a tiny incision in the skin. The uterus, fallopian tubes, and ovaries can be visualized clearly. A diagnostic laparoscopy helps to identify any tubal, pelvic, or ovarian condition causing infertility. These conditions can range from uterine fibroids, endometriosis, duplication of the uterus (bicornuate uterus or uterus didelphys), to adhesions due to pelvic inflammatory conditions such as genital TB, polycystic ovaries, ovarian cysts, and inflammation of the intestines and the appendix. An operative laparoscopy can normalize the conditions of the pelvis. It calls for the skilled use of many instruments. The cutting of tissues and adhesions is done either by electric current, harmonic scalpel; which works on the principal of sound waves or laser. Laparoscopic procedures have made surgery for many painful pelvic conditions, painless, involving less morbidity and a shorter stay in the hospital.

A laparoscopy is useful in cases of acute or chronic ectopic pregnancy (see pp 58–9).

Hysteroscopy

A hysteroscopy involves placing a telescopic instrument into the uterine cavity. In normal circumstances, the uterine cavity appears velvety and reddish, due to good blood supply, and shows the two inner openings of the fallopian tubes. In case of genital TB, the uterine cavity is narrow, with scarring and adhesion formation.

Hysteroscopy can also detect and treat an intrauterine septum. Polyps and submucous fibroids can impinge on the uterine cavity and can be visualized and removed effectively through a hysteroscope.

Alanha had a pregnancy termination seven years ago. She took almost two months to recover from it. She continued to bleed and had low-grade fever. She settled down eventually but found difficulty in conceiving. Although clinical examination revealed a normal-sized uterus, a sonography showed bright calcified spots inside the uterine cavity. A hysteroscopy revealed a white structure embedded deep inside the uterine cavity. On further exploration it turned out to be a forgotten IUCD. Since she did not want to conceive right away, the doctor had placed an IUCD, at the time of the pregnancy termination. Alanha had completely forgotten about it. She conceived naturally soon after the IUCD was removed through a hysteroscope.

Endometrial biopsy

An endometrial biopsy involves removing a piece of endometrial tissue by a non-traumatic metallic tube. The pathologist uses special techniques and staining to evaluate the cells. Although genital TB is a common cause for infertility in women and men, its diagnosis often remains elusive. An endometrial biopsy looks out for signs of TB infection, and can also spot the TB bacillus. The TB bacilli are also cultured and made to grow on a special medium, designed to support their growth. We rely on several tests to confirm the diagnosis of TB. A molecular biology test, called TB detection by polymerase chain reaction (PCR), amplifies the protein coding for the TB bacillus, so that even if a few bacteria are present in the uterus these can be detected. A recently introduced molecular biology test called pathogen associated molecular pattern (PAMP) can pick up the disease in case the TB bacillus is not active in the body (see Figure 17.22 in insert pages). The other tests include gamma interferon, ELISA, and immunologic tests.

Our immune system protects us from disease and harmful organisms. This is done with the help of specialized white blood cells. However, sometimes these cells turn rogue and attack the body's defenses. In some women there is an increased activity of natural killer cells in the uterine cavity. This makes the uterine cavity hostile to implantation, and reject the embryo. With special staining techniques called immunohistochemistry, these cells can be identified (see Figure 17.23 in insert pages). These cells also secrete substances called tumor necrosis factors alpha (TNF α), which are harmful to the embryonic growth. These can be measured by a technique called immunocytochemistry.

In special circumstances, an endometrial biopsy is performed around day twenty-one of the menstrual cycle—the usual day of implantation—to figure out if substances called integrins are being secreted. Integrins help the embryo to adhere to the uterine wall. The amount of activation of receptors for progesterone—a key hormone for implantation—is also noted.

CT scan and MRI

On a few occasions there may be a need for a detailed study of the anatomy of the pelvic organs. A CT scan and

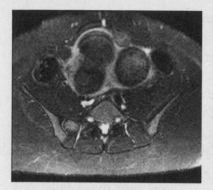

Figure 17.24 MRI outlining
fibroids

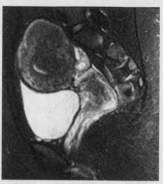

Figure 17.25 MRI outlining
adenomyosis

MRI are generally useful in diagnosing complicated cases of ovarian cysts, endometriosis, fibroids (Figure 17.24), adenomyosis (Figure 17.25), absent vagina, absent uterus, and some conditions of ambiguity of the genitalia.

A detailed history and physical examination are important steps towards successful treatment. However, there are many conditions which call for thorough investigation. The tests for male fertility are simpler and less taxing, and hence should generally be done prior to those for the female. In both partners, one should avoid unnecessary tests and always begin with the less invasive and less expensive tests. Finally, it is important to always remember that laboratory reports can at best supplement clinical diagnosis and never replace it. Good doctors are not yet an extinct species!

18

Becoming Pregnant Step by Step

Part I

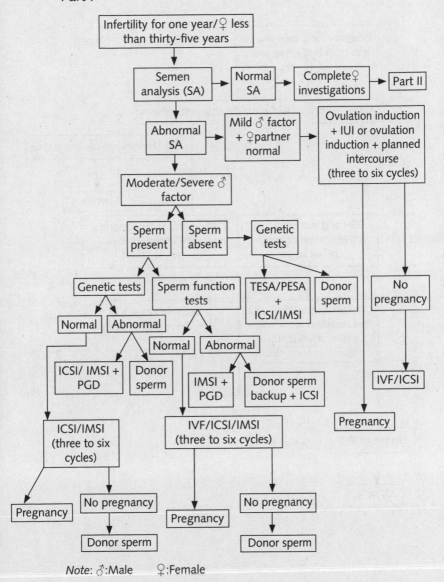

Note: ♂:Male   ♀:Female

Part II

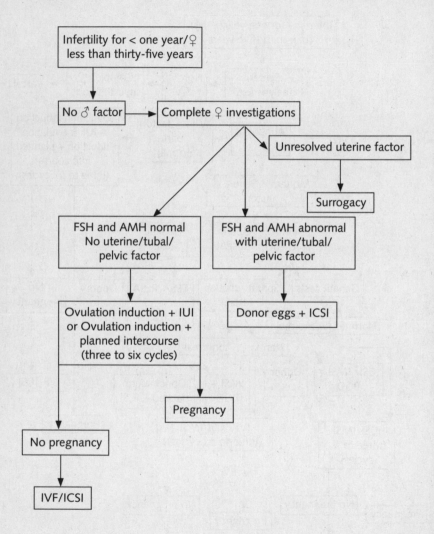

Part III

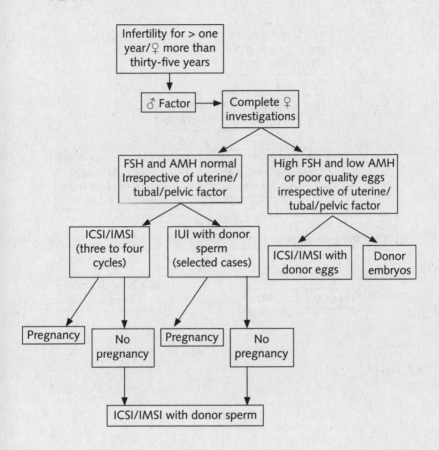

Part IV

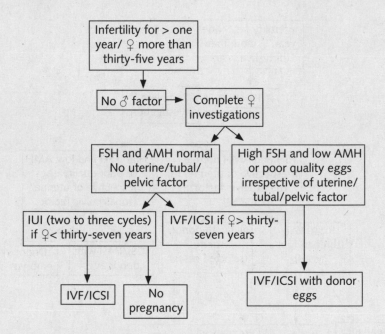

Part V

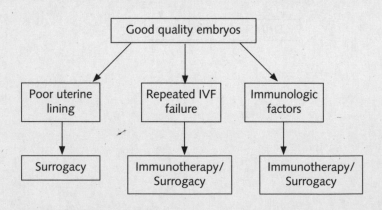

Part VI

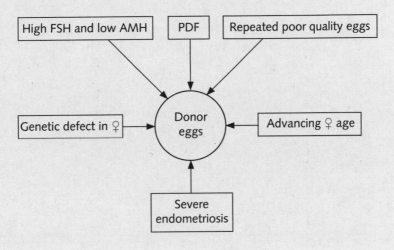

Part VII

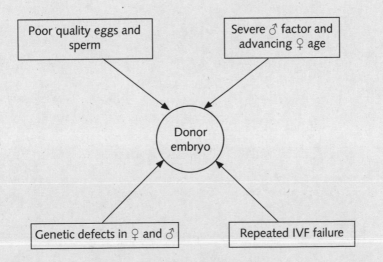

19

The Director's Cut: Farah Khan's Story

I believe in angels because I have three beautiful angels at home who surround my life with love and happiness. However, there was one particular angel who was responsible for giving me my children, and she is Dr Firuza Parikh.

Giving birth to triplets at the age of forty-three is no walk in the park, but I had little choice. I got married at the young age of forty, and both my husband, Shirish, and I were keen to start a family soon. God bless IVF because it's never too late to conceive any more. However, having said that, I have to point out that going through IVF is a gruelling procedure; maybe that's why only a woman can go through it!

My first meeting with Dr Firuza Parikh changed my life. I knew at once that I was in the best possible hands. Dr Firuza Parikh was my guiding light through it all. She was always encouraging and positive. And, most importantly, always honest. When I finally conceived triplets, she put forth the pros and cons in front of me. But Shirish and I were so determined to have them that I agreed to all her terms and conditions.

Today my life is beautiful, it has meaning and I'm almost always happy. And I know Dr Firuza Parikh gives this happiness to thousands of women every year, to many who can't afford it, and who have nothing but the will to desire a child. And just like me, thousands of women remember Dr Firuza Parikh in their prayers everyday and thank the angel for their little angels.

I was also fortunate to have a very supportive and actively involved husband. When I meet women who complain that they are just not getting pregnant, more often than not, they are going alone for the sessions to the doctor. My wedding to Shirish was like a whirlwind. He had threatened me that if I had no intentions of getting married to him, then he would opt out of the relationship. It was primarily because of him that things fell into place. Otherwise I would have been happy to carry on the way we were.

After we were married, Shirish and I knew we had to start trying to have a baby immediately since I was already forty. I had never thought about having children when I was younger and unmarried. I was not even fond of children. But when I started the IVF treatment, I realized how much I wanted to be a mother. In fact, I was desperate to have a baby! I now know that I had always harboured this desire deep within me, when I replay some of the past interviews that Shirish and I had done together. One in particular is revealing. It was an interview with Simi Garewal soon after we had got married and Simi had asked me, 'Where do you see yourself five years from now?' I had said, 'I will be sitting here with three babies and an Oscar in my hand.' My answer then had been completely spontaneous, but it was Simi who recently reminded me about my statement. I have my three babies but the Oscar, however, is still pending!

When we started planning a family, I did not think I would require any special help as my gynaecologist then, seemed to think I would get pregnant naturally. But two years passed by and I did not get pregnant. It was at a chance meeting with Haseena Jethmalani (who was pregnant with twins) at a friend's party where she gave me her doctor's number. It was as if it had been planned that I would meet Haseena that day and that she would direct me to meet Dr Firuza Parikh.

The next morning I called Dr Firuza Parikh.

Firuza tells me that when I walked into her office for the first consultation, I carried an air of urgency about me. She perceived me as being organized and ready to start the treatment without wasting time. She says that she was struck by my positive attitude towards having a baby and life in general.

Our first session included a detailed history, a thorough examination, and a comprehensive review of all my past treatments. In view of my age and history, she suggested that we try ICSI. I had asked her, 'Doc, can we start today?' She then explained to me how the cycle starts with a month of preparation. I looked at my diary for my commitments to *Om Shanti Om*, made the necessary changes, and said, 'I am ready.'

No sooner had I left her office that a thought struck me and I went back. 'Well, I am disposing my sanitary napkins today as I won't need them for the next nine months,' I declared. Dr Firuza Parikh told me much later that at that very instant she knew that I would become pregnant. However, she had cautioned me that IVF is not always successful, and that for me, the chances of failure were more than the chances of success. But I was not thinking about failure at all.

The treatment consisted of a round of injections, blood tests, ultrasound scans, and a periodic review of the findings. Although I was neck deep in the production of *Om Shanti Om*, I kept every appointment, was on time on all days, and would sometimes request for a night appointment. I loved chatting with all the couples while waiting to see Dr Firuza Parikh. Sometimes her staff would end up chatting with me as well.

I sincerely believe that if you do not have a positive

attitude towards the procedure it is not going to work. Complaining doesn't help and if you think that you are not getting pregnant, then you won't. I know that many women worry about going through the process of IVF, mainly due to the injections that have to be administered. I hate injections just as much as anybody but it is only an injection. Dr Firuza Parikh is not asking you to climb Mount Everest! Every morning I would go all the way to the clinic at Jaslok for my shot from Firuza. After my shot, I would head for my shooting to Film City.

Now when I look back at all I had to go through, it is something forgotten and done with, and it seems worthwhile to see what I have got back. Twenty to thirty years ago if you were above forty, there was no way you were going to have a baby. IVF is a wonderful thing. One has to ignore the injections as the reality is that nobody is going to invent a pill that you can take to get a baby.

Firuza was always very gentle and encouraging. You need that, especially because IVF is a very emotional kind of treatment. I never thought about going to any other doctor other than her, how much ever time it took to get me pregnant.

Shirish was a pillar of support. He had a scientific approach to the treatment and would ask some of the most intelligent questions related to the procedure. He would always carry his laptop with him and would be working on his script while I was occupied with the blood tests and scans. The support from your husband while undergoing IVF is very essential. For me just to know that Shirish would drive all the way with me, for an appointment with Firuza, for my scan or my injection, was reassuring. Just to know that he was there with me all the way, made such a difference. It is so much easier when you go through the procedure of IVF together as a couple.

By the third beta HCG test, Firuza had subtly hinted that we may be looking at a multiple pregnancy but said that she would only confirm it after a scan. She told me over the phone, 'This looks like twins or triplets!' After giving us all instructions for pregnancy care, she also warned me that I might have to slow down my whirlwind activities. I called her ten minutes later and said, 'Doctor, Shirish and I are sure that I am carrying triplets. I think it's going to be a boy and two girls.' Don't ask me how I knew it. Somethings a woman just knows.

Twenty days later, a sonography confirmed the beating of three tiny hearts. By then I was immersed in the making of *Om Shanti Om*. Firuza was apprehensive about how I was going to manage the bed rest and the demands that a triple pregnancy would put on me. She drew out a strict regimen for me and told Dr Anahita Pandole—her assistant and the obstetrician who would be directly responsible for my pregnancy—to take charge and spell out the rules. These included no late nights, bed rest, a healthy diet, and minimum work.

One night at around 11:30 pm, Dr Anahita called Firuza frantically, saying that I was on a live television programme when I should have been in bed. What if my uterus became weak and could not bear the weight of three babies? She pleaded with Firuza to talk to me. When Firuza called me, I told her that I was expecting her call, and asked her if she was worried about my being on television.

I reassured her that the shooting had actually occurred in our living room at home. Months later, when Firuza visited our home, she looked around the living room suspiciously and asked me, 'Are you sure that television programme was shot here?' I smiled enigmatically.

The one time I do recollect Firuza freaking out, was when I was five months into the pregnancy. I had invited Firuza and her husband, Dr Rajesh Parikh, to the *Om Shanti Om* fashion show. As I was walking down the ramp, along with the entire cast, during the finale I could see Firuza turn pale as though she were about to faint. After everybody had finished congratulating us, she took me aside and said, 'What are you doing, Farah?' She kept worrying about my cervix and I kept reassuring her that my cervix wasn't going to dilate. It was as if my mother had caught me at a naughty act and I was covering up for it!

It was a good thing that she was strict, and I told her that I would follow the rules. However, the truth was that I felt the worst when I was suggested complete bed rest, one month prior to the delivery. That was the time I bloated, my legs were swollen, and I couldn't walk, when on the other hand I was very active till my baby shower.

During the shooting of my film, they had arranged for a Lazyboy so that I could lie there and shout out directions to my cast and crew. I would need to use the bathroom every few minutes and I am almost certain that the cause of this was Czar sitting on my bladder, or rather jumping on it. I think Anya was the one who would kick me, and Diva had these long nails when she was born, so I realize that she was the one scratching me from the inside.

If I got paid a rupee for every time someone on the set said my triplets would be named 'Om', 'Shanti', and 'Om', my children's education would be taken care of. The other running joke was that my kids would be named 'Amar', 'Akbar', and 'Anthony'. I kept arguing that the triple 'As' were not triplets. And to top it off, the male members of the crew joked if I would develop a third breast to feed all three babies.

Towards the end of my pregnancy, the people on the set were so protective that every time I walked or came across a hurdle they would shout, 'Look down, look down!' to which I would respond, 'I'm pregnant not blind. I can see what is in front of me!' But they looked after me very well and I was a very good patient. I was told that it was dangerous to carry triplets, especially with my hectic schedule, and both Firuza and Dr Anahita were worried about the weight of the babies.

I had terrible morning sickness for two months and sometimes it seemed more like an all-day sickness. During the filming of the song 'Dard e Disco' with Shahrukh Khan, I would throw up every time he took his shirt off, although everyone else could not get over his six-pack! I even developed a pregnancy rash. There was a point in the pregnancy when I could not lie down and had to sleep propped up on the Lazyboy, as my stomach was so big that it would come right under my chin when I lay down. Having a bath seemed a chore equal to climbing ten floors, and I would be panting after my bath. But till the day I delivered, I was able to cross my feet and sit much to the amazement of both the doctors. I constantly reassured them that I would give them three healthy babies. During my pregnancy I also became a vegetarian because I could not tolerate the smell of non-vegetarian food. The three kids, however, love non-vegetarian food.

Firuza had told me to admit myself in the hospital as soon as the film was released. When I did, I was so bored that I was constantly giving live interviews to news channels. I think she was fed up with me by then.

A caesarean was planned. Shirish was in the operation theatre with four cameras. Dr Pandole was swift with the knife, and Dr Fazal, our paediatrician, had kept three incubators ready. I knew from the moment I saw them, that Diva would be the crowd puller, Czar would be in control, and Anya would be the beauty.

The news of the babies was out, and every now and then I would hear a roar from the sixteenth floor of Jaslok; it was the crowd outside the hospital and in the lobby. Everyone was excited at the news of the triplets. However, it was when Shahrukh and Gauri Khan visited us that the crowd went berserk. Dr Firuza Parikh told me that in its entire history, the hospital had never witnessed such commotion. Women and men, children and grandparents had all rushed to the hospital when word got out that Shahrukh was with us. With his impeccable manners, Shahrukh met every one of Firuza and Rajesh's staff individually and thanked each one of them. He had won them all.

Around ten days later, Shirish and I took the babies home. Life has never been the same again. Before I had my babies, I would tend to be self-absorbed, and worry about little things, but now I am a changed person. I am calmer and in a happier space. I have a lot more empathy for people, though I am not sure if I have developed enough patience yet. The little things don't upset me anymore. They don't seem to matter much because the bigger picture has been put into place. Life has been good to me after the babies. Everything has changed for the better.

My message to the readers of this book is that don't see the procedure as a hardship and look at the larger picture to see what you will gain in the long run; it will help you to succeed. Embrace IVF as a wonderful procedure. You will forget the pain once your babies are born.

Since the baby is for the couple, and not just for the mother, the husband's support is extremely essential during the treatment. The best part about having triplets is that when the grandparents visit, there is a child for each to play with and one for us as well, and nobody fights over the children!

20

The Mind–Body Connect in Fertility

The mind plays a significant role in human reproduction. Over the past few years research from all over the world, including that from our centre, has reiterated the importance of the mind–body connect in the treatment of infertility.

Twenty-five years ago, our centre was one of the first in the world to offer psychological evaluation and counselling services to all our patients. Today, the ASRM recommends that all fertility centres across America should have psychological evaluation and counselling services integrated into their treatment programmes. However, since these are voluntary guidelines, they are not always adhered to by many centres.

We started our own counselling facilities in a rather curious manner. In 1989, the success rate with IVF worldwide was 10 to 15 percent. At our centre, it was around 14 percent. This was before the advent of ICSI and other advances in treatment. Thus, if a man had a semen count of less than 5 million per ml, we could not offer the couple much by way of treatment other than recommending donor insemination.

Sometimes, I had to inform the couple that there was little that I or anyone else in the world could do for them and perhaps they were better off adopting a baby rather than taking treatment from us. Patients would find it difficult to accept that there was not much by way of medical treatment and even more difficult to accept the idea of adoption.

Ours was the only IVF centre in a private hospital in the country. Those unwilling to go to one of the couple of private clinics or the one public hospital in the country that offered IVF, would either travel abroad for an opinion or take recourse to non-medical treatments. Often, they came back to us to enquire if any developments had taken place in the preceding few weeks. Adoption was an option that most couples were unwilling to consider.

I had recently returned to India from Yale and found it difficult to handle the immense resistance to adoption. So I requested Rajesh, who had recently started the first neuropsychiatry clinic in India and among the first few in the world, to talk to these patients. He agreed.

On listening to our patients' stories, he soon realized that while many of them were depressed and anxious at the thought of adoption, in some patients, the anxiety and depression clearly preceded their infertile status. One of the couples conceived naturally after Rajesh treated the wife's depression. Another conceived naturally after they had adopted a baby. Soon we discovered that there were many more such couples. Clearly, when they were less stressed their fertility improved even without any ART treatment.

Rajesh, who is always oriented towards research and a firm believer in evidence-based medicine, began a study on our patients to examine the relationship between stress and infertility. In one of the first studies conducted in 1990, he and his team discovered that in over 60 percent of infertile couples, at least one partner was clinically depressed. Some of these patients harboured suicidal ideas, yet denied that they were depressed. His team also observed that while the majority of patients attributed the cause of their depression to their infertile status, the next major cause of stress in our patients was the nature of our treatment protocols such as sex on schedule.

Initially, our team found it hard to accept that our treatment was a contributor to their stress. After all, we saw ourselves offering a solution to their problems. Besides, how could a simple procedure such as IUI be stressful? Rajesh persuaded us that this was largely from our point of view. But if we listened carefully to our patients, we would find that the simplest of procedures could indeed be very stressful from their perspective. Soon we accepted his team's findings that the majority of our patients experienced high degrees of stress and that our treatment sometimes added to it. We resolved to be more understanding of our patients' needs and, with his guidance and the assistance of his team, we improved our skills in empathetic listening. Just then, came the next big challenge.

Rajesh and his team would advise about 15 percent of our patients not to undergo IVF at the time that they were seeing us. They felt that these patients were already depressed and our treatment, instead of helping them, would make them more depressed. My team and I found this very difficult to handle. After all, we were convinced that our patients were depressed because they did not have babies and once we solved their problems, they would be just fine. Our patients firmly believed that too. And here was a team advising us and our patients not to go further with the treatment.

Yet, within months, we discovered that our patients were more than happy to see him and his team. Those who became pregnant without our treatment such as Purnima and Mitesh (the stock broker), the couple that we have described on pages 39 and 40 started telling everybody they met that seeking and accepting psychological support would certainly help the treatment.

A few patients began asking us if they could meet Rajesh even before we suggested it. Soon, our centre and I were no longer perceived by some as arrogant in refusing treatment to patients who were very keen to move forward. In fact, the feedback we received from referring doctors was that, more often than not, we were also perceived as being ethical enough to refuse treatment to those who did not need it. Most important, ever since we started the psychological evaluation and treatment of our patients, our success rate went up and, within a year of inception, we were on par with the best centres in the world. We also started receiving patients from over 60 countries, including the United States, England, China, and Brazil.

The research data that came out of these studies was received very well at national and international meetings. After a session, it was not unusual to see Rajesh surrounded by IVF specialists from all over the world with their queries. I remember this most vividly after a long session at the European Congress in Vienna in 1994. We had to wait patiently for Rajesh for over an hour while he was rapt in discussion with international IVF specialists.

To summarize our research findings of the past twenty-five years, most couples presenting with infertility experience some form of stress or clinical depression. Recognizing and addressing this is of paramount importance. The success rate is higher in non-depressed couples compared to depressed couples. Among depressed couples, those who opt for treatment and benefit from it succeed significantly more often than those who do not accept treatment. It seems as though stress and infertility have a reciprocal relationship and addressing it is an important aspect of successful treatment.

The effect of stress on reproduction is mediated through stress hormones such as corticosteroids, epinephrineine, and norepinephrine. These affect every aspect of reproduction as they affect FSH, LH, Prolactin, and other hormones that have a key role in human reproduction. In males, they affect the quantity and the quality of sperm and their fertilizing potential. In females, they affect not only the ova but also the implantation of the embryo.

Harvard psychologist Dr Alice Domar has done more research on the psychological aspects of fertility treatments than anyone else in the world. She established the world's first 'Mind–Body Program for Fertility' in Boston. She has this to say, 'I just did a literature review on the subject and found 20 research studies from around the world; all looked at whether or not psychological distress had an impact on IVF success rates. Fifteen of these found that increased levels of psychological distress before or during the IVF cycle were associated with decreased pregnancy rates, three found no relationship, and two were inconclusive. Several of the studies found strong relationships between distress and outcome—in one study, depressed women were only half as likely to conceive as nondepressed women.'

We advise our couples to undergo psychological evaluation prior to starting treatment. The evaluation may include psychological tests such as the Minnesota Multiphasic Personality Inventory (MMPI), the Rorschach Inkblot Test (ROR), and the Thematic Apperception Test (TAT). Those who are anxious, depressed, or stressed are offered counselling and/or medication to ensure their emotional well-being during our treatment. Some are advised to defer treatment until they are better. We are convinced that this evaluation and emotional support contributes to the success of our programme.

21

Our Research Goes On

- The role of factors secreted by cumulus cells on embryo development and implantation
- Oocyte cryopreservation
- The use of FISH in slowly cleaving and arrested embryos
- The association of human polymorphic chromosome variants with subfertility
- In vitro maturation of germinal vesicle oocytes
- The impact of sperm apoptosis on pregnancy
- Intracytoplasmic morphologically selected sperm injection (IMSI)
- The use of FISH on follicular fluid to detect gonadal sex chromosome mosaicism in women undergoing IVF/ICSI
- PGD for thalassemia
- Stress and reproductive failure
- The role of pollution in male and female infertility

Our centre has been at the forefront of basic and clinical research since its inception twenty-five years ago. It is our constant endeavour to improve pregnancy rates, in order to offer better care to our patients. Over the years, our research has resulted in more than two hundred and fifty national and international publications, four hundred lectures and academic presentations, thirty-two workshops for doctors, and eight dissertations for MD, MSc and PhD. Some of our current research areas are described in this chapter.

The role of factors secreted by cumulus cells on embryo development and implantation

Cumulus cells are in close proximity to the oocyte. These cells secrete growth factors and sticky substances called integrins, which help the embryo adhere to the uterine lining. We are studying some of these factors in order to understand what contributes to the success of implantation in IVF, ICSI, and IMSI. Our research has resulted in the technique of CAT, which has improved pregnancy chances with ART. We have not patented this technique but published it in *Fertility and Sterility* (see Figure 21.1 in insert pages). We continue advancing our research on CAT and have had over 2,000 babies through the procedure.

Oocyte cryopreservation

Our team is currently concentrating on oocyte cryopreservation—a procedure which can help women with some types of cancer to freeze their ova before radiation of the ovaries, chemotherapy, or surgical removal of the ovaries.

The use of FISH in slowly cleaving and arrested embryos

One of the causes of the failure of ART is the production of embryos with abnormal chromosomes. In our research project, cells are biopsied by slowly cleaving and arresting embryos which are not used in IVF, and subjected to FISH (see Figures 21.2 and 21.3 in insert pages). Our study shows that such embryos have chromosomal abnormalities such as aneuploidy and mosaicism. In all these conditions the number of chromosomes is abnormal. We are in the process of publishing our research.

The association of human polymorphic chromosome variants with subfertility

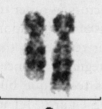

9

Figure 21.4
Variation in the size
of Chromosome 9

Chromosome variation can affect fertility. Slight variations in shape and size, are sometimes seen in chromosomes 1, 9, 16, and Y. We have observed an increase in the size of chromosome 9(qh+) (Figure 21.4) and Y (yqh+) in infertile patients. We are researching their contribution to repeated miscarriages and male infertility.

In vitro maturation of germinal vesicle oocytes

During an IVF cycle, a small percentage of oocytes are immature or in the germinal vesicle stage (see Figure

21.5). Such oocytes do not get fertilized into embryos. We have used cumulus cells to mature these oocytes in the laboratory so that they can be used for ICSI/IMSI, and can result in embryos capable of implantation. We are in the process of analyzing this data.

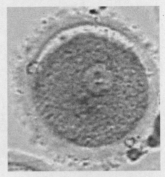

Figure 21.5 A germinal vesicle stage oocyte

The impact of sperm apoptosis on pregnancy

We are researching sperm apoptosis (see Figure 21.6 in insert pages) in men with diabetes, or severe male factor following chemotherapy. Our preliminary conclusion is that the chances of pregnancy decrease in the presence of increased sperm apoptosis. We are considering possible treatment options for such couples. Our research on sperm apoptosis was presented at the Annual Conference of the American Society for Reproductive Medicine in Boston in 2013.

Intracytoplasmic morphologically selected sperm injection (IMSI)

IMSI is an advanced technique of ICSI where we magnify the sperm which are being used for ICSI about seven thousand times (Figure 21.7). This allows us to select sperm which are viable and have the most potential to produce healthy embryos. We are currently examining the sperm of

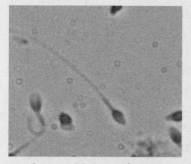 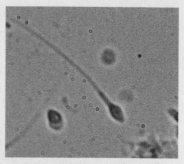

Sperm at 20 X magnification   Sperm at 40 X magnification

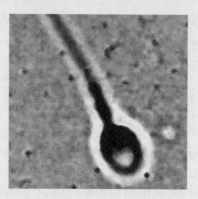

Figure 21.7 The same sperm enlarged seven thousand times with the help of differential interference contrast (DIC) micrography

men with severe male factor infertility to study the common defects that are present, and are also conducting a study of the sperm of diabetic men.

The use of FISH on follicular fluid to detect gonadal sex chromosome mosaicism in women undergoing IVF/ICSI

We are studying the cells in the fluid surrounding the egg, known as the follicular fluid, for chromosomal abnormalities. Women whose follicular cells show higher chromosomal abnormalities on FISH, have higher chances of miscarriages following IVF.

PGD for thalassemia

We are setting up facilities for testing couples at risk of having children affected by thalassemia, by the procedure of PGD. Using ICSI and PGD, we will be able to identify those embryos which are affected by thalassemia, and those that are not. Only embryos that are not affected by thalassemia will be transferred, to ensure the birth of healthy babies.

Stress and reproductive failure

Our research into this aspect of infertility has been ongoing for the past twenty-five years. We are evaluating the impact of various stress-reducing techniques involving counselling, meditation, yoga, behaviour therapy, and medication in improving the chances of pregnancy.

Our research, thus far, emphasizes the importance of a holistic approach to help couples attain successful pregnancies.

The role of pollution in male and female infertility

Pollution adds endocrine disruptors to the environment. These are chemicals which disrupt the male and female reproductive system. They are present in DDT, industrial chemicals, plastics and varnishes. They accumulate in the body causing early puberty, early menopause, diminished ovarian reserve and decreased sperm counts. We are currently researching the contribution of endocrine disruptors to male and female infertility."

Glossary

Abortion: The premature termination of a pregnancy, either spontaneously or voluntarily. Spontaneous termination is also called a miscarriage.

Absent Vagina: A congenital defect in which a baby girl is born without a vagina. During fetal development, the vagina does not form as it should, but the external genital area appears normal.

ACA: See under Anti Cardiolipin Antibodies.

Acanthosis Nigricans: The darkening of the skin characterized by dark wart-like patches in the body folds.

Acrosome: A caplike structure at the anterior end of a spermatozoon that produces enzymes aiding in penetration of the ovum.

Acupressure: A form of complementary treatment administered by applying pressure with the fingers to specific pressure points on the body.

Acupuncture: A system of complementary medicine that involves pricking the skin or tissues with needles.

Adenomyosis: A glandular tissue found in the musculature of

the uterus. Its proliferation causes abnormal enlargement of the uterus.

Adhesions: Bands of scar tissue which form between organs. Usually they occur because of infection but can also form after surgery.

Adoption: The procedure which allows people to become the legal parents of a child.

Adrenal Glands: Hormone producing glands situated on top of the kidneys.

AFP: See under Alpha Fetoprotein.

Agonist: A substance which mimics the action of a naturally occurring substance.

Alpha Fetoprotein (AFP): A protein produced by the foetus. It is measured in pregnant women using blood or amniotic fluid as a screening test for developmental abnormalities.

AMA: See under Anti Microsomal Antibodies.

American Society for Reproductive Medicine (ASRM): A multidisciplinary non-profit organization dedicated to the advancement of the art, science and practice of reproductive medicine.

Amenorrhoea: Absence of menstruation. Primary amenorrhoea is when a woman has never menstruated. Secondary amenorrhoea is when a woman has stopped menstruating after having her periods in the past.

AMH: See under Anti Mullerian Hormone.

Amniocentesis: The sampling of amniotic fluid using a needle, which is inserted into the amniotic cavity through the uterus, to screen for developmental abnormalities in a fetus.

Amniotic Fluid: The fluid surrounding the fetus in the womb.

ANA: See under Anti Nuclear Antibodies.

Androgens: Male hormones such as testosterone. They are naturally present in both men and women. In men, they are responsible for puberty, maturation of sex organs, and formation of sperm. Male hormones are in less concentration in women. Excess of these in women can cause weight gain, hairiness and thickening of voice.

Aneuploidy:An abnormality in the number of chromosomes, for example trisomy or monosomy.

Angelman Syndrome: This is caused by the deletion of some genes on the maternally inherited Chromosome 15. It is also known as Happy Puppet syndrome, and is occasionally associated with IVF pregnancies. The affected child has intellectual disability and has frequent laughing spells.

Anovulation: Absence of ovulation even though menstruation may occur.

Antagonist: A compound which blocks the production of gonadotrophins (FSH & LH) in the pituitary. Used for ovarian stimulation for ART.

Antibodies: Proteins produced by the immune system when it detects harmful substances in the body.

Anti Cardiolipin Antibodies (ACA): These are associated with recurrent miscarriages besides other disorders.

Anti Microsomal Antibodies (AMA): The presence of these antibodies is an indication of thyroid inflammation and dysfunction.

Anti Mullerian Hormone (AMH): A protein released by the ovaries related to the reserve of follicles in the ovary.

Anti Nuclear Antibodies (ANA): They can attack structures within the nucleus of one's own cells and are seen in some autoimmune disorders.

Anti Ovarian Antibodies (AOA): They have been reported in women with premature ovarian failure and unexplained infertility.

Anti-phospholipid Antibodies (APA): Antibodies which attack phospholipids. The presence of Antiphospholipid antibodies may indicate there is an underlying process that results in recurrent pregnancy loss. Phospholipids hold dividing cells together, and are necessary for growth of the placenta into the wall of the uterus. They also filter nourishment from the mother's blood to the baby and filter the baby's waste back through the placenta. Individuals with high APAs have a propensity to produce blood clots.

Antiphospholipid Syndrome: A disorder in which the immune system mistakenly produces antibodies against certain normal proteins in the blood which can cause blood clots to form within the arteries or veins as well as cause pregnancy complications, such as miscarriages and stillbirths.

Antithyroglobulin Antibody (ATA): An antibody that adversely affects the normal functioning of the thyroid gland.

Antral Follicles: Small sacs (2–8 mm in size) seen on the ovaries via ultrasound, also known as resting follicles. The antral follicles, under hormonal stimulation, will mature and finally form the Graafian follicle containing the mature egg.

Anulom Vilom: A Yogic technique of breathing alternately through a single nostril, retaining the breath and breathing out through the other nostril.

AOA: See under Anti Ovarian Antibodies.

APA: See under Anti Phospholipid Antibodies.

Appendicitis: An inflammation of the appendix, which is the tube-shaped pouch attached to the cecum, the beginning of the large intestine.

Apoptosis of Sperm: A type of programmed cell death caused by the fragmentation of sperm DNA.

Array Comparitive Genomic Hybridization (CGH): An advanced molecular technique by which the sample DNA is tested against normal control DNA. Gains or losses in the DNA can be studied.

ART: See under Assisted Reproductive Technologies.

Aseptic: Free from contamination caused by harmful microorganisms.

Ashtanga Yoga: The eight fold path of yoga as outlined by Patanjali: yama, niyama, asana, pranayama, pratyahara, dharana, dhyana and samadhi.

Aspermia: Absence of ejaculated semen.

ASRM: See under American Society for Reproductive Medicine.

Assisted Hatching: A procedure which involves making an opening in the zona pellucida (shell) of the embryo in order to improve implantation. Lasers are used for hatching.

Assisted Reproductive Technologies (ART): It refers to any fertility treatment that involves eggs, sperm and embryos.

Asthenozoospermia: Poor sperm motility.

ATA: See under Antithyroglobulin Antibody.

Autistic Features: Characteristics of a pervasive developmental disorder marked by severe deficits in social interaction and communication and by a limited range of activities and interests. It is frequently accompanied by the presence of repetitive, stereotyped behaviours.

Autoimmune Disorders: Any large group of diseases characterized by abnormal functioning of the immune system that causes it to produce antibodies against the body's own tissues. In this condition, the immune system mistakenly attacks and sometimes destroys healthy body tissues.

Autonomic Nervous System: The part of the peripheral nervous system that acts as a control system, functioning largely below the level of consciousness and controls involuntary functions affecting the heart rate, digestion, respiratory rate, salivation, perspiration, pulpillary dilation, micturition (urination) and sexual arousal.

Autosomal Dominant: A pattern of inheritance where there is a 50-percent chance of recurrence of a genetic disorder in males and females.

Autosomal Recessive: A pattern of inheritance where there is a 25-percent chance of recurrence of the genetic disorder in males and females.

Ayurveda: The traditional Indian system of medicine which uses diet, herbal treatment and yogic breathing.

Azoospermia: Complete lack of sperm in the semen.

Balanced Translocation: An interchange of parts of chromosomes detected on karyotyping, usually in cases with a history of repeated miscarriages.

Bartholin's Glands: A pair of small glands at the base of the vagina that secrete a lubricating mucus.

Basal Body Temperature: The body's temperature at rest.

Charting basal body temperature is a way to track ovulation.

Beckwith-Wiedemann Syndrome: A genetic disorder resulting in overgrowth, a large tongue and an increased risk of tumours.

Benign Prostatic Hypertrophy (BPH): It is a non-malignant (noncancerous) enlargement of the prostate gland, a common occurrence in older men.

Bhujangasana (Cobra pose): A yoga asana in which the chest is lifted from a prone position with palms and legs on the floor.

Bicornuate Uterus: A uterus with two horns. It is a birth defect where the two horns of the uterus have not united to form one.

Blighted Ovum: An early pregnancy in which the gestational sac grows to a point that the pregnancy does not sustain. Also known as an anembryonic gestation.

BPH: See under Benign Prostatic Hypertrophy.

Bromocriptine: A drug used to treat high levels of prolactin.

Buserelin: A medicine which is a long-acting gonadotropin-releasing hormone analogue which downregulates the pituitary-gonadal axis; blocks testosterone production in the testes. It is used to treat metastatic prostate cancer.

Caesarean Section: A surgical procedure in which incisions are made through a woman's abdomen and uterus to deliver her baby.

CAM: See under Complimentary and Alternative Medicine Therapies.

Candida: A yeast infection of the female and male genital tract.

Capacitation: Sperm acquire this ability to penetrate and fertilize the ovum as they travel through the female genital tract.

CAT: See under Cumulus Aided Transfer.

Cauterizing: To burn the skin or flesh of a wound with a heated instrument or caustic substance, typically to stop bleeding or prevent the wound from becoming infected.

CAVD: See under Congenital Absence of the Vasa Deferentia.

CBAVD: See under Congenital Bilateral Absence of the Vasa Deferentia.

Central Nervous System: The part of the nervous system that integrates the information that it receives and coordinates it with the activity from all parts of the body. It consists of the brain and the spinal cord.

Cervicitis: Inflammation of the cervix.

Cervix: Part of the genital tract located between the vagina and uterus.

Cervical Cerclage: Also called cervical stitch. It is done for the management of an incompetent cervix.

Cervical Mucous: Mucous secreted by glands found in the inner folds of the cervix.

Chakrasana (Wheel pose): A Yogic asana in which the hands and feet are placed on the floor while the abdomen arches upwards.

Chemical Pregnancy: A pregnancy only confirmed by slightly elevated BhCG levels in the blood. The BhCG values do not rise consistently and start falling.

Chlamydial Infection: A sexually transmitted infection in humans caused by Chlamydia trachomatis.

Chocolate Cysts: Accumulation of dark brown fluid in the ovary resulting from endometriosis. Also known as endometrioma.

Chorionic Villus Sampling (CVS): A technique of prenatal diagnosis done at around ten to eleven weeks of gestation. A small part of early placental tissue called chorionic villi is removed. This tissue consists of foetal cells and can be used for genetic analysis by karyotyping, FISH, or PCR.

Chromosome: Thread-like structures within the nucleus which contain the hereditary material called DNA.

Chromosomal Abnormalities: Aberrations in either the number or structure of the chromosome.

Cleavage: The division of the zygote into two or more cells. The cells keep dividing until they reach a ball of more than hundred cells.

Clinical Pregnancy: A pregnancy that is confirmed by both high and consistently rising levels of BhCG, and ultrasound confirmation of a gestational sac followed by heartbeats in the embryo.

Clitoris: Part of the female genitalia consisting of a small elongated highly sensitive erectile organ at the front of the vulva which is responsive to sexual stimulation.

Clomiphene: A fertility drug that stimulates production of FSH, which in turn brings about ovulation.

Clomiphene Citrate: A fertility drug that is used to stimulate ovulation.

CODA Tower: An air purifying system innovated by and named after Drs Cohen and Dale.

Coenzyme Q: Any of several quinones found in living cells. They function as coenzymes that transfer electrons from one molecule to another in cell respiration. They are powerful antioxidants.

Coitus: Sexual intercourse.

Colour Doppler: Sonographic study of blood flow in various organs represented in different colours.

Complementary and Alternative Medical Therapies (CAM): A group of diverse medical and health care systems, practices, and products that are not a part of conventional medicine.

Conceptus: The products of conception at any point between fertilization and birth. It includes the embryo or the foetus as well as the extraembryonic membranes.

Congenital Absence of the Vasa Deferentia (CAVD): A condition in which the vasa deferentia fail to form prior to birth.

Congenital Bilateral Absence of Vasa Deferentia (CBAVD): This is seen in cases of azoospermia and can be associated with cystic fibrosis mutations.

Cornu: The 'horns' of the uterus where the fallopian tubes meet the uterus.

Cornual Block: A blockage of the part of the fallopian tubes which attach themselves to the uterus.

Corpora Cavernosa: Tissue on both sides of the penis consisting of a pair of columns of erectile tissue that, together with the corpus spongiosum, produces an erection when filled with blood.

Corpus Luteum: The Graafian follicle converts into this organ after ovulation. It is yellowish in colour and juts out from the ovary. It secretes progesterone.

Corpus Luteum Cyst: A cyst which occurs after an egg is released from the follicle during ovulation. Fluid builds up in the follicle creating a cyst which resolves by itself in a few weeks.

Corpus Spongiosum: A mass of spongy issue on the bottom of the penis that, with the corpora cavernosa, forms the erectile tissue of the penis.

Cortex: The outer layer of any organ or part.

Corticosteroids: Medication that suppresses the immune system and reduces antibody production.

Cortisol: An adrenal hormone produced in response to stress.

Counselling: A process which enables people to talk about their feelings and how to deal with certain situations.

Count (or density): The number of sperm present in millions per millilitre.

Cowper's Glands: Two small glands that discharge a component of seminal fluid into the male urethra during sexual excitement and lubricate the penis.

Creative Visualization: The practice of seeking to affect the outer world by changing one's thoughts and expectations; the basic technique underlying positive thinking.

Cryogenic Containers: Containers which maintain very low temperatures (-180 degree Celsius) due to liquid nitrogen.

Cryopreservation: The process of preserving tissue by freezing it in liquid nitrogen. The process stops all metabolic activity of the cells. The technique is used to preserve sperm, eggs, embryos, and testicular and ovarian tissue.

Cryptorchid: A developmental defect marked by the failure of the testes to descend from the abdomen into the scrotum.

Cryptorchidism: Undescended testis.

CT Scan: A medical imaging procedure that uses computer-processed X-rays to produce tomographic images or 'slices' of specific areas of the body.

Culture Medium: The liquid solution in which the sperm and eggs are processed and the embryos are allowed to grow for up to five days.

Cumulus Aided Transfer (CAT): A procedure where the cumulus cells along with the embryos are transferred into the uterus. This procedure enhances the chances of pregnancy as the cumulus cells secrete substances promoting growth and stickiness of the embryos.

Cumulus Cells: The nutrient cells that surround the ovum.

Cumulus Complex: A group of cells consisting of the oocyte in the Graafian follicle surrounded by tightly packed layers of cumulus cells.

Cumulus-oocyte Complex: The oocyte which leaves the follicle at the time of ovulation is surrounded by a large number of cumulus cells, forming the cumulus-oocyte complex.

Cumulus Oophorus: A cluster of cells that surround the oocyte, both in the ovarian follicle and after ovulation.

CVS: See under Chorionic Villus Sampling.

Cystic Fibrosis: A genetic condition which particularly affects the lungs and is associated with azoospermia due to CBAVD.

Cystic Hygroma: A congenital condition in which the lymph vessels form a cystic growth; usually occurs in the groin, neck, or axilla.

Cytokines: Chemicals made by cells that act on other cells to stimulate or inhibit their function.

Cytomegalovirus: A virus found in body fluids, including urine, saliva, breast milk, blood, tears, semen and vaginal fluids. It can cause disease in unborn babies and in people with weak immune systems.

Danazol: Medication used to suppress endometriosis.

Dehydroepiandrosterone (DHEA): An androgenic steroid secreted largely by the adrenal cortex in both males and females.

Delayed Ejaculation: Delay in ejaculation despite the presence of normal sexual desire and stimulation.

Delinking: A procedure to disconnect the fallopian tubes from the uterus.

Deslorelin: These are synthetic versions of a hormone called gonadotropin-releasing hormone analogue that are released from the hypothalamus gland in the brain used for the treatment of precocious puberty and prostate cancers. These are also used in suppressing the ovaries prior to starting ovarian stimulation.

Dexamethasone: A synthetic glucocorticoid used primarily in the treatment of inflammatory disorders.

DGS: See under DiGeorge Syndrome.

DHA: See under Docosahexaenoic Acid.

Dhanurasana (Bow pose): A yogic asana in which the body assumes the shape of a bow with the arms being used like a bowstring. The person practicing the asana lies down on the stomach and arches the spine by using the hands to hold the ankles.

DHEA: See under Dehydroepiandrosterone.

Diabetes: A metabolic disease characterized by high blood sugar levels.

DiGeorge Syndrome (DGS): An illness characterised by a birth defect that is caused by an abnormality in chromosome 22. It affects the baby's immune system.

Dilation & Curettage (D&C): It is a procedure to widen the cervical canal in order to remove products of incomplete or missed abortions.

Diminished Ovarian Reserve: A condition of low fertility characterized by low number of oocytes in the ovaries with impaired recruitment.

Dizygotic Twins: Twins that develop from two separate eggs.

Docosahexaenoic Acid (DHA): A member of the omega-3 family of fatty acids. It is one of the breakdown products of alpha-linolenic acid (ALA) and is essential for the development and maintenance of the nervous system.

Donor Ova: Mature female reproductive cells obtained from a female other than the one who will carry the pregnancy.

Double Marker Test: A screening test that measures the serum levels of AFP and estriol and reflects genetic abnormalities in the fetus.

Douching: Instilling fluids into the vagina in order to irrigate it.

Down Regulation: A process by which the pituitary gland in the brain is desensitized so that the body's natural production of FSH and LH is temporarily suppressed. This is achieved by using either GnRh antagonists or GnRh agonists.

Down's Syndrome: A genetic disorder—Trisomy 21 or Mongolism where the children have very low IQ, typical upslanting eyes, low set ears, and a Simian crease or a single transverse palmar crease. The risk of having a child with Down's syndrome increases with advanced maternal age.

Duchenne Muscular Dystrophy: The most common form of muscular dystrophy, in which fat and fibrous tissue infiltrate muscle tissue, causing eventual weakening of the respiratory muscles and the myocardium. The disease, which almost exclusively affects males, begins in early childhood and usually causes death before adulthood.

Ductus Arteriosus (Ductus): A blood vessel that allows blood to bypass the baby's lungs before birth. Once the infant is born and the lungs fill with air, the ductus arteriosus is no longer needed and shuts down. If it stays patent, there is an abnormal flow of blood between the aorta and the pulmonary artery - the two major blood vessels that carry blood from the heart. This causes respiratory distress and weakness in the newborn and can be fatal if untreated.

Dysmenorrhea: Pain or cramping that occurs during menstruation. Late onset dysmenorrhea is usually associated with the presence of endometriosis.

Dyspareunia: Painful intercourse.

Ectopic Pregnancy: An abnormal pregnancy where the embryo implants itself outside the uterus. The common sites of implantation are the fallopian tubes, the ovaries, the cervix, and sometimes the pelvic cavity.

Edward's Syndrome: A genetic disorder due to Trisomy 18, characterized by low-birth weight, club feet, receding chin, low-set ears and other malformations.

Efferent Ductules: Small seminal ducts approximately 12 in number leading from the testis to the head of the epididymis.

Egg Donation: The process by which a woman, who is fertile, donates her eggs (oocytes) to another who is not producing good quality and/or quantity of eggs.

Egg Retrieval: The removal of the oocytes from the ovaries by an ultrasound technique after maturing the eggs.

Eicosapentaenoic Acid (EPA): An omega-3 fatty acid found in fish oils.

Ejaculatory Duct: Either of the paired ducts in males through which semen is ejaculated. They are formed by the junction of the seminal ducts with the vas deferens, that pass through the prostate and empty out through the urethra.

ELISA: Enzyme-linked immunosorbent assay; a rapid immunochemical test that involves an enzyme used for measuring a wide variety of body fluids. ELISA tests are sensitive and specific and are used to detect substances that have antigenic properties, primarily proteins.

Embryo: A fertilized egg within the first eight weeks of conception.

Embryologist: A scientist with training and skills in handling sperm, eggs and embryos in the laboratory.

Embryo Biopsy: A process involving the taking of one or more cells (blastomeres) from an embryo at the eight cell stage for genetic analysis.

Endocrine Disorders: Disorders of the hormonal system, which include those of any of the glands that secrete hormones directly into the bloodstream : the pituitary, pineal, thyroid, parathyroid, adrenal, testes, ovaries, and the pancreatic islets of Langerhans.

Endocrine Function: The secretion of hormones into the blood stream by the endocrine glands.

Endometrioma: Ovarian cysts filled with blood. Also known as 'chocolate cysts'.

Endometriosis: A condition in which endometrial tissue grows in abnormal places.

Endometrium: The inner lining of the uterus.

Endometrial Biopsy: A test involving the taking of a small sample of the endometrium for examination for histopathology or TB testing.

Endoscopy: The visualization of the interior of the body using telescopic instruments such as the laparoscope and the hysteroscope.

Enzymes: Proteins produced by cells in the body. These induce and hasten chemical changes in the body.

EPA: See under Eicosapentaenoic Acid.

Epididymis: A part of the male reproductive system. It is made up of thin tubules which carry the sperm from the testes to the vas deferens.

Epinephrine: A stress hormone produced by the adrenal gland. It affects important bodily functions such as the flow of blood, breathing and heart rate. It also affects other hormones associated with fertility.

Erection: The state of the penis when it is turgid, enlarged and rigid.

Estradiol: An important female hormone produced by the ovary. It is the hormone most often measured during IVF treatment.

Estriol: One of the three main estrogens produced by the human body and found in high concentration in the urine of females. It is a female sex hormone that increases during pregnancy.

Estrogen: A hormone secreted primarily by the ovaries but also secreted by the adrenal glands and from fatty tissue. Estrogens are a group of hormones, that is, estrone, estradiol and estriol. Of these, estradiol is the most active form.

Estrogen Replacement Therapy: The therapeutic administration of estrogen to postmenopausal women in order to reduce the symptoms and signs of estrogen deficiency, such as hot flashes and osteoporosis. Estrogen Replacement Therapy in the context of fertility treatments is related to the preparation of the uterine lining prior to the transfer of the embryo created from donor eggs or preparation of the uterine lining prior to the transfer of frozen thawed embryos.

External Os: The vaginal opening of the cervix.

Factor V Leiden Mutation: A genetic disorder of blood coagulation (clotting) that carries an increased risk of venous thromboembolism (the formation of clots in veins that may break loose and travel through the bloodstream to the lungs or brain).

Fallopian Tubes: A pair of tubular structures on each side of the uterus which help lead the fertilized eggs from the ovaries to the uterus.

Fecundability: The probability that a couple will get pregnant. The fecundity rate is the likelihood of pregnancy per monthly cycle.

Female Factor Infertility: A term used when the cause of infertility is specific to the woman.

Fertile Window: The time period where sex is likely to lead to pregnancy.

Fertility: Refers to the ability to conceive and have children.

Fibroids: Usually benign (noncancerous) tumours that grow from the muscular layer of the uterus.

Fibromyoma: Benign (noncancerous) growths of fibrous tissue and muscle cells inside the uterus.

Filariasis: A group of tropical diseases caused by various thread-like parasitic worms and their larvae characterized by fever, chills, headache, and skin lesions in the early stages. If untreated, it can progress to include gross enlargement of the limbs and genitalia. The larvae transmit the disease to humans through a mosquito bite.

Fimbriae: Fringe or fringelike margin or border, especially at the opening of the Fallopian tubes.

FISH: See under Fluorescent In Situ Hybridization.

Fluorescent In Situ Hybridization (FISH): This is a DNA-based technique of studying chromosome abnormalities from nuclei of undividing cells, without actually seeing the chromosomes by karyotyping.

Foetal Reduction: The procedure in which one or more foetuses are aborted by injecting potassium hydrochloride, in order to improve the outcome of the remaining foetus / foetuses.

Foetus: The developing conceptus that has reached the twelve-week stage.

Follicle: A fluid filled sac that contains an egg or oocyte.

Follicle Stimulating Hormone (FSH): A hormone secreted by the pituitary gland, which is responsible for stimulating the growth and development of eggs in women, and stimulating the growth and development of sperm in men.

Follicular Cyst: A cyst which occurs when a follicle does not complete its maturation. The ovum is not released. The follicle develops into a cyst. This cyst resolves by itself within 1-3 menstrual cycles.

Follicular Phase: It begins on Day 1 of the menstrual cycle (the day the period starts) and ends when a hormone called luteinizing hormone peaks and ovulation occurs. During this phase, the oocytes begin the maturation process which is completed at the time of ovulation.

Fragile X: A genetic disorder mainly affecting males who display hyperactivity and autistic features. Women with premature ovarian failure may be carriers of this condition and should be tested before IVF.

FSH: See under Follicle Stimulating Hormone.

Gamete: Refers to either the egg or sperm cell.

Gamma Interferon: A small, species-specific glycoprotein produced by T-cells. It possesses antiviral activity and plays a central role in the immunoregulatory processes. Elevated levels of gamma interferon may be seen in individuals suffering from tuberculosis.

Genetic: Of an inherited basis.

Genetic Counselling: A process where the genetic problem in the family is explained, other people at risk identified, and ways of circumventing the disorder through assisted reproduction or other means discussed.

Genital Tuberculosis: Tuberculosis affecting the genital tract leading to infertility.

Germ-cell Aplasia: A condition in which the testicles have no germ cells. Since men with this condition have normal Leydig cells producing testosterone, they will develop secondary sex characteristics. May also be caused by large and/or prolonged exposure to toxins or radiation.

Gestational Surrogacy: An arrangement wherein a woman carries the baby for a couple.

Giemsa Banding: Special staining of chromosomes to identify individual pairs and detect anomalies during karyotyping.

Ginseng: A plant tuber credited with various tonic and medicinal properties especially in Traditional Chinese Medicine.

Glans Penis: The sensitive bulbous structure at the distal end of the penis.

Glycosylated Haemoglobin: A form of haemoglobin used to identify the average blood sugar concentration over a prolonged period of time.

GnRH: See under Gonadotrophin Releasing Hormone.

GnRH Agonist Analogue: An artificially prepared hormone that mimics the body's natural hormone, gonadotrophin releasing hormone (GnRH). It desensitizes the pituitary. This is required for downregulation prior to controlled ovarian hyperstimulation.

GnRH Antagonists: An artificially prepared fertility hormone that suppresses the production of the hormone LH and FSH.

Goitre: Enlargement of the thyroid gland causing swelling in the neck.

Gonadotrophins: These are fertility drugs which contain the hormones LH or FSH or a combination of both. They are processed from human urine or prepared by recombinant genetic techniques.

Gonadotrophin Releasing Hormone (GnRH): A hormone

released from the hypothalamus which stimulates the pituitary gland to produce FSH and LH.

Gonorrhoea: A sexually transmitted disease caused by a bacterium called Neisseria gonorrhoeae, acquired through sexual contact characterized by a burning sensation when urinating and a mucopurulent discharge from the urethra or vagina.

Goserelin: It is a synthetic version of a hormone called gonadotropin-releasing hormone analogue that is released from the hypothalamus gland in the brain used in the treatment of precocious puberty, prostate and cancer.

Graafian Follicle: A mature ovarian follicle containing an oocyte and a large fluid-filled cavity.

Granulosa Cells: Cells present in the follicles of the ovary that surround the oocyte.

Guided Imagery: The use of relaxation and mental visualization techniques to improve mood and physical well-being.

Gynaecomastia: The development of abnormally large breasts in males.

Hatching: The process by which the blastocyst emerges from the zona pellucida before implantation.

Haemoglobin: A protein present in red blood cells. It carries oxygen to the different parts of the body.

Haemophilia: A congenital illness characterised by a tendency to uncontrolled bleeding. It usually affects males and is transmitted from mother to son.

Haploid: (of a cell or nucleus) Having a single set of unpaired chromosomes.

Harmonic Scalpel: An ultrasound-powered cutting tool that simultaneously cuts and seals human tissue.

Hatha Yoga: A yogic system of physical exercises and breath control.

Hb Electrophoresis: A blood test that can detect different types of haemoglobin.

HCG: See under Human Chorionic Gonadotrophin.

HEPA: See under High Efficiency Particulate Air Filters.

Heparin Therapy: Daily injections of low molecular weight heparin used in the treatment of women suffering from recurrent miscarriages, blood clotting and repeated implantation failure.

Herpes: Any of several diseases caused by the herpes virus, characterized by the eruption of blisters on the skin or mucous membranes.

High Efficiency Particulate (HEPA) Air Filters: Filters composed of a mat arranged with fibres which can filter out 99.99 percent of airborne particles of 0.3 mm diameter. Particles containing bacteria, viruses, dust and fungal spores are filtered out.

Hirsuitism: The growth of hair in abnormal places in women caused by excess male hormones circulating in the body. Hirsuitism is commonly seen in women with PCOS and sometimes in women with adrenal tumours.

HLA: See under Human Leukocyte Antigens.

HMG: See under Human Menopausal Gonadotropin.

Homeopathy: A system of alternative medicine based on the concept that substances that produce symptoms of sickness in healthy people have a curative effect when given in highly dilute quantities to sick people exhibiting those symptoms.

Hormones: Chemicals produced by a cell that send out messages to other parts of the body.

Hormone Replacement Therapy (HRT): The use of the female hormones, estrogen and progesterone, in menopausal situations.

Hostile Cervical Mucous: A term used to describe cervical mucous which does not allow the sperm to survive within it.

HRT: See under Hormone Replacement Therapy.

HSG: See under Hysterosalpingogram.

Human Chorionic Gonadotropin (HCG): A hormone secreted by the placenta during pregnancy that prolongs the life of the corpus luteum. It is used to trigger ovulation.

Human Leukocyte Antigens (HLA): A collection of human genes on chromosome 6 that encodes proteins that function in cells to transport antigens from within the cell to the cell surface. These proteins are sometimes referred to as the MHC, or major histocompatibility complex.

Human Menopausal Gonadotropin (HMG): A pituitary hormone, initially obtained from the urine of postmenopausal women, now produced synthetically. It is used to induce ovulation.

Hybridization: The use of a DNA or RNA probes to detect complementary genetic material in cells or tissue.

Hydramnios: A condition in which there is excessive fluid around the foetus.

Hydrocele: A swelling of the scrotum due to an accumulation of fluid below the covering of the testes.

Hydrosalpinges: Blocked, dilated, fluid-filled fallopian tube.

Hydrosalpinx: A blocked fallopian tube filled with tubes.

Hymen: A membrane that partially closes the opening of the vagina.

Hyperandrogenism: Abnormally high levels of androgens.

Hypertrophy: A non-tumorous enlargement of an organ or a tissue as a result of an increase in the size rather than the number of constituent cells.

Hypnotherapy: The treatment of a variety of health conditions by hypnotism.

Hypogonadotropic Hypogonadism: Absent or decreased function of the male testes or female ovaries due to a problem with the pituitary gland or hypothalamus.

Hypospermatogenesis: The condition of having decreased sperm production.

Hypothalamus: A master structure in the brain which controls the activity of the pituitary gland.

Hysterosalpingogram (HSG): A test to evaluate the shape of the uterus and patency of the fallopian tubes. The test involves injecting an iodine-based dye through the cervix and taking X-Rays to see if the dye spills through easily from the fallopian tubes. In cases of blockage, the fallopian tubes do not get outlined well.

Hysteroscope: An endoscope that is inserted through the cervix into the uterus to enable the surgeon to view the inside of the uterus in order to diagnose and treat problems within the uterine cavity.

Hysteroscopy: Inspection of the uterine cavity by a telescopic instrument through the cervix.

ICSI: See under Intracytoplasmic Sperm Injection.

IgG: See under Immunoglobulin G.

IgM: See under Immunoglobulin M.

IMSI: See under Intracytoplasmic Morphologically selected Sperm Injection.

Intracytoplasmic Sperm Injection (ICSI): A procedure which involves taking one sperm cell and injecting it directly into the cytoplasm of an oocyte. This technique has revolutionized the treatment of male factor infertility.

Immunocytochemistry: The range of microscopic techniques used in the study of the immune system.

Immunoglobulin G (IgG): One of the five major classes of immunoglobulins; the main antibody defence against bacteria.

Immunoglobulin M (IgM): The class of antibodies found in circulating body fluids and the first antibodies to appear in response to an initial exposure to an antigen.

Immunoglobulins: Any of a class of proteins present in the serum and cells of the immune system that function as antibodies.

Immunological Conditions: Conditions resulting from altered immunity of an individual.

Immunomodulation: The adjustment of the immune response to a desired level, as in immunopotentiation, immunosuppression, or induction of immunologic tolerance.

Immunotherapy: A treatment that helps the body to fight infection and immunological problems. It is helpful to some women who suffer recurrent miscarriages. The most common form of immunotherapy is IVIg, which is a protein that absorbs harmful antibodies.

Implantation: A process by which the embryo adheres to the wall of the uterus.

Impotence: The inability to achieve or maintain a penile erection for successful intercourse.

Incompetent Cervix: A condition in which the cervix is weak and begins to open before a baby is ready to be born.

Infantile Uterus: A uterus that has failed to develop adult characteristics.

Infertility: The inability of a couple to produce a pregnancy after one year of intercourse with no contraception. One in six couples is affected by this condition.

Infusions of Intravenous Immunoglobulins (IVIG): A liquid containing antibodies used to treat immune related conditions such as repeated miscarriages and implantation failures.

Inhibin: A hormone which downregulates FSH synthesis and inhibits FSH secretion.

Inhibin A: A glycoprotein hormone in the blood made by the placenta of a pregnant woman. It is used for detecting Down's Syndrome in the baby.

Injectables: Drugs taken via injection either subcutaneously, intramuscularly or intravenously.

Insulin: A hormone that regulates glucose metabolism in the body.

Integrins: Proteins that mediate interactions between two cells as well as between a cell and the extracellular matrix. Integrins secreted in the endometrium help with implantation.

Interleukins: Substances extracted from white blood cells that stimulate their activity against infection and may be used to combat some forms of cancer. They are involved in many immune reactions of the reproductive and endocrine systems.

Interstitial Cells: The cells between the seminiferous tubules of the testes (Leydig cells) that produce the male hormones.

Intra Cytoplasmic Morphologically selected Sperm Injection (IMSI): A technique of ICSI in which the sperm is enlarged 7,000 times for the selection of the healthiest sperm.

Intra Cytoplasmic Sperm Injection (ICSI): An advanced form of IVF wherein the sperm is injected into the cytoplasm of the egg. This practically ensures fertilization as the seven steps to fertilization that occur in nature are completed in the lab. ICSI is particularly useful in male factor infertility.

Intrauterine Contraceptive Device (IUCD): A plastic device which is inserted into the uterus as a form of contraception.

Intrauterine Insemination (IUI): A fertility treatment which involves placing specially processed sperms directly into the uterus with the help of a special catheter.

Intraventricular Haemorrhage: A condition in which blood vessels within the brain rupture and bleed into the hollow chambers (ventricles) normally reserved for cerebrospinal fluid and into the tissue surrounding them. It can occur in premature babies.

Introitus: Entrance or opening to a hollow organ or tube (especially the vaginal opening).

In-Vitro Activation: A technique that involves removing the ovaries, cutting them into small one to two millimetre square cubes, and treating the fragments with special stimulating drugs.

In Vitro Fertilization (IVF): A fertility treatment in which fertility drugs are used to stimulate the ovaries. The eggs are retrieved and placed together with sperm in a special, nutrient rich medium. After fertilization takes place, the embryos are placed inside the uterus with the help of a catheter.

IUCD: See under Intrauterine Contraceptive Device.

IUI: See under Intrauterine Insemination.

IVF: See under In Vitro Fertilization.

Karyotyping: The process of obtaining chromosomes for analysis, by grouping them in pairs, to detect abnormalities which may be responsible for infertility, repeated miscarriages, and other conditions.

Kapalbhati: An important part of Shatkarma (sometimes known as Shatkriya), the yogic system of body cleansing techniques. It involves forceful exhalation, removing all toxins. Its literal translation is 'glowing' or 'shining skull.'

Keyhole Surgery: Surgery that utilizes a laparoscope with a video camera and surgical instruments inserted through small incisions. It is also called minimally invasive surgery.

Klinefelter's Syndrome: A numerical chromosome abnormality (47,XXY) where a male has an extra X chromosome, resulting in infertility due to absence of sperm. Other features include increased height, breast development, and small genitalia.

Labia Majora: The outer folds of skin of the external female genitalia.

Labia Minora: The inner folds of skin of the external female genitalia.

LAH: See under Laser Assisted Hatching.

Laparoscopic Electrocauterization of the Ovarian Surface (LEOS): This is a laparoscopic procedure cauterizing the multiple unruptured follicles seen in the Polycystic Ovary Syndrome. It reduces the androgens of the ovaries, thereby facilitating ovulation.

Laparoscopy: A procedure in which abdominal and pelvic organs are visualized using a telescopic instrument introduced through the abdominal wall.

Laser: Used in surgery to cut or destroy harmful tissue such as endometriosis and adhesions.

Laser Assisted Hatching (LAH): Used to help the embryo hatch from its protective outer shell, the zona pellucida, and promote implantation in the uterine wall after embryo transfer. Laser-assisted hatching uses a highly focused diode laser beam to remove a very small section of the zona pellucida (the outer wall of an embryo) in precise increments.

Lateral Metroplasty: A surgical procedure which helps to increase the volume of the uterus and broaden the walls by making slit-like incisions in the lateral walls of the uterus.

LEOS: See under Laparoscopic Electrocauterization of the Ovarian Surface.

Letrozole: A non-steroidal aromatase inhibitor drug used to treat breast cancer in postmenopausal women and also used to stimulate ovulation.

Leuprolide: A potent medicine which is a synthetic long-acting agonist of gonadotropin-releasing hormone that regulates the synthesis and release of pituitary gonadotropins, luteinizing hormone and follicle stimulating hormone.

Level III Sonography: A specialized ultrasound examination of the fetus in order to visualise various organs and systems in the fetus.

LH: See under Luteinizing Hormone.

LH peak: The high level of luteinizing hormone that occurs in response to the estrogen peak in the middle of the menstrual cycle and triggers ovulation.

Libido: The desire for sexual pleasure.

LIT: See under Lymphocyte Immunization Therapy.

Liquor Folliculi: The fluid surrounding the ovum in the ovarian follicle.

Lupus Anticoagulant: Antibodies against substances in the lining of cells that prevent blood clotting in a test tube. These substances are called phospholipids. Persons with these antibodies may have a high risk of blood clotting.

Luteal Phase: Second half of the human menstrual cycle, beginning with ovulation and ending, in the absence of fertilization, with the menstrual phase. During this phase, estrogen and progesterone increase, and work together to create changes in the lining of the uterus that prepare it to accept an embryo, should conception occur.

Luteal Phase Defect: A condition due to the dysfunction of the ovaries or due to improper ovulation.

Luteal Support: A process in which medicines are given after ovulation or embryo transfer to help implantation and later maintain pregnancy.

Luteinizing Hormone (LH): A hormone secreted by the pituitary gland which helps the eggs to mature and develop. In males, it is responsible for the maturation of sperm.

Lymphocyte Immunization Therapy (LIT): A procedure in

which white blood cells from the prospective father are injected into the skin of the prospective mother to prepare the maternal immune system for pregnancy. LIT assists the mothers immune system in the development of immunologic tolerance to the genetically foreign pregnancy tissues.

Lymphocyte: A type of white cell that is of fundamental importance in the immune response of infectious microorganisms and other foreign substances.

Maca: A root which has nutritional and health value and has been used for treating infertility.

Magnetic Resonance Imaging (MRI): An imaging technique that uses a magnetic field and pulses of radio wave energy to visualize internal structures of the body.

Makler Chamber: A flat counting chamber with a thickness of 10 µm, used for sperm analysis. It was invented by an Israeli scientist, Dr. Makler.

Male Factor Infertility: A term used when the cause of infertility is specific to the man.

Masturbation: Sexual gratification by stimulating the genitals often resulting in orgasms. It is the most common method of obtaining sperm for ART treatment.

Medroxyprogesterone: A progesterone compound used to treat menstrual disorders.

Medulla: The inner region of an organ or tissue, especially when it is distinguishable from the outer region or cortex.

Meiotic Spindle: The structure within a cell that segregates chromosomes between daughter cells during genetic cell division.

Menarche: The beginning of menses and puberty in a girl.

Menopause: The cessation of menstruation which occurs around the age of forty-five to fifty. It is said to be premature when it occurs in a woman under the age of forty.

Menstruation: The shedding of the uterine lining in the form of bleeding through the vagina.

Mesterolone: An androgen hormone (male sex hormone) used as replacement therapy in hypogonadism because testosterone cannot be given orally. Side effects can include prostate problems, headache and depression.

Metabolic Syndrome X: A condition characterized by obesity, with elevated cholesterol, triglycerides, sugar and blood pressure. It can cause infertility due to polycystic ovaries.

Metformin: An antidiabetic medicine prescribed for Type II Diabetes.

Methotrexate: A drug that interferes with cell growth and is used to treat rheumatoid arthritis as well as various types of cancer. It is used for the medical management of an ectopic pregnancy.

Methylenetetrahydrofolate reductase (MTHFR) Mutation: A rare genetic defect that can lead to complications in pregnancy due to the inability to efficiently metabolize folic acid and vitamin B9, which are both essential to the development and health of the fetus. The disorder has been linked to a variety of pregnancy complications such as chromosomal abnormalities, Down syndrome and congenital malformations.

Micro-manipulation: In fertility treatments, a procedure which involves manipulating the egg and injecting the sperm into the egg. It is done on the platform of a microscope.

Minnesota Multiphasic Personality Inventory (MMPI): The most widely used and researched psychological test. It is often used to assess personality traits, emotional and thought disorders, as well as to develop treatment plans.

Miscarriage: The loss of a pregnancy before the foetus is twenty-eight weeks old. It is further classified as inevitable, incomplete, missed, or recurrent miscarriage.

Mitochondria: Units within cells that convert energy into forms that can be used by the cell. They are also involved in other cell processes such as cell division and growth, as well as cell death. They are the storehouses of energy.

Mittelsmerz: One-sided, lower abdominal pain that occurs in women at or around the time an egg is released from the ovaries (ovulation). Also called 'ovulation pain' or 'midcycle pain'.

MMPI: See under Minnesota Multiphasic Personality Inventory.

Molar Pregnancy: An abnormal form of pregnancy in which a non-viable fertilized egg implants in the uterus and converts a normal pregnancy into an abnormal one. The mole indicates a clump of growing tissue, or a 'growth'; the placental cells form clusters of grape like structures.

Monosomy: Absence of one chromosome from a pair.

Monozygotic Twins: Also called identical twins. They develop from one zygote that splits into two.

Mons Veneris: A mound of fatty tissue covering the pubic area in women.

Morphology: Refers to the shape or form of cells.

Morula: An embryo at an early stage which consists of cells in a solid ball.

Mosaicism: Presence of both normal and abnormal karyotypes

of varying percentages in an individual.

Motility: It is used to describe the percentage of sperm that move under their own power.

MRI: See under Magnetic Resonance Imaging

MTHFR: See under Methylenetetrahydrofolate reductase Gene Mutation.

MTHFR Mutation Analysis: The methylenetetrahydrofolate reductase (MTHFR) mutation test is used to detect two relatively common mutations in the MTHFR gene that are associated with elevated levels of homocysteine in the blood.

Mucous (cervical): Fluid produced by glands in the cervix. Mucous production is under the influence of hormones. At the time of ovulation, the mucous appears clear, thin and stretchy.

Mumps: An acute, inflammatory, contagious disease caused by a paramyxovirus. It is characterized by swelling of the salivary glands, especially the parotids, and sometimes of the pancreas, ovaries, or testes.

Muscular Dystrophy: A hereditary condition marked by progressive weakening and wasting of the muscles.

NACE: See under Non-Invasive Analysis for Chromosomal Examination.

Nafarelin: These are synthetic versions of a hormone called Gonadotropin-releasing hormone analogue that is released from the hypothalamus gland in the brain used in the treatment of precocious puberty, prostates and cancers. These are also used in suppressing the ovaries prior to starting ovarian stimulation.

Natural Cycle IVF: The natural pattern of ovulation without hyperstimulation. It allows the IVF cycle to be as close to nature as possible and also reduces the cost of the cycle.

Natural Killer Cells: Lymphocytes (white blood cells) which constitute a major part of the immune system. They play a major role in the rejection of tumours and virus infected cells. When in excess in the uterine lining, they may cause miscarriages.

Naturopathy: A system of alternative medicine based on the theory that diseases can be successfully treated or prevented without the use of drugs, by techniques such as control of diet, exercise and massage.

Necrozoospermia: A condition in which sperm in the semen are dead or motionless.

Neural Tube Disorders (NTD): These include spina bifida where a part of the spinal cord protrudes from the back, anencephaly or severe underdevelopment of the brain, and encephalocoele, where the brain tissue protrudes through openings in the skull.

NIFTY: See under Non-Invasive Fetal Trisomy Testing.

Nocturnal Penile Tumescence: A normal condition of penile erection that occurs during sleep through the majority of the male lifetime.

Non-Invasive Analysis for Chromosomal Examination (NACE): A test that is less invasive than amniocentesis and is used to detect common chromosomal abnormalities such as Trisomies 21, 18 and 13.

Non-Invasive Fetal Trisomy Testing (NIFTY): A test that is less invasive than amniocentesis and is used to detect common chromosomal abnormalities such as Trisomies 21, 18 and 13.

Norepinephrine: A stress hormone produced by the adrenal

gland. It affects important bodily functions such as the flow of blood, breathing and heart rate. It also affects other hormones associated with fertility.

NT: See under Neural Thickness Scan.

NTD: See under Neural Tube Disorders.

Nuchal Thickness (NT) Scan: Ultrasound scanning performed in early pregnancy to investigate the nuchal fold; an area of skin at the back of the neck. Excessive thickness of the skin is an indicator of possible chromosomal abnormalities such as Down's syndrome.

Nuchal Translucency: Sonographic assessment of the amount of fluid behind the neck of the foetus. It is a screening test for Down's syndrome. Foetuses at high risk of Down's syndrome have a higher amount of fluid in the neck region.

Nutritional Therapy: A health care specialty area based on attaining better health through diet.

Obstructive Azoospermia: A condition in which the tubes which carry sperm in the ejaculate are obstructed leading to a negative sperm count.

OHSS: See under Ovarian Hyperstimulation Syndrome.

Oligoasthenoteratozoospermia: A condition with low count, poor motility and abnormal shape of sperm.

Oligospermia: A condition of low sperm count.

Oocyte: An egg or ovum. The female gamete.

OPK: See under Ovulation Predictor Kit.

Orchidectomy: The surgical removal of one or both testes.

Orchiditis: Inflammation of the testes.

Orgasm: Sexual climax. It is usually accompanied by ejaculation of semen in men.

Osteopenia: A condition where bone mineral density is lower than normal. It is considered to be a precursor to osteoporosis.

Osteoporosis: A condition in which bones become porous and fragile due to depletion of calcium, and prone to fractures due to age and a decrease in estrogen levels.

Ostia: The opening of the fallopian tubes.

Ovarian Cyst: A part of the ovary that swells up like a sac containing fluid. The fluid is usually separated from the rest of the ovary by a wall of tissue.

Ovarian Hyperstimulation Syndrome (OHSS): A painful and potentially dangerous side effect of fertility drugs. In OHSS, the ovaries become swollen with fluid leaking into the abdominal cavity causing discomfort.

Ovary: The ovum producing reproductive organ in the female. It secretes estrogen, progesterone, and other hormones such as inhibin, androgens and Anti-Mullerian hormones.

Ovulation: A process by which a mature egg or ovum is released from the ovary.

Ovulation Predictor Kit (OPK): A kit that detects a surge of the hormone LH, which peaks twenty-four to forty-eight hours prior to ovulation. It is conducted through a urine test.

Ovum: Mature female egg cell.

PAMP: See under Pathogen Associated Molecular Pattern.

Pancreas: The gland which secretes digestive enzymes and hormones such as amylase, lipase and insulin.

Papaverine: A drug which causes blood vessels to expand,

thereby increasing blood flow. Papaverine can be used to produce erections in men with erectile dysfunction.

Paschimottanasana (Seated Forward Bend pose): A yoga asana which involves an intense dorsal Stretch, wherein the yogi sits on the floor with legs flat on the floor, straight ahead then bends forward from the hips to bring the trunk parallel with the legs.

Patau Syndrome: Also called trisomy 13. It is a congenital disorder associated with the presence of an extra copy of chromosome 13. The extra chromosome 13 causes numerous physical and mental abnormalities, especially heart defects.

Patent Ductus Arteriosus (PDA) : A condition in which the ductus arteriosus remains open after birth. It is potentially fatal.

Pathogen Associated Molecular Pattern (PAMP): Patterns in cells associated with specific bacteria such as the TB bacterium.

PCOS: See under Polycystic Ovary Syndrome.

PCR: See under Polymerase Chain Reaction.

PCT: See under Post-coital Test.

PE: See under Premature Ejaculation.

Pedunculated Fibroid: An uterine fibroid (a benign growth of fibrous tissue and muscle cells inside the uterus) that has a stalk (called a pedicle) attached to it.

Pelvic Area: The lower part of the female abdomen containing the uterus, fallopian tubes, ovaries, urinary bladder and rectum.

Pelvic Inflammatory Disease (PID): An infection of the pelvic organs—uterus, ovaries and fallopian tubes. It can result in infertility.

Pelvic Tuberculosis: Tuberculosis affecting the pelvic organs

& the reproductive organs, often referred to as Genital TB.

Penis: The male organ responsible for intercourse, ejaculation and urination.

Pentoxyfyline: A drug (similar to caffeine) which has been shown to enhance sperm motility. It also appears to have the added benefit of promoting fertilization.

Percutaneous Epididymal Sperm Aspiration (PESA): Aspiration of the sperm from the epididymis.

Perineal Muscles: Muscles in the floor of the pelvis that are important for labour and delivery.

Peritubal Adhesions: Fibrous bands of scar tissue that form between internal organs and tissues around the fallopian tubes.

PESA: See under Percutaneous Epididymal Sperm Aspiration

Pessary: A medical device which is inserted into the vagina or rectum.

PGD: See under Pre-implantation Genetic Diagnosis.

PID: See under Pelvic Inflammatory Disease.

Pituitary: A pea-sized endocrine gland situated in the brain. It is the master gland that controls the other glands.

Placenta: The thick pad of tissue inside a pregnant woman's uterus that provides nourishment to and disposes waste from the growing fetus.

Placental Hormone Secretions: Some of the hormones produced by the placenta, including human placental lactogen, chorionic gonadotropin, estrogen, progesterone and thyrotropin-like hormone.

POC: See under Products of Conception.

POF: See under Premature Ovarian Failure.

Polycystic Ovary Syndrome (PCOS): A condition where multiple small cysts appear in the ovary. Abnormal hormone imbalance can cause problems in ovulation in this condition.

Polymerase Chain Reaction (PCR): A technique in molecular biology used to amplify a single copy of DNA into multiple copies.

Polymorphisms/Variants in Chromosomes: Small changes in the shape and size of chromosomes that are usually considered as a variation from normal looking chromosomes. However, some of these may be responsible for infertility and repeated miscarriages.

Polyps: Abnormal growth of glandular tissue.

Polyvinylpyrrolidone (PVP): A synthetic polymer used in the ICSI procedure for the preparation of sperm samples.

Poor Ovarian Reserve: A low number of oocytes available in the ovaries.

Post-coital Test (PCT): A diagnostic test which allows observation of the interaction of semen and cervical mucous. A sample of mucous is taken from the cervix during ovulation, sexual intercourse having taken place some hours earlier. This sample is then viewed under the microscope for sperm number and activity.

Prednisolone: A glucocorticoid medicine used to treat inflammatory conditions.

Pre Eclampsia: A condition in which the blood pressure rises in pregnancy with significant amount of proteins in the urine. It is frequently seen in the first pregnancy and in older women, and is potentially dangerous for the mother and baby.

Pre-implantation Genetic Diagnosis (PGD): An additional step in IVF to identify genetically normal embryos by studying one to two cells of the embryo prior to embryo transfer.

Premature Ejaculation (PE): A condition in which ejaculation occurs within two minutes of sexual penetration.

Premature Menopause: A condition in which the ova get depleted before the age of forty. It can occur due to genetic reasons when the ovaries are surgically removed or following chemotherapy.

Premature Ovarian Failure (POF): The cessation of menstrual periods due to failure of the ovaries before age 40; it is also termed early menopause.

Prepuce: The fold of skin surrounding and protecting the head of the penis, also known as the foreskin.

Presacral Neurectomy: A surgical procedure in which nerves at the back of the uterus are severed in an attempt to eliminate or reduce pain due to periods or due to pathology of the pelvic organs.

Primary Oocyte: An oocyte that is in its early growth phase.

Primordial Follicle: An immature ovarian follicle consisting of an oocyte enclosed by a single layer of cells.

Products of Conception (POC): The tissues present in a fertilized gestation. This term is usually used for tissue coming from a failed pregnancy.

Progesterone: A hormone secreted by the corpus luteum of the ovary after ovulation.

Prolactin: A hormone secreted by the pituitary gland in both men and women. Prolactin is responsible for triggering the production of breast milk in women. It is also required in small amounts for the menstrual and reproductive cycle. Excess amounts of prolactin cause inappropriate secretion of milk from the breasts (galactorrhoea), and can block ovulation.

Prolactinoma: A condition in which an overactive pituitary gland in the brain overproduces the hormone prolactin. This can cause secretion of milk from breasts.

Pronuclei: The stage immediately after fertilization before the gametes fuse. It is seen sixteen to eighteen hours after fertilization. After fusion, the pronuclei are no longer visible and shortly after that stage, cell division commences.

Prostate: A walnut-sized gland found in men. It surrounds the urethra as it leaves the base of the bladder. It produces an alkaline fluid essential for sperm survival.

Prostate Specific Antigen (PSA): A protein manufactured exclusively by the prostate gland. PSA is produced for the ejaculate where it liquefies the semen and allows sperm cells to swim freely. Elevated levels of PSA in blood serum are associated with benign prostatic hypertrophy and prostate cancer.

Prostatitis: Swelling and inflammation of the prostate gland, a walnut-sized gland located directly below the bladder in men, often causing painful or difficult urination.

Prothrombin: A protein present in blood plasma that is a factor needed for the normal clotting of blood.

PSA: See under Prostate Specific Antigen.

Puberty: The age at which the reproductive organs commence activity.

PVP: See under Polyvinylpyrrolidone.

Quadruple Marker Test: A screening test similar to the triple marker. This test also measures the levels of inhibin along with AFP, estriol and BhCG.

Receptor Sites: Sites on the surface of cells which respond to particular hormone signals delivered in the blood.

Reciprocal Translocation: An interchange of parts of the short or long arms of different chromosomes.

Recombinant DNA Technology: It allows DNA to be produced by artificial means. It takes DNA from two different sources and combines that DNA into a single molecule. It is used in infertility treatment to create hormones that have the same DNA structure as the ones in the body.

Recurrent Spontaneous Abortion (RSA): The occurrence of more than two spontaneous abortions.

Relaxin: A peptide hormone produced by corpus luteum in the female and the prostate in the male, known to enhance the motility of sperm.

Renal Transplant: A surgical procedure to remove a healthy, functioning kidney from a living or brain-dead donor and implant it into a patient with non-functioning kidneys.

Respiratory Distress Syndrome: An acute lung disease of the newborn (especially the premature newborn) in which layers of tissue called hyaline membranes impede the oxygen that is breathed in from passing into the blood.

Rete Testes: An anastomosing network of delicate tubules exiting from the testes and carrying sperm outwards from the seminiferous tubules to the efferent ducts.

Retinoblastoma: A rare malignant tumor of the retina of the eye affecting children.

Retinopathy: Refers to non inflammatory damage to the retina.

Retrograde Ejaculation: A condition in which semen enters the bladder during orgasm instead of leaving the body via the urethra.

Retroverted Uterus: A condition in which the uterus is tipped backwards towards the rectum instead of forward. Some women may experience symptoms including painful sex. A retroverted uterus does not necessarily to affect a woman's fertility.

Rh Incompatibility: A dangerous condition that occurs during pregnancy in which a woman has Rh-negative blood with a baby with Rh-positive blood.

Rh Isoimmunization: A condition which develops with Rh negative women, where the fetus's father is Rh positive, resulting in a Rh positive pregnancy. The disease is generally preventable by treating the mother during pregnancy or soon after delivery with an intramuscular injection of anti-RhD immunoglobulin. It is one of the causes of hemolytic diseases in newborns (HDN). Also known as Rh (D) disease, Rhesus incompatibility, Rhesus disease, RhD Hemolytic Disease of the Newborn, Rhesus D Hemolytic of the Newborn or RhD HDN.

Robertsonian Translocation: A genetic disorder which results from the fusion of the long arms of two satellite chromosomes (for example 13/14, 13/15, 14/21 or 14/22). A Robertsonian translocation results when the long arms of two acrocentric chromosomes fuse at the centromere and the two short arms are lost. In this case, the long arms of Chromosomes 13 and 14 fuse but no genetic material is lost so the person is normal despite the translocation.

ROR: See under Rorschach Inkblot Test.

Rorschach Inkblot Test (ROR): A widely used psychological test in which a person's perceptions of inkblots are recorded and then analyzed by a trained psychologist. The test examines personality characteristics and emotional functioning.

RSA: See under Recurrent Spontaneous Abortion.

Rubella: A contagious viral disease with symptoms like mild measles. It can cause major abnormalities in the baby including heart defects, deafness, cataracts and brain abnormalities.

Salpingectomy: An operation in which one or both of the fallopian tubes are removed.

Salpingitis: Inflammation of the fallopian tubes.

Salpingostomy: The surgical unblocking of a blocked fallopian tube.

Sarvangasana (Shoulderstand): An inverted asana in hatha yoga.

SCO: See under Sertoli-Cell Only Syndrome.

Scrotum: The bag of skin that lies below the penis. It holds the testes, epididymis, and a part of the vasa deferentia.

Sebaceous Glands: Microscopic glands in the skin that secrete oily/waxy matter, called sebum, which lubricates and waterproofs the skin and hair.

Secondary Infertility: A condition of infertility where the couple has had a pregnancy in the past but is unable to conceive again.

Semen: The fluid ejaculated from the penis at orgasm. The seminal fluid contains sperm, proteins and carbohydrates.

Semen Analysis/Sperm Count: The analysis of semen under the microscope to count the number of sperm in million per millilitre, as well as to assess their shape and motility.

Seminal Vesicles: A pair of glands approximately 5 centimetres in length, located close to the urinary bladder, which secrete fluid that contributes substantially towards semen.

Seminiferous Tubules: Thousands of thin tiny tubes found within the testes which produce sperm.

Seminoma: A malignant tumor of the testis.

Septate Uterus: A congenital uterine malformation where the uterine cavity is partitioned by a broad longitudinal band of tissue.

Serial Transvaginal Ultrasonography: A procedure by which the development of the follicles during ovulation induction is checked serially to observe their growth.

Sertoli-Cell Only Syndrome(SCO): An inherited condition in which the testicles have no germ cells. Since men with this condition have normal Leydig cells producing testosterone, they will develop secondary sex characteristics. May also be caused by large and/or prolonged exposure to toxins or radiation.

Shatavari: Asparagus root, roots and leaves used as an ayurvedic herb.

Shirodkar's Stitch: An eponymous procedure of a purse string stitch around the cervix. It helps conserve the pregnancy in some patients.

Shirshasana (Head stand): A yogic asana in which the body is completely inverted and held upright supported by the forearms, while the crown of the head rests lightly on the floor.

Sickle-Cell Anaemia: A chronic hereditary blood disease, primarily affecting indigenous Africans and their descendants, in which an accumulation of oxygen-deficient fragile red blood cells results in anemia, blood clotting and joint pain.

Because of their shape, the cells can cause blockage of small blood vessels in the organs and bones, reducing the amount of available oxygen.

Single Gene Disorders: Disorders arising from abnormal changes in a single gene.

Speculum: An instrument used to examine the vagina and cervix.

Spermatic Cord: The cord-like tubular structure in males formed by the vas deferens and surrounding tissue that runs from the abdomen down to each testicle. The two spermatic cords support the testes in the scrotum. Each cord is sheathed in connective tissue and contains a network of arteries, veins, nerves and the first section of the ductus deferens, through which semen passes in the process of ejaculation.

Spermatids: Immature male sex cells formed from a spermatocyte that can develop into spermatozoa without further division.

Spermatogenesis: The process of sperm cell development; immature sperm cells undergo successive mitotic and meiotic divisions (spermatocytogenesis) and a metamorphic change (spermiogenesis) to produce spermatozoa.

Spermatogonia: Male germ cells that give rise to spermatocytes early in spermatogenesis.

Spermatozoa: Generative cells in the semen that cause fertilization of the female egg or ovum. They consist of round or cylindrical nucleated cells with a short neck and a thin motile tail.

Spermatozoon: Sperm; the reproductive cell or gamete of the male carried in semen that fertilizes the ovum to produce the zygote.

Sperm Morphology: The shape and/or form of the sperm cell.

Spina Bifida: A birth defect which occurs when the bones of the spine (vertebrae) do not join and unite properly around part of the baby's spinal cord.

Spironolactone: A steroid medicine that promotes sodium excretion and is used in the treatment of certain types of edema and hypertension.

Stein Leventhal Syndrome: A condition where multiple small cysts appear in the ovary due to hormonal imbalance and cause problems in ovulation. This term is rarely used and is now being replaced by the term PCOS.

Steroids: Any large group of fat-soluble organic compounds such as the sterols and sex hormones, most of which have specific physiological actions.

Stimulation of Ovaries: This involves increasing the size and number of ovarian follicles with the help of medicines for IUI/IVF/ICSI treatment.

Stress Hormones: They are released in the body in response to stress. They affect most bodily functions such as the flow of blood, breathing and heart rate. They also affect other hormones such as those associated with reproduction. Corticosteroids, epinephrine and norepinephrine are the common stress hormones.

Subfertility: Decreased fertility or a decreased chance of getting pregnant.

Submucous Fibroids: Growths arising from the wall of the uterus inwards to distort the endometrial cavity. It can be a cause of menorrhagia (heavy periods), intermenstrual bleeding, premenstrual spotting, infertility and miscarriage.

Superovulation: A term used to describe the hormone-induced production of multiple eggs for use during ART.

Suppression: A process resulting from medicines given during and prior to an IVF stimulation cycle to prevent ovarian cysts from occurring and to block spontaneous unplanned ovulation during IVF stimulation cycle.

Surrogacy: A condition in which a woman carries and gives birth to a baby for another woman.

Syndrome: A particular disease or condition with a pattern of signs and symptoms.

Synechiae: Adhesions within the uterine cavity. These are usually due to past infection, trauma or surgery.

TAT: See under Thematic Apperception Test.

Tay Sachs Disease: An autosomal recessive genetic disorder resulting from Hexosaminidase deficiency causing destruction of nerve cells in the brain, and occurs due to a mutation on the HEXA gene on Chromosome 15.

TB: See under Tuberculosis.

TCM: See under Traditional Chinese Medicine.

Teratozoospermia: A condition in which the majority of sperm are abnormally shaped. The abnormal shape may be in the head, midpiece, or the tail of the sperm.

TESA/TESE: See under Testicular Sperm Aspiration/Extraction.

Testicular Biopsy: A minor surgical procedure, which involves the removal of a small sample of testicular tissue.

Testicular Sperm Aspiration/Extraction (TESA/TESE): A minor surgical procedure, which involves the removal of a small sample of testicular tubules in order to retrieve sperm for use during the ICSI procedure.

Testosterone: A male hormone produced in the testes. It stimulates the development of male sex characteristics and is essential for sperm production.

Thalassemia: A form of anaemia where those affected patients need regular blood transfusions.

Theca Cells: Lutein cells derived from the theca interna of the graafian follicle.

Thematic Apperception Test (TAT): A psychological test intended to evaluate a person's patterns of thought, attitudes, observational capacity, and emotional responses to ambiguous test materials.

Thrombophilia: An abnormality of blood coagulation that increases the risk of thrombosis (blood clots in blood vessels).

Thyroid: A large endocrine gland found in the neck. It controls the body's metabolism.

Thyroxine: A hormone produced by the thyroid gland.

Titliasana (Butterfly pose): A yoga asana in which the legs are folded at knees, bringing the soles of feet together.

T Mycoplasma: An infection which possibly causes fertility problems and miscarriages.

TNF α: See under Tumour Necrosis Factor alpha.

TO Masses: See under Tubo-ovarian Masses.

TORCH Testing: A category of blood tests also known as the TORCH PANEL involving infectious-disease antibody tests which measure the presence of antibodies (protein molecules produced by the human immune system in response to specific disease agents such as Toxo plasma, Rubella, Cytomegalovirus

& Hepatitis virus) and their level of concentration in the blood.

Torsion of the Ovary: Twisting of the ovary resulting in pain.

Totipotent Cells: These are cells which are capable of developing into a complete organism or differentiating into any of its cells or tissues.

Toxoplasmosis: An infection caused by Toxoplasma gondii. If contracted in pregnancy, it may damage a foetus or cause a miscarriage.

Traditional Chinese Medicine (TCM): A range of traditional medicine practices originating in China, based on the notion of harmony and balance.

Triple Marker Test: Blood test performed at seventeen to eighteen weeks of pregnancy to classify a patient as at, either high risk, or low risk for chromosomal abnormalities and neural tube defects. This test measures serum levels of AFP, estriol and BhCG.

Triploidy: Presence of 69 chromosomes in each cell instead of 46.

Triptorelin: These are synthetic versions of a hormone called Gonadotropin-releasing hormone analogue that is released from the hypothalamus gland in the brain used in the treatment of precocious puberty, prostates and cancers. These are also used in suppressing the ovaries prior to starting ovarian stimulation.

Trisomy: The presence of an extra chromosome in a karyotype.

Tubal Ectopic Pregnancy: A condition in which a fertilized egg attaches (or implants) itself in one of the fallopian tubes rather than the uterus.

Tubercular Salpingitis: Tuberculous infection affecting the

genital tract.

Tuberculosis (TB): A communicable disease caused by infection with the tubercle bacillus, most frequently affecting the lungs and sometimes the uterus.

Tubo-ovarian Masses (TO masses): Adhesions between the tubes and the ovaries due to a past or present infection or inflammation. In India, the commonest cause of it is Genital TB.

Tumour Necrosis Factor alpha (TNFα): A protein, produced by white blood cells that is destructive to cells showing abnormally rapid growth. Also produced in large amounts in the presence of Genital TB.

Turner's Syndrome: A congenital condition in which a woman has one X chromosome instead of two resulting in infertility.

Ultrasound: The use of ultrasonic waves for diagnostic or therapeutic purposes, specifically to image an internal body structure and monitor a developing foetus.

Umbilicus: A medical term for the navel.

Unbalanced Translocation: A condition resulting from the fertilization of a gamete containing a translocation chromosome by a normal gamete, in which a segment of the translocation chromosome is represented three times in each cell and a trisomic state exists even though the individual has 46 chromosomes.

Undescended Testicle: A term used to describe a testis which has not descended into the scrotum from the abdomen.

Unicornuate Uterus: A uterine malformation where the uterus has a single horn instead of two and is banana shaped.

Urethra: The passage which takes urine from the bladder to

the outside. In men it also carries semen during ejaculation.

Urinary Bladder: An elastic, muscular sac situated in the anterior part of the pelvic cavity in which urine collects before excretion.

Urologist: A doctor who specializes in disorders of the genitourinary system.

Uterine Fibroids: Benign (noncancerous) growths of fibrous tissue and muscle cells of the uterus.

Uterine Polyps: Growths attached to the inner wall of the uterus that extend into the uterine cavity. They are usually noncancerous (benign) and range from a few millimetres— no larger than a sesame seed—to several 'centimetres—golf ball sized or larger.

Uterosacrals: Ligaments connecting the uterus to the sacrum. They hold the uterus in position.

Uterus: The female reproductive organ in which the foetus grows during pregnancy.

Uterus Didelphys: A congenital defect resulting in a double uterus with a double cervix and a double vagina.

Vagina: The muscular canal extending from the cervix to the outside of the body.

Vaginal Septum: A congenital partition within the vagina.

Vaginismus: Painful spasmodic contractions of the vagina in response to physical contact or pressure (especially sexual intercourse).

Vaginitis: Inflammation of the vagina.

Varicocele: An abnormal enlargement of the veins in the testicles.

Varicocele Ligation: A surgical procedure to correct a varicocele. Varicoceles are varicose or dilated veins within the scrotum that can cause infertility in some men.

Vasa Deferentia: A thin muscular tube which carries the sperm from the testes to the urethra. There are two vasa deferentia.

Vas Aplasia: A birth defect where the tubes which carry sperm from the testes to the penis remain undeveloped.

Vasectomy: A surgical procedure during which the vasa deferentia of a man is severed and tied to prevent sperm from entering the ejaculate. It is a means of birth control.

Vaso Vasostomy: The joining together of two cut surfaces of the vas deferentia after the blockage has been removed.

Vascular Endothelial Growth Factor (VEGF): This is stimulated by LH and it has an influence on the granulosa cells.

VDRL: A serological screening test for syphilis developed by the former Venereal Disease Research Laboratory in London.

VEGF: See under Vascular Endothelial Growth Factor.

Vitrification: A technique of rapid freezing of oocytes and embryos.

Vulva: The external genital organs of the female.

Xenoestrogens: Estrogens present in pesticides and plastics that can cause infertility and miscarriages.

X Linked: A pattern of inheritance where the abnormal gene is on the X chromosome. Males have a 50-percent risk of being affected and females have a 50-percent chance of being carriers.

Y Chromosomes: Chromosomes which determine masculinity.

Y Microdeletions: Small chromosomal deletions which are

not visible through the microscope. They occur on the active part of the Y chromosome. They can be detected by multiplex PCR, and are responsible for male infertility.

Yoga: A spiritual and physical discipline which includes breath control, simple meditation, and the adoption of specific bodily postures for health and relaxation.

Zona Pellucida: A membrane surrounding the oocyte or egg.

Zygote: The stage after the sperm fertilizes the egg but before the cell division commences.

Index

A Note on the Author

Dr Firuza R. Parikh is the Director of Assisted Reproduction and Genetics at Jaslok Hospital and Research Centre. She completed her undergraduate as well as postgraduate medical education at the KEM Hospital and the Seth GS Medical College, Mumbai and trained at Yale University School of Medicine in reproductive medicine for four years. She returned to India in 1989 to set up and head the first private IVF centre at the Jaslok Hospital. Within a year of its inception, the centre was recognized as an international centre of excellence and started receiving patients from over 40 countries across the world. In recognition of her accomplishments she was appointed Visiting Associate Professor at the Yale University School of Medicine in 1992 and thereafter as Professor. In 2005, she was listed by India Today as one of the 50 most powerful people of India.

Dr Parikh is a pioneer and the leading fertility specialist in India. She is responsible for the birth of more than 7500 ART babies, and her pioneering research on CAT (Cumulus Aided Transfer) has significantly improved the chances of pregnancy in IVF. She is a global pioneer in stem cell research and has been featured in over 1100 newspaper and magazine articles worldwide including the *New York Times*, *Washington Post*, *Time*, and *Newsweek*.

Currently, she is Editor-in-Chief of Fertility and Sterility, Indian edition and Visiting Professor of Obstetrics and Gynaecology at the University of California, Los Angeles, UCLA. Married to internationally renowned neuropsychiatrist Dr Rajesh Parikh, she lives in Mumbai with her three children Swapneil, Manish, and Nikita.

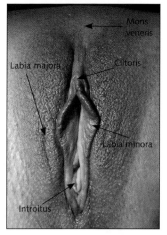

Figure 4.1 The female external genitalia

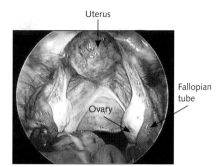

Figure 4.3 Laparoscopic photograph of the female internal genitalia—uterus, fallopian tubes, and ovaries

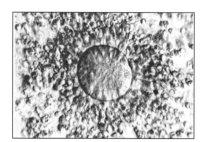

Figure 4.4 Microphotograph of an oocyte surrounded by granulosa cells

Figure 4.6 The cervix

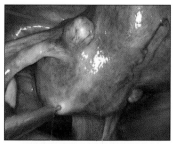

Figure 4.7 Laparoscopic photograph of multiple uterine fibroids

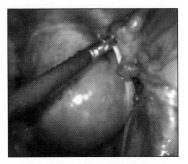

Figure 4.8 Laparoscopic photograph of the right fallopian tube swollen due to TB

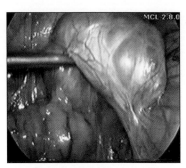

Figure 4.9 Laparoscopic photograph of a hydrosalpinx due to genital TB

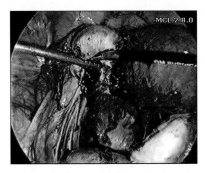

Figure 4.10 Laparoscopic photograph of endometriois affecting the left fallopian tube, left ovary, uterosacral ligaments, and the bowels

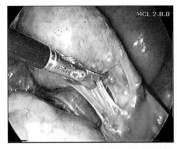

Figure 4.11 Laparoscopic photograph of adhesions between the right fallopian tube and the intestines

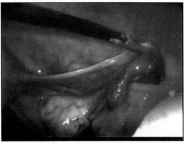

Figure 4.12 Laparoscopic photograph of right tubal ectopic pregnancy about to burst

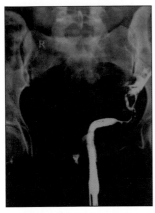

Figure 6.1 Unicornuate
uterus outlined on HSG

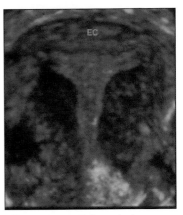

Figure 6.2 A T-shaped uterus on
3D sonography

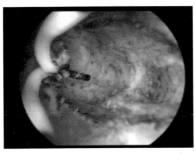

Figure 6.3 Hysteroscopic
photograph of lateral metroplasty
for a T-shaped uterus

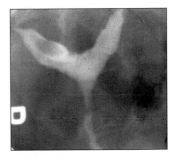

Figure 6.4 A septate uterus
outlined on HSG

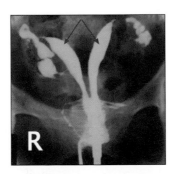

Figure 6.5 A bicornuate uterus on
hysterosalpingogram

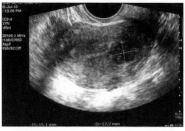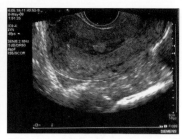

Figure 6.6 An intramural fibroid impinging on the uterine cavity on sonography

Figure 6.7 A sonographic view of a uterine polyp causing irregular bleeding

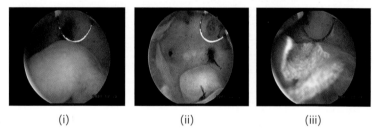

(i) (ii) (iii)

Figure 6.8 Ritika's large uterine polyp being removed by hysteroscopy

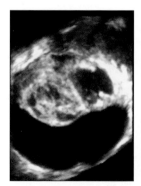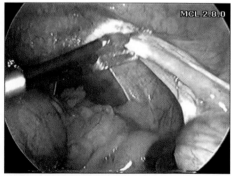

Figure 6.9 A sonographic view of a hydrosalpinx

Figure 6.10 A laparoscopic view of delinking of a hydrosalpinx

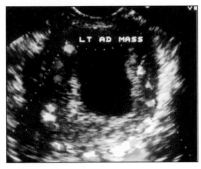

Figure 6.11 Ipshita's ectopic pregnancy
outlined in 3D sonography

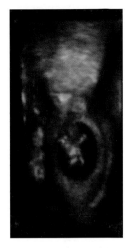

Figure 6.12 A sonographic view
of a cervical ectopic pregnancy

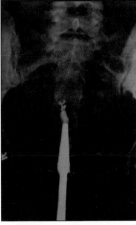

Figure 6.13 Intrauterine
adhesions outlined on HSG

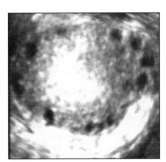

Figure 6.14 A sonographic view
of the necklace appearance of
the polycystic ovary in PCOS

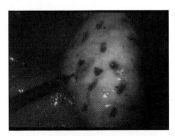

Figure 6.15 LEOS for polycystic
ovaries

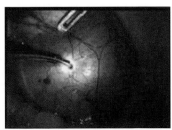

Figure 6.16 A laparoscopic viewof
a benign simple ovarian cyst

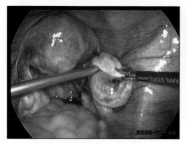

Figure 6.17 A laparoscopic view
of a simple ovarian cyst

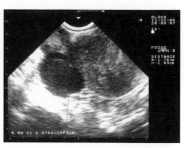

Figure 6.18 A sonographic view
of a chocolate cyst of the ovary
(endometrioma)

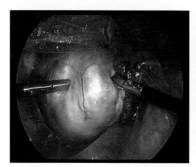

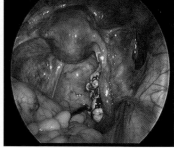

Figure 6.19 A laparoscopic view of Ratna's ovary before and after the
removal of the dermoid cyst

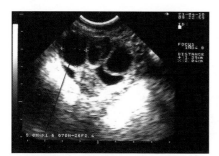

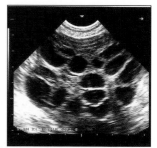

Figure 7.1 A sonographic image
of ovarian follicles on day nine of
controlled ovarian stimulation

Figure 7.5 A sonographic
image of an ovary likely to
hyperstimulate

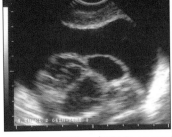

Figure 7.6 and 7.7 Sonographic images of the ovaries showing moderate hyperstimulation and ascitic fluid

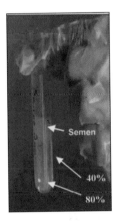

Figure 8.1 Swim-up technique for IUI

Figure 8.2 Swim-down technique for IUI

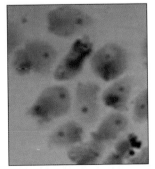

Figure 8.4 Hunting for the oocytes

Figure 8.5 The oocytes are placed in the carbon dioxide incubator

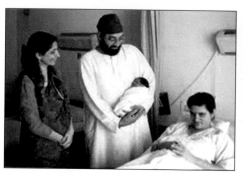

Figure 8.11 Luv Singh—Southeast Asia's first ICSI baby as a newborn in 1994, with his parents Gita and Kiranjit Singh; (right) as a teenager

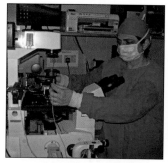
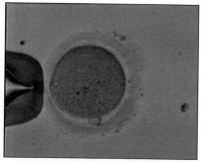

Figure 8.12 The micromanipulation system

Figure 8.13 The micropipette holding the egg

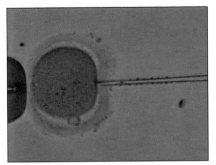

Figure 8.14 The injection micropipette
puncturing the zona

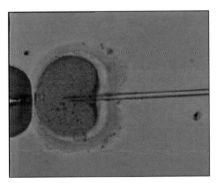

Figure 8.15 The micropipette injecting
the sperm

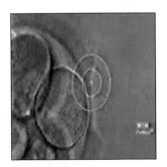

Figure 8.17 The laser beam makes an opening in the zona

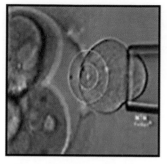

Figure 8.18 A single cell is removed from the eight-celled embryo

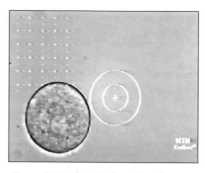

Figure 8.19 The single cell undergoes genetic analysis

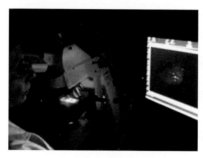

Figure 8.20 FISH on the blastomere

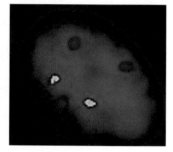

Figure 8.21 PGD by the FISH method

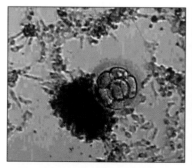
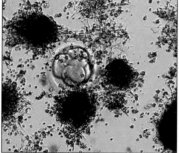

Figure 10.1 and 10.2 Clusters of expanded cumulus cells surround the developing embryos

Figure 10.3 Cumulus cells engulfing the embryo

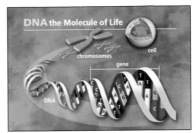

Figure 12.3 A diagrammatic representation of DNA—the molecule of life

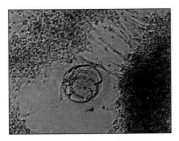

Figure 12.4 Our cover story on the first successful pregnancy in India by PGD for Robertsonian translocation

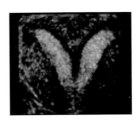

Figure 12.5 A sonographic picture of a bicornuate uterus

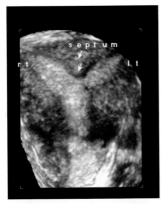

Figure 12.6 A sonographic picture of a septate uterus

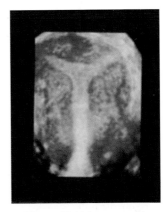

Figure 12.7 A sonograhic picture of a T-shaped uterus

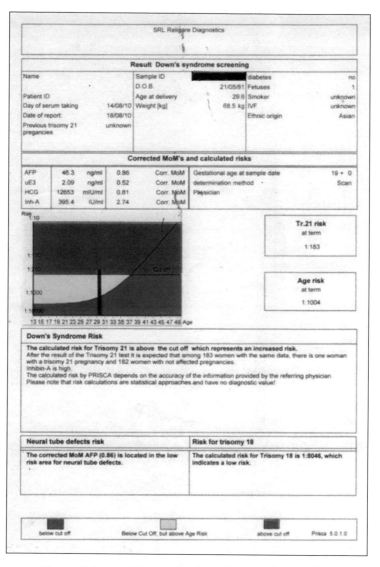

Figure 13.1 A positive quadruple marker test showing low levels of estriol in the maternal blood suggestive of Down's Syndrome in the foetus

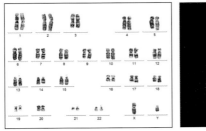
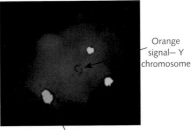

Orange signal— Y chromosome

Green signal—X chromosome

Figure 13.2 Photograph of a normal male karyotype and a normal FISH

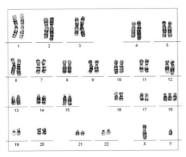
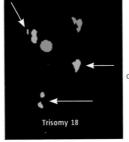

3 Aqua signals—3 chromosomes 18

Trisomy 18

Figure 13.3 Photograph of an abnormal karyotype and FISHFigure

13.2 Photograph of a normal male karyotype and a normal FISHNote: Figure 13.2 shows a picture of a male with 23 pairs of chromosomes on karyotyping and normal signals for the X and Y chromosomes on FISH, whereas Figure 13.3 shows a male with an extra chromosome 18. This is confirmed by three signals for chromosome 18 on FISH.

Figure 16.2 Shirshasana or head stand

Figure 16.3 Sarvangasana or shoulder stand

Figure 16.4 Chakrasana or the
wheel pose

Figure 16.5 Titliasana or the
butterfly pose

Figure 16.6 Bhujangasan

Figure 16.7 Paschimottasana

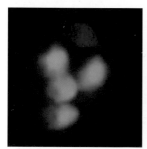

Figure 17.17 Normal
(blue) and apoptotic
sperm (green)

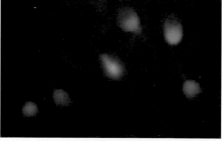

Figure 17.18 Partial apoptosis
(blue-green)

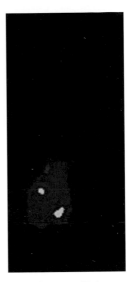

Normal haploid sperm with only one chromosome of each pair

Figure 17.19 Sperm FISH showing normal signals

Abnormal sperm with two sex chromosomes (XY) leads to a sex chromosome abnormality called Klinefelter's syndrome (XXY) in the foetus

Figure 17.20 Sperm FISH showing abnormal signals

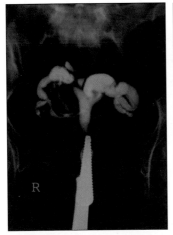

Figure 17.21 Outline of a hydrosalpinx on HSG

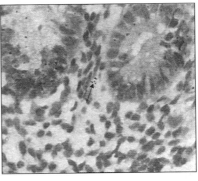

Mycobacterium Tuberculosis (Positive)

Figure 17.22 Immunohistochemistry—identification of mycobacterium TB PAMP in the endometrium courtesy: Double Helix Labs

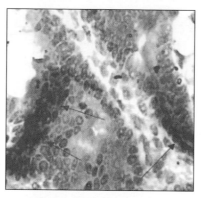

Figure 17.23 Microscopic photograph of endometrial cells being attacked by Natural Killer cells
Courtesy: Double Helix Labs

Figure 21.1 Our cover story showing cumulus cells surrounding the developing embryo

Figure 21.2 Triploidy on FISH

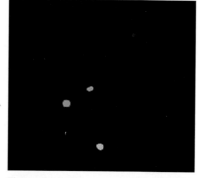

Figure 21.3 Monosomy 18 with XXY

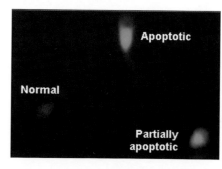

Figure 21.6 Sperm apoptosis

Interpretation Apoptotic sperm < 13 percent = high fertility potential Apoptotic sperm 13 to 40 percent = good to fair fertility potentialApoptotic sperm > 40 percent = poor fertility potential
Figure 20.6 Sperm apoptosis